THE HOUSE MATE

NINA MANNING

Boldwood

First published in Great Britain in 2020 by Boldwood Books Ltd.

Copyright © Nina Manning, 2020

Cover Design: Nick Castle Design

Cover Photography: Shutterstock

A CIP catalogue record for this book is available from the British Library.

Paperback ISBN 978-1-83889-150-3

Large Print ISBN 978-1-83889-780-2

Ebook ISBN 978-1-83889-151-0

Kindle ISBN 978-1-83889-152-7

Audio CD ISBN 978-1-83889-240-1

MP3 CD ISBN 978-1-83889-777-2

Digital audio download ISBN 978-1-83889-149-7

Boldwood Books Ltd
23 Bowerdean Street
London SW6 3TN
www.boldwoodbooks.com

For My Mum, Lee Taylor.

PROLOGUE

I crouch under the table and desperately try to control my ragged breathing. How the hell did I end up here? Curiosity or just pure bloody-mindedness? I think back to the simplicity of my life, before all this. I was on a path to recovery; things had become a little easier. I had my routines; life had a structure. Now all of my senses are working on overdrive. I am thrust back to my cognitive behavioural therapy classes, and so I begin to think outside of myself to distract from the fear and panic. The '5-4-3-2-1' technique. Right, let's do this. Okay, five things I can see: a chair leg; a table leg; a length of brown-and-orange tablecloth, matted and greasy at the corner; a dent in the wooden floor, where something heavy had been dropped; a small handmade wooden bear the size of my hand, wearing a hessian jacket.

Four things I can touch. Stay calm, stay calm. The hard floor beneath my knees, sweat on my forehead, a sticky patch next to my knee where someone has dropped some jam or something similar, a cut on my right leg.

Three things I can hear: a clock ticking, a fan oven cooling... footsteps. I hear footsteps.

Two things I smell: the putrid stench of vomit mixed with a cleaning product.

One thing I can taste: There is blood in my mouth. I can taste blood.

* * *

Instagram post: 25th April 2019

Wow, guys, I cannot believe a whole year has passed and I'm still here. I started this Instagram account because I enjoy cleaning and showcasing the results to other people and you guys have shown me such great support, I feel grateful.

One year in and I can hardly believe I have one million followers. And I love every single one of you – even though I can't see you in person, I feel all your love and support for what I do.

I hope I can keep offering you great cleaning advice and that you will continue on this journey with me.

Keep up the cleaning, guys.

Mrs C x

#cleaning #cleanstagrammer #anniversary #mrsclean
76,378 likes

1

I piled four coins on top of one another on the mantlepiece in my bedroom, turning each one a fraction so the tiny indentations on the side of each coin were in perfect alignment. Then I took two steps to the left and turned my attention to the locks on the window. I pulled each latch back and forth six times until it was back on lock again. I headed to the bedroom door, let myself out and shut it behind me. Once on the other side, I locked and unlocked the bedroom door six times, then I left it locked and put the key in my back pocket. I walked down the stairs, silently counting each step as I descended. An even ten every time. I arrived in the hallway and stole a brief look at myself in the oval mirror on the wall.

Once upon a time I would have relished showing off my taut cheekbones, delighted in the looks of intrigue people would give when they saw the greenness of my eyes against my pale skin and thank the hairdressers who would reliably inform me my shoulder-length black hair was the sleekest they had ever styled. I used to take time over my appearance, but these days I simply slipped my purple fabric tie-dye scarf around my neck and pulled on my boho slouch hat with a peak so I could shade my eyes and hide my face from the world. I pulled on my denim jacket over my slight frame, aware that I no longer worried about dieting; any excess weight had fallen off years ago and had made no attempt to creep back on.

I slid into my black Doc Martens and hit the concrete outside. I refrained from opening and reopening the front door due to the imposition on my house mates, even though it pained me not to do so; instead I closed it with one click. The act brought little satisfaction. So I compensated by walking only inside the lines of the pavement stones for a gratifying ten steps.

Today was one of my worst days. Usually I could get away with performing only one or two compulsions, but today I carried out my full repertoire of compulsions to ease the fear. To balance out the scales so nothing bad would happen.

These compulsions, behaviours, are a force that come on quickly and sometimes from nowhere. It's a monster I must feed. I don't consider myself ill. It doesn't bring any inconvenience to my life. So long as I can just do some or all these small acts each day, everything will be okay. Nothing bad will happen. At least not again.

This morning I had woken with a weight on my chest I couldn't shift. Today was the anniversary. Three years had passed. Yet still here I was, a mere shell of the woman I once was.

I looked back at the five-bed, three-storey Victorian house I had been living in with three strangers for the last few weeks and looked up at a cloudless blue sky and the tall imposing buildings that cocooned me, protected me. People say they are drawn to the ocean to heal; the gentle lap of the waves are melodic and can repair your soul. But moving to a town like Richmond was the only option. Here, there were no spaces wide enough to expose my true fears. When I heard the roar of an ocean wave, I would always hear the screams carried by the wind. Here, all I needed to do was close my eyes and remind myself that I was safe and that everything was going to be okay.

The sounds of the streets can be imposing; sometimes I feel as though they are about to crush my skull. I have learned how to block things out. I choose to focus on one sound at a time, and hear only that until it is no more, then my mind weaves itself around another sound, and so it continues until I reach my destination. Of course blocking out everything but one sound can often be mistaken for rudeness, nonchalant. Snidey even.

But sometimes you have no choice. When you have been screamed at enough times, are forced to hear it, that's when it's the hardest; when I am reminded of the past.

Some sounds are supposed to be so beautiful, like the gentle tone of a child's voice, innocent and pure. Yet they can fill my every fibre with terror.

Walking is a sort of therapy. 'Anxiety struggles to hit a moving object,' I was told during one of my Steps2Wellbeing seminars; just one of the forms of therapy I have had over the years so I can carry on existing in the world. But is it worth it when it's only yourself you have to keep alive? We aren't meant to be solitary creatures despite my desire to keep hiding away from the world, and the person I can no longer bring myself to think about.

I now share a house with three other girls, all students like me, but over a decade younger. I have to do as much as I can each day to keep face; to show my house mates that all is well in the mind of Regina Kelly. Referring to myself as a student feels strange. It's been a long time since I last studied. This short introductory course will see me through to the end of the summer term, then I begin my degree in September.

I know my house mates watch me, that they see me repeat basic actions. A simple chore becomes a maddening act, repeated over and over until my mind is temporarily satisfied. But they stay quiet. Offer me a cup of tea as though everything is exactly as it should be and there isn't a thirty-five-year-old woman standing in our shared kitchen turning the oven knob on and off an even amount of times.

I am thankful for their ignorance, for turning a blind eye, especially on the harder days when the images fly through my mind like a freight train and I feel the impenetrable dark clouds gather around me, as though I'm walking through a black fog.

I had developed a routine already in just a few weeks since I moved to Richmond upon Thames and had quickly embraced the leafy borough with its parks and wide tree-lined avenues. I was so confined for so long, it was a relief to be able to walk to the local mews.

I entered the café and was hit by tantalising caramel and nutty aromas. Each day there was a slightly different scent in the air but always the same member of staff was waiting for me and that made me feel as though the world wasn't about to implode. The door made a loud sucking noise as it opened.

My eyes scanned the room. It was busier than usual. I tried to spot Heather, the confident young girl who had been serving me the last few weeks, when someone pushed past me quite abruptly.

I froze. Terror spiked through me.

In the time I had been away I had forgotten that I had to share walkways with others, that the small spaces I inhabited were not for my sole purpose only. When I realised I was safe and no one was trying to grab me, I looked up and saw a young man with a beard and a black Puffa jacket, holding a huge camera over his arm. I caught his eye, then quickly looked away.

'I'm so sorry,' he said. I knew he wanted to touch me, to emphasise his apology, but thankfully his hands were full; my arm still buzzed from the collision. I forced my gaze upon my destination and hurried towards the counter.

Finally, I could see Heather and my tense body slackened momentarily. Another piece of the day's jigsaw slotted into place. Heather smiled at me, but it was tainted with stress.

'It's busy in here today,' I said in her direction, hoping but knowing she would serve me. She nodded at me with wide eyes as she pulled cardboard disposable cups from a sheath of plastic wrapping.

'Can I help?' A barista I had never seen before spoke at me in a monotone voice, and I quickly averted my eyes towards Heather.

'I've got it, Tom,' Heather called and winked at me as she finished wrestling with the cups and headed over to the counter. Tom shrugged and headed out onto the café floor and started clearing tables.

'They've been shooting a TV commercial out there this morning. They were here at five! They just stopped for a tea break, hence the chaos. And the mess,' Heather said as she pointed out towards the café floor.

I glanced backwards, but the disarray made me quickly turn away and think happier, cleaner thoughts.

'Usual?' she asked, heading to the coffee machine. She began making my preferred coffee; one and a half shots of decaf coffee, half oat milk, half soya heated to just before boiling with a shot of caramel. I smiled as I felt a flutter of satisfaction that I had already earned my status as a regular.

As Heather worked on my coffee, I glanced back over my shoulder out into the mews through the window. The low-hanging trees were aesthetically pleasing and framed the quadrangle like a picture, dappling the concrete with light and making it the perfect location for shooting scenes. There were cosy, well-presented shops, two cafés and a deli where rich middle-class families hung out with other rich middle-class families at the weekend, all tending to their rainbow-colour-cladded toddlers and young children in Boden boots. At the weekends I would have to jerk my legs aside as I heard the sound of a scooting child arriving precariously close to my shins followed by low, unthreatening calls of 'Jet!' or 'Milo!' from a full-bearded father, wearing his baby in front of him like this year's latest accessory. I'd never purposefully avoid the mews on the weekend, but I found it a lot harder when there were more children around. Today was a Thursday and it was pretty quiet, although I didn't need to be in a heavily populated area to hear the lingering echoes of children playing. It had been playing on loop in my mind for three years.

Heather presented me with my coffee in a takeaway cup. I paid and thanked her and headed to the door just as the TV crew and cast were beginning to spill back out into the mews. I pulled my cap down over my eyes and walked outside. In the street, the mews was buzzing with bodies. Some of the pavement had been cordoned off, and people were flocking to grab a glimpse of what they were shooting today.

I jolted aside as a young lad on a scooter sped past me. The wheel of his scooter clipped my heel. Suddenly my heart was drumming against my chest. I breathed in for three and out for six; just a short, sharp reset as my therapist had taught me, as I leant into the wall, hoping I could morph into it and that no one could see how small, seemingly inconsequential incidents could throw me off track.

I pushed myself off the wall and went to walk on, but, from the corner of my eye, I caught a glimpse of a dark jacket and a black baseball cap partially covering a face I thought I recognised. There was a shift in the atmosphere around me, like a surge of an electric current that was urging me to run. I felt my blood run cold and my hands became clammy. The short, breathless episode a moment ago was a mere prelude to the terror that began to tear through my body.

I began to walk at a pace. Three smartly dressed women blocked my way on the corner, their synchronised laughs sounded demonic in my ear as I skimmed past them. Their words morphed into the words I had heard him say so often: *you can't run away*.

I looked across the road again, but the man was nowhere to be seen. His words were evaporating and becoming the breeze around me once more.

I slipped into the grocery shop where I could take a moment to breathe and shake the image of the man out of my head. It couldn't have been him. I was safe here.

I slowly sipped my coffee whilst I perused the neatly stacked aisles. A jar of pickles was slightly out of line so I nudged it back in with its suitors; the order restored a small amount of calm within me.

I found my way to the next lane; non-perishables, toilet rolls, sanitary products and the likes. I was just nudging some wet wipes back in line on the shelf when the sound of a raspy, raised voice alerted my attention to the till. I walked to the end of the aisle and saw a woman dressed in a dark overcoat, with her back to me.

'You don't understand – I will return later, but I need this now.'

'I'm sorry. If I did this for you, then I would have to do it for all my customers. Please come back later when you have enough money.' The cashier, a man in his twenties with a disproportionately long neck, was leaning forward and speaking quietly to the woman.

I edged my way closer to the till, my hand already in my

pocket, ready to be of assistance. I moved closer still so that I was right behind the woman, her clipped Eastern European accent was punctuating through the cashier's protests.

'I'm really sorry.' The cashier said again. I was so close behind the woman I could smell her perfume, it smelt like Parma violets. Tufts of peroxide-blonde hair were poking from under her black bobble hat.

The cashier's eyes met mine. The woman, who sensed his attention, wavered and turned abruptly. Her green eyes bore into me, urgent and accusing. She scowled, then turned and headed for the door, rushing through it and back out into the street.

I approached the counter and saw what she had been trying to buy. It was a bottle of liquid paracetamol, the stuff you usually bought for kids. Just looking at it brought back a tsunami of memories of little hot heads and feverish nightmares, small bodies tossing and turning between the covers in the dead of night. Bodies that no longer existed in my world, yet I would never be free of their memories.

I shook the images from my head and looked at the cashier.

'How much?'

As I stepped out of the shop, I scanned the area, desperately trying to see the woman. I spotted her, her head hunched, hands in her pockets, heading away from the mews. I increased my pace to a light jog, weaving in and out of people who seemed to be coming at me in waves, until I was next to her.

'Excuse me,' I said as I arrived at her side.

She jumped as though I had given her an electric shock, then she turned to me with that same scowl. I handed her the bottle of paracetamol.

'Please, take it – it's on me.'

She went to walk away and I touched her arm, instantly regretting the sort of action that would make me recoil. She stopped in her tracks. I edged my way back to her side and pushed the paracetamol bottle into the large pocket of her coat. She watched me, briefly looked up at my face, mumbled something in her native language and hurried on down the street. I stood amongst the sea of people and watched her as she disappeared around the corner.

* * *

I didn't stop thinking about the woman all the way home. I played the scenario over in my mind. I imagined the child or children who were waiting for the medicine, what their ages were and if they were boys or girls. I had wanted to follow her to see where she lived, to see why a woman who was shopping in an affluent area couldn't afford a bottle of paracetamol. The walk that was supposed to alleviate my racing mind had achieved the opposite. I counted the lamp posts on the way home to calm my cluttered thoughts, tightening my grip on my shoulder bag until I reached the steps that lead up to the house that I was just coming round to the idea of calling home.

I had become accustomed to a solitary existence, so being greeted when I arrived home was a real novelty. Yet again I was surprised that one of my three house mates was just reaching the bottom of the stairs as I came through the front door.

'Oh, hey,' Mini said as I closed the door behind me and began to unwind the scarf from around my neck. She eyed me in that way I was becoming familiar with. Being assessed was not unusual to me and Mini always looked slightly alarmed by my presence, as though she wasn't entirely sure what to do with me. I imagined she thought I was always on the edge and might do something crazy at any moment, my strange routines adding an almost nervousness to the house. Mini, as her name suggested, was the youngest house member at just twenty. At fifteen years her senior, I had yet to shake the notion that she saw me as a slightly crazy distant auntie or cousin rather than a house mate she could confide in.

I took my cap off and hung it on the coat stand by the front door. Ignoring the mirror, which in the past would have encouraged me to check my hair for post-hat frizz.

'I was just going to get some lunch.' Mini began walking into the kitchen.

'Okay.' I followed her because I constantly felt the need to compensate for my inability to be *that* house mate; the one who sat up until dawn, chatting and giggling, offering to paint nails, plait hair and listen to endless stories of near misses with 'the one'.

I tried to ignore the chaos of the kitchen and sat down at the huge table that could seat at least eight. I was still getting used to eating with others again after spending so much time taking my meals alone.

I was still struggling with the size and openness of the house: five bedrooms, a huge kitchen, two reception rooms and three bathrooms between four of us.

One lonely room had cocooned me for the last year where sounds would arrive uninvited, an echo of an infant yelping or screaming, but always, I heard the cries. They say you never stop hearing them. I was forever alert; ready to run to the slightest whimper.

Even in a house this size, there was nowhere I could hide that would drown out the sounds that ran through my mind on a loop.

Mini's uncle owned the property and let it out for a price that would choke a Yorkshire man, but made London renters nod with enthusiasm whilst daring to utter the word *bargain*. I looked around at the kitchen with its large surfaces and random scattered items: bleach, washing-up liquid and an array of utensils were out on the surface next to the sink, which was deep, white ceramic and stained with tea. The Aga was greasy and a pan left over from breakfast was still perched on top of the insulating lid; the fat congealed to a sticky, yellow mass. The huge wooden kitchen table had a general tacky feel to it that didn't seem to lift no matter how many times it was wiped.

Up until now I had managed to not let the mess get to me, but I wasn't sure how much longer I could leave it. The lack of order in here brought everything to the surface. Even now in the kitchen with Mini, I began to look around for something I could open and shut an even amount of times to satisfy the monster who I knew would not rest.

Perhaps if I offered to clean the kitchen? I imagined this as a way I could bring a little bit of me to the house; up until now I hadn't felt confident enough to take the initiative and show the girls some level of basic domesticity. I had little else to offer in the way of sparkly wit or entertaining anecdotes about my day. I looked around and thought perhaps I could assert my role as the older and wiser house mate and draw up a cleaning rota. Perhaps I would be the one who would instil some basic home skills into these girls, something they would look back upon in later life, remember me and be thankful for.

Mini pulled open the fridge, and I caught a glimpse of the salad tray with its dying leaves stuck to the clear shelf and a mass of jars that had left rings that could be seen through the glass underneath. I averted my eyes; I didn't need to see it to know it was there. In the last few years, cleaning had become a compulsion; something I needed to do and do well. Looking around, I felt something new growing inside me: an uncontrollable need to cleanse the house from top to bottom.

Mini opened a tub of prawns in Marie Rose sauce and

emptied the contents over half an avocado. She left the remnants on the side and sat down opposite me on the kitchen table, giving me one of her half-smiles, showing off her perfectly pinched pink cheeks and petite lips. I could see why her parents named her Mini; with her sleek black hair, she was like a perfect china doll.

'How are you finding it all, are you feeling settled?' she asked before she took a mouthful of her salad. A little sauce spilled from her lips and she emitted a squeak like a small animal, then dabbed her mouth with a piece of kitchen roll.

Settled. I pondered over the word, which had so many connotations. I didn't think I would ever feel settled, in fact, I was forever teetering on the edge of uncertainty. But I imagined Mini was curious to know if the bed was comfy enough and had I found enough bathroom space to keep my toiletries.

'I am now, yes. You know what it's like, it takes a while.'

'And your course? Textiles, isn't it? Has it started yet?' Mini reached over and edged yesterday's newspaper closer to her; it was open on the crossword where someone had abandoned it halfway through.

'Erm, yes. Next week, after the Easter holidays,' I said, trying to sound keen, but I felt burdened with guilt at being able to start again, learning a new skill, which I hardly felt I deserved. But I needed the distraction. I also needed something to spend my money on. The money that was fairly mine. An even split down the middle. It was what I was entitled to, so I took it. There hadn't and wouldn't be any lavish expenditures, I would simply exist with it. I had reached a point where I was functioning, and that was all I needed to do.

I watched in awe as Mini rapidly filled in the blank spaces of the crossword with only a moment's pause after reading each clue.

'Have you always loved art?' she asked.

I thought back to my late teens, when most girls my age were out experiencing everything they could. By the time I was twenty, I had already become a mother.

I reached for a stray paper napkin and folded it over six times until it was a neat, tight square wad.

'I loved design at school,' I said, pressing the napkin square down until my finger turned a deep shade of pink.

I noticed Mini staring at my finger and I quickly pushed the napkin away. I knew she saw what most did; a woman with a bunch of obsessive compulsions.

What she didn't know was what I did to become her.

2

THEN

The room was filled with dancing bodies and people slouched in sofas and chairs. A block of three disco lights flashed beneath a makeshift DJ booth where a pale, skinny guy with a ginger afro was mixing vinyl records. I looked across to my right and my eyes stopped on a guy a few feet away. I could tell he was older than me as he danced amongst the chaos, busting out some moves to a Michael Jackson hit. There was something alluring about him, something about the way he smiled. He had a slight gap in his teeth, but it suited him. He wore a faded black T-shirt; his tanned arms were muscly with wisps of light-blonde hair. His hair was cut short and I wanted to run my fingers across it, to feel the brittle follicles on my fingertips. I watched him for what felt like forever until finally his eyes met with mine. We shared a moment and in that look was a sentiment that said, 'I know you.'

Even though we hadn't met before, it was as if we had known each other all our lives. When he finally found his way over to me, he began the conversation as though we were halfway through it.

'That vodka won't drink itself, you know.' He pointed at the full bottle next to me. I had bought it from the off-licence on the way here, along with a bottle of Diet Coke. But I didn't fancy drinking either of them.

It had been another friend's birthday two nights previously, and I had gone at it pretty hard, so was still feeling the after-effects.

I was only at this party because I was staying with my cousin, forty miles from my house. He rang on the off-chance and said one of his friends was having a party and did I fancy coming up and staying the night? There was a moment when I thought to myself, I won't go, I'll stay at home and keep an eye on Mum.

My mum was having another one of her turns. The 'black dog', as she preferred to call it, had come back to visit. I thought the term was more depressing than *depression* itself. I would be turning eighteen in the summer, but I would probably still stay living with Mum. I needed to keep an eye on her, even though all she did was sleep during these episodes.

But there was another part of me that was interested to go to the party, to see what the night could bring. I was still young and ready to grab what life offered with both hands. And if I was being totally honest, I was looking for love. I had grown up watching too many films: *Sleepless in Seattle*, *When a Man Loves a Woman*, *Indecent Proposal*. Mum would always have a love film on any time of the day or night. She referred to them as her 'weepies'. I never saw her weep at them though. Instead, by the end of the film she would have more of a scowl on her face, as though she knew she had been dealt an injustice. But still she played them. And I watched. And I learned that no matter what life threw at you – alcoholism, bankruptcy or the death of spouse – there would always be someone else there to save you; to pick up all the pieces and put you back together again.

Standing at this party with this stranger in front of me, I felt as though I had been saved.

I told him that I didn't fancy drinking the vodka, that I was feeling a bit worse for wear, then I laughed and told him that all I actually wanted was a cup of tea.

'Then that is what you shall have,' he said with a twinkle in his eye. We left the party that I had been at for just over an hour together, hand in hand.

He told me to call him D. 'Everybody does,' he said.

* * *

He took me to a McDonald's and bought me a cup of tea and a doughnut and told me anecdotes of nights out and holidays that made me feel like I had barely lived a life at all; which, of course, I hadn't.

'What will folk think when I tell them I took a girl to McDonald's on a first date?' He tucked into a burger with fries, apparently not conscious of eating in front of strangers.

'So this is the first date?' I asked quietly as I attempted to sip scalding-hot tea from a polystyrene cup as graciously as I could.

'Many more to come, I hope.' He raised his eyebrows and flashed a cheeky grin, exposing that tooth gap.

* * *

He dropped me off at my cousin's house an hour later. Time seemed to stand still as his lips met mine, unfurling all of my senses. I could smell alcohol on his breath, but beyond that, there was a scent about him that was hypnotic.

He left me with my knees weakening and a promise of another date.

'Once I've shown you a good night out and how I treat a lady, you'll never want to let me go,' he called as he walked off down the path and back to the waiting taxi.

I watched the car drive away and felt the pang in my gut; this was just like the films I had watched.

I was already missing him.

3

NOW

I was alone in the house again. I still had hours to go to make it to the end of this day. I still felt the tension rising through my body, the thoughts layering themselves one over another, each becoming entwined with the next. I heard a voice, a voice I recognised. I looked around the hallway where I was standing alone.

'Don't do it,' the voice said. I was being pulled back in time.

I looked behind me again. 'Don't do it,' they said, and suddenly they were there with the same kindness in their eyes; behind their veil of sadness they too were trying to overcome their difficulties, and they wanted me to try as well. If I just unlocked and locked the front door an even six times, everything would be okay, no one would get hurt. No one would die. Why couldn't they just understand that?

I felt the actual presence of someone behind me, a voice that was very real; not from the past. I spun around and there was Sophia, another house mate.

She had put her shoulder-length blonde, curly hair in bunches and was wearing dungarees; she looked like a children's

TV presenter and reminded me of all those years I spent hours watching children's TV programmes.

'That one's a bit tricky, huh?' She smiled at me, her blue eyes twinkled. I realised I had found my way to the front door and my hands were on the doorknob.

I felt a wave of shame flood over me. Sophia was the eldest of the three house mates, but still so young at only twenty-three. I was drawn to her more than the other two, yet I still felt like a small child who had been caught with their hand in the cookie jar. The noise of the door must have brought Sophia from her room, where she spent an inordinate amount of time studying hard. She had told me on the first night I was here how studying had been inbuilt into her from a young age by her parents, who were both head and shoulders above everyone else in their chosen careers. I knew they put too much pressure on Sophia to be better than she was. Sophia was being kind and patient with me – a trait I had recognised in her from the first day – but I was sure all three of the girls would be sick of me once they began to hear me opening and closing doors over and over. But I was beginning to enjoy being around others again. I had spent far too long solitary. I was glad Sophia had appeared when she had. When someone else was in the house, it felt nice. It felt right. Perhaps I could start to appreciate having someone there for me again. I had pushed away everyone from my past a long time ago.

I thought about calling them from time to time, my cousins, or even my mother. I was an only child. My father had passed away when I was just fifteen, so I had the guilt of the unanswered calls from my mum to deal with. In the three years that had passed, I still couldn't bring myself to pick up the phone and reach out even though so many people had texted me after it happened, telling me they were there for me. What was the point of reaching out to those whose lives were so far removed from me now? It would only stir up all the memories; people were very good at forgiving, but I knew no one would ever forget what I did.

'You have to just twist it like this.' Sophia leant in past me. I could smell her coconut conditioner; the one I had seen on the bathroom shelf on my first day in the house and inhaled so I could get a sense of who I was going to be sharing a house with. I looked at Sophia's hand on the doorknob as she tried to demonstrate how sometimes the lock would get stuck. I smiled at her vain attempt to make my behaviour appear normal.

'Thank you,' I said, and I knew from the way her smile reached her eyes that she was genuine.

'Look, tell me to do one if you think I'm being rude,' Sophia said. 'As you still have a few days to go until your course starts, I wondered if you fancied a little project to keep you busy?'

* * *

We stood next to one another outside the large green wooden summerhouse. It ran about ten feet along the back edge of the garden in front of the fence and hedge that divided the gardens. All along the side facing us were large floor-to-ceiling windows. The rest of the garden was square. A few small slabs of concrete passed for a patio just outside the back door, then it was mostly grass with modest borders of small, easy-to-manage plants with the summerhouse perched right at the top end.

'It's such a great little unit, it seems a shame to let it go to waste just sitting there filled with junk. I thought, maybe if you were not too busy and you fancied the challenge, you might enjoy emptying it out and giving it a spruce? We could all chip in for some new furniture or accessories. It could be a really nice spot to come and sit now it's getting warmer.' Sophia turned to me with a grimace. 'What do you think? I don't want to overload you.'

'I'll do it,' I said with a small smile. Inside, I felt a wave of relief. Much like the kitchen, I'd had my eye on the summerhouse since I had arrived, but I hadn't wished to sound impertinent by offering to give it a once over.

'Oh wow, that's amazing. Really, the others will be so pleased. I'd love to do it myself, but my workload is fierce at the moment – I barely have enough time to eat and sleep.'

'It's fine – it will keep me busy for a few days. Plus, the weather is picking up – I'll enjoy being outside.'

'Great! Just chuck all the stuff we don't want on the lawn and I'll send a photo of it to Mini's uncle and see what he wants to do with it.'

'Well, no time like the present,' I said as I headed back to the house to fetch Marigolds, bin bags and spray guns, feeling for the first time in a long time a flurry of enthusiasm and a sense of purpose.

* * *

Once I was alone and inside the summerhouse, I felt the relaxation come in waves, but each time I acknowledged it, it dispersed, and the aggressive butterflies crept back into my gut. Cleaning was a welcome distraction and brought back a swell of relief. I looked around at the dusty interior of the summerhouse, with its stacked boxes and stuffy furniture. Sophia was right; this would make a nice place to hang out. I could imagine myself sat here on a warm day, reading or sketching some ideas.

I began dragging the furniture outside. It was all old stuff that probably once belonged in the main house. It was just about good enough for a charity shop. Once I had dragged the last chair outside, I collapsed into it. It was a brown velour lounger with a chrome base and looked like it had come straight out of the seventies. I imagined once it would have been fashionable, but it had seen better days. I squinted up at the spring-afternoon sun, and I allowed myself a moment to close my eyes. As I did, I felt a surge of tiredness engulf me.

* * *

I opened my eyes and gulped in a breath. I looked around and tried to establish where I was. Looking up at the sky, the clouds had enveloped the sun. I felt a chill and grasped around for my cardigan, but it was still inside the summerhouse. I stood slowly, trying to shift the fog in my head and reconnect with my surroundings. I turned back towards the summerhouse when I heard a tiny voice, saying something I couldn't quite make out. It seemed to be coming from the other side of the fence. It was the sort of sound that would skim past the eardrums of others, but the sound of a small child's voice was so familiar that it would never pass me by. The butter-like velvet tone carried by the slight breeze had me floored. It was as though I knew the voice. *Mama*, the word floated across the fence.

Suddenly I was no longer in a garden in Richmond, but miles away, in another time, in another place where I was reciting from a favourite book. The words come back at me, muddled and broken through a tiny mouth. I laughed because of the unadulterated joy as their words skipped along like a song. It was music to my ears, but a sonnet that was so painfully nostalgic I wanted to crawl into a ball.

The gut-wrenching reality hit me as I was snapped out of the daydream; that voice had gone and would never return. And the voice from across the fence, only a vivid reminder of the colossal mistake I was still repenting for.

Up until now I had not seen or heard anything come from

next door, and my bedroom window looked straight into their garden, but I felt that I needed to get a look at the neighbours. I wondered if they had been away somewhere or perhaps had just moved in.

I looked towards the end of the garden and I could see the shrubbery parted as it curved to the right. Could there be a way into the neighbour's garden from ours? I wasn't ready to start crawling about on my hands and knees just yet, and I remembered there was a stepladder in the summerhouse. I set it up as close to the fence as I could get it, then I cautiously walked up, one step, two, three until my head was just peeping over the fence. I listened with intent and anticipation for the child to show itself, my mouth dry and my palms damp with sweat.

Why did I torture myself like this? Maybe because today, the anniversary, was so significant and the voice sounded so familiar. A voice that would forever stay that way in my mind because it never had a chance to evolve and change and grow. As I conjured up an image in my mind, the child appeared in the garden. A fleeting moment. He or she? I couldn't quite tell.

Their hair was a shock of untameable brown curls, much like the ones I had tried to train, but to no avail. Yet there were those curls again, floating past me, as if time had rewound. The child seemed to coast past in slow motion, their feet just on the patio, heading for the patch of grass.

Then suddenly, I saw a flash of blonde hair. A hand stretched out and grabbed the child's arm. The child threw their head back in protest. The innocent calls of, 'Mama,' turned to a blood-curdling yell as they were dragged backwards and out of my sight. I heard a door slam so hard it ricocheted around my chest, and all I was left with was the echo of the child's screams.

As I stood on the stepladder, the scream continued, but became fainter as though they were falling, falling, falling...

My foot became air as I struggled to find somewhere to place it. Before I knew where I was, I was looking up at the sky with my leg twisted backwards and a sharp pain resonating from my ankle to my waist.

'Regi, are you okay?' I turned my head to my right and Karen, my other house mate, was standing over me inquisitively, yet without too much concern in her tone or her face. She always had such a serious aura about her from the way she dressed, always blue skinny jeans and long-sleeve T-shirts, to the way she wore her hair tied back so tightly in a neat, sleek ponytail, it seemed to pull the skin up from around her eyes.

'I think so.' I looked up at the stepladder. I had slipped just three steps. I could feel tenderness on my shin where I knew a large bruise would form later.

'Well, okay, then let's get you up.' She reached out her hand, which I ignored, pushing myself up instead. I went to put the weight on both legs and pain shot through my ankle. I sucked in my breath through my teeth.

'Right, erm, okay. Let's get you sat down, shall we?' Karen said uneasily and looked impatiently around before grabbing the lounger I had been sat on when I fell asleep. I watched as she awkwardly manoeuvred it over to me, its weighty legs protesting against the overgrown grass. After painfully observing her efforts, I refrained from telling her I could have walked to it quicker.

'I see you've started on the summerhouse.' Karen took out a tissue and blew her nose. 'Bloody hay fever.' She wiped her nose and shoved the tissue into the back pocket of her jeans. I turned to look at the array of furniture scattered on the lawn.

'Yes, I was, and then I kind of got distracted.' I sat down.

'Spying on the neighbours?' she said as though it was the kind of thing she expected from me.

'Just. Interested.' I scuffed at the grass with my healthy foot.

'Well, their gardens aren't nearly as good as ours,' she said.

'Do you know much about the neighbours then?' I tried to sound nonchalant.

Karen shook her head. 'Not really, I've lived here for a year almost and I haven't met anyone yet.' She sucked in a breath and closed her eyes, then let out a huge sneeze. Another tissue was ripped from a packet. 'Speaking from experience, I also think it's quite possible to live next door to someone and never ever see them.' Karen dabbed her nose and pushed the wet tissue into her back pocket with the other one.

'So have you ever seen the neighbours on this side? Did you know they have a child?'

'I've never seen a child. This street is mainly professionals and students, not very family friendly. I only know that information from Mini's uncle. He rents out about six houses on this street.'

'Right.' I remembered them all telling me this when I came to look at the house. I scratched my neck and looked around at the furniture scattered around on the grass. 'I'll ring the charity shop to see if they can come and pick any of this up.'

'Good idea. Fancy a brew?' Karen began walking back to the house.

'Yes, great.'

I hobbled through to the kitchen and Karen presented me with a nettle tea at the kitchen table. I had stopped drinking real, caffeinated tea and coffee years ago, believing that caffeine was the source of my insomnia. It took me many more therapy sessions before it was revealed to me that because my mind was in hyper-vigilant mode in the day, by night my brain was reminding me it wasn't safe to sleep.

'Shit, we're out of milk,' Karen said and went to head out of the kitchen door.

'It's okay, I'll go.' I stood up to test the pressure on my ankle. The pain had begun to subside.

'No, stay, it's for my coffee – you've just got your tea.'

I needed to walk; the shock and stress of the fall and the child's voice and that image of the mother, or whoever it was, pulling them back with such force meant I could not relax. I needed to do something or I wouldn't rest. Karen looked perturbed as she followed me into the hallway, where I pulled on my purple tie-dye scarf and slouch hat.

I looked over my shoulder. 'It's fine, I'll be back in ten minutes.'

She looked on with a perplexed expression.

'It's fine,' I assured her. 'I need the walk to clear my head after the fall.'

'You could be concussed!'

'I'm fine.' I batted away her comments with my hand. I stood for a second as she pulled out another tissue and let out an almighty sneeze.

'Want me to pick you up some antihistamines?'

'No, hate them. They make me drowsy.'

'Okay then.' I opened the door and walked down the steps and onto the street. A slight wave of calm washed over me, but before long the nagging sensation was back. I needed to perform some sort of compulsion; I wasn't sure just walking would suffice. As I passed next-door's house, I looked up at it. It was the same as ours, a three-storey Victorian building. I could see no sign of life through any of the windows.

I counted each step I took until I reached a hundred, which brought me almost to the end of the street.

I turned right and headed towards the mews, carefully avoiding all the cracks.

* * *

Inside the grocery shop, I rearranged three jars of pickled onions and two cans of tomato soup on the shelf, picked up two pints of semi-skimmed milk and headed to the counter. It was the same guy who had been serving me earlier, and he eyed me with some sort of recognition or curiosity. I barely managed a smile as by now the day's events had caught up with me. The woman with the medicine this morning, the child next door and then my fall. I could feel my body slowing down for the day, and I was already thinking about my bed and how sleep came a little more easily now. In the beginning, when I was walking through each day like a zombie, sleep was a form of torture. I would exhaust myself in the day, only to nod off for twenty minutes at a time, waking in a blind panic. This would go on all night and for weeks at a time.

I thanked the shopkeeper and stepped outside into the mews. The light was starting to fade as the afternoon came to an end. I was just comforting myself with the knowledge that I had my bedtime routine to complete – put on clean bedsheets, shower, brush my teeth for thirty-four seconds – when I saw a glimpse of a figure out of the corner of my eye.

I recognised the frame immediately.

I began walking hurriedly towards home. I touched my wrist, where there was now a burning sensation, as though someone had been holding it tightly just a moment before. Flashes of a face to accompany the figure were suddenly in my mind's eye and I became riddled with compulsive thoughts, all firing at me like bullets one after another. I hurried away from the mews, stopped and caught my breath. I took a moment to lean on a wall, and as I did, a man came out of his house and bent down to get a look at me.

'You okay, love?'

I looked down the street, towards the mews where I had just come from. There was no one there. I touched my wrists. I could still feel a slight sensation, but it was fading.

'Yes, yes, just a bit tired.' I stood up. The man stood back and watched me warily for a moment before going back into his house.

I snatched a look down the street behind me again and the figure appeared on the corner. A tall man, wearing dark clothes. A black cap was pulled down over his face, his head slightly tilted so only he could see me.

Although I couldn't see his eyes, I recognised everything else about him. I pulled my cardigan around me and began walking away from him at speed, I tripped on a crack in the pavement and stumbled forward. I righted myself, then stole a look down the street to the corner, only to see it was empty.

The man was gone. I looked around to see if he had made it across to the other side of the road when I had been racing along, but that was empty too. I suddenly doubted myself. Had I imagined it?

I wanted to believe I could come here and stay hidden and anonymous. But I knew on this occasion my mind wasn't playing tricks on me.

I was no longer hidden.

He had found me.

4

The weekend began, and I found myself drawn to the sanctuary of the summerhouse again, my notebook and pencil in hand, ready to prep ideas for textiles projects. Mini's uncle had given the all clear for the old furniture to go to the charity shop, so a van had been round and took the lot early that morning. I looked around at the blank canvas, feeling a sense of anticipation of what it could become and, for a moment, a slight butterfly sensation in my stomach. I was so unused to the subtlety of those kinds of butterflies compared to the fierceness of the anxiety that could take my gut hostage on a daily basis. But as I had been told many times before by countless therapists and counsellors: receive any amount of positivity you can and hold on to it.

But my brain had a funny way of tricking me into thinking I still did not deserve happiness, and no sooner had the light relief arrived, than the darker feelings chased it away.

Mini popped her head around the summerhouse door at lunchtime, assessing the room from the safety of the threshold, not wanting to dirty the brand-new duck-egg-blue brogues she was sporting.

'How's it going? Thought I'd remind you to eat!' She smiled sweetly. 'Oh, and to show off these babies.' She wiggled her foot through the door.

'They're beautiful,' I said sincerely. I remembered the pleasure gained from a brand-new pair of shoes and how they made everything you wore look great again.

I stood up and wiped my forehead just below my Alice band. I had been wiping the floor with a cloth, and dust coated my jeans.

'Wow, you should have done a tap-to-tidy on this place.'

I furrowed my brow.

'What's a tap-to-tidy?' I stood up and felt my muscles ache where I had been crouched.

'Oh, it's all over Instagram. These "cleanstagrammers", they post a photo of their disorganised kitchen counter then ask you to tap the screen, which takes you to the next picture, where – *voilà!* – the kitchen counter is tidy. Like a before-and-after photo.' Mini looked longingly round the space. 'This would have made an awesome tap-to-tidy post.'

I still was not entirely sure what she was talking about. Technology hadn't been a part of my life for so long. I had only recently opened an Instagram account with the intention of using it to showcase my artwork, and so far I had posted precisely three photos. One of an autumn sunset that had inspired me to create something similar in textile-form, and the other two were some preliminary sketches of a piece I wanted to create with recycled rubbish.

Mini stepped aside to let me out of the summerhouse.

'Look.' Mini was at my side, precariously close. I felt my body clench up. She brought up her Instagram account on her phone then held it close to my face; I could smell strawberry hand cream and mint chewing gum as she began scrolling.

'This woman is a cleanstagrammer. I follow a few of them – some of these women aren't just cleaners, they are accidental interior designers.' Mini shook her head. 'I mean, it's great and all, but I do get a tad jealous that these women are getting paid thousands a year in sponsorship and given endless free products when I have to fork out to pay to learn how to be an interior designer. Sometimes I just think I should do this instead.'

I looked on in amazement as Mini scrolled through wall after wall of little tiny squares, all showcasing perfect symmetrical images with impeccably clean surfaces and immaculately made beds. I looked on at the incredible neatness in each photo, and a sublime sense of calm washed over me.

'I mean look at this woman, Clean and Bright, seven hundred and fifty thousand followers, and now she's launching her own home fragrance.' Mini carried on relentlessly scrolling. 'And this woman, Heather Duster. I mean, that's clever, right? Well, she has almost a million followers. A million people, Regi – it's insane, isn't it?'

'Wow, it's a whole other world I had no idea about,' I said, itching to see more of the symmetry and orderliness.

'It's a clever little app. But then all clever things come in small packages.' She giggled, looking down at herself. 'I mean, look at some of these accounts – they all must have massive OCD to keep their houses that spotless...' Mini trailed off and looked at me with slight panic in her eyes. Her phone fell to her side and she took a step backwards. I felt relief to get my personal space back. 'I mean, that's not a bad thing – if it gets their houses looking that clean, I wouldn't complain.'

I gave Mini a reassuring smile. 'It's fine, Mini, like all people with OCD, I don't consider myself to have a problem. We're all absolutely fine.' I made my eyes go a bit funny and Mini laughed.

The tension between us washed away. I had told all the girls
when I came to view the house that I had what had been classi-
fied by a doctor as OCD, and that it manifested itself in the daily
behaviours I had to do. Sophia was the only one who really took
an avid interest; she had sat up with me on the first night, long
after the other two had gone to bed, and asked me all about it.
She was always careful not to tread too close to the crux of the
problem, where my behaviour originated from; that part was
never going to be open for discussion.

'Anyway, enjoy the cleanstagrammers, but don't overdo it.
Studies have been done into the overall mental health of Instagram users and found that it can actually trigger depression and
anxiety.' Mini pointed over at the summerhouse. 'It's looking
good in there already.' And she sashayed away in that dreamy way
of hers, her mind already on something else.

I looked over at the summerhouse. Yes, it had potential, but it
needed a good clean-up and a sort-out. I found myself drawn to
my phone, to my Instagram account, and before I knew it, I had
begun searching for cleanstagrammers and interior design
accounts. I clicked and clicked furiously until I found an account
that really caught my eye. Heeding Mini's words, if I limited the
amount of accounts I followed, I wouldn't be doing any more
damage to my mental health.

As I looked through, I took the notebook and pen I brought in
with me, in case I had any brainwaves for my textile designs, and I
started noting down ideas, ways to hang photos and how to position plant pots, things I initially thought I would use for the
summerhouse but before I knew it I was discovering tips and
techniques that I could take into the house with me: where to get
labels from to label jars, ways to clean a sink without harsh chem-
icals and which products to use on the floor. Some of the

cleanstagrammers even had links to printable worksheets that you could work to on a weekly basis and I thought about the satisfaction I could gain from the organisation and how soothing that could be.

I was drawn to an account called Mrs Clean. Her Instagram profile was hundreds of squares of simplicity, elegance and symmetry. I couldn't get enough of it.

I scrolled all the way back to her very first post, which showed an image of her standing next to her mop and bucket, with only her legs in shot and one pink-Marigold-cladded hand by her side. The background was blurred but I could see she was standing in a very bright and stark-white kitchen.

Under the photo she had given a short introduction to herself. From then on every photo was exceptionally shot, accompanied by relevant content. Comparing her account to others, it appeared to me that Mrs Clean had gone into this Instagramming lark with a clear business head. Other accounts had clearly evolved from dodgy grainy photos with busy backgrounds to the polished images they were producing now. Mrs Clean's were all professional-looking from the outset. Hers was the one I chose to follow.

Filled with inspiration for the house, I wandered back inside to see what I could get started on.

The back door led into the kitchen, and as I arrived inside, I could see the coast was clear. My body was saying, 'Do it, do it,' although words from another time told me, 'Don't.' But still, I did it anyway. I closed and locked then unlocked the back door with the key six times.

I heard a shuffle behind me as I locked the door for the final time. I turned around and there was Karen's boyfriend, Steve. I stopped statue still as Steve's eyes bore into me. Instantly, my palms felt clammy and I felt my chest go tight. My breath became laboured. I stole a look across the kitchen at the only other exit.

Steve followed my look. 'My cousin has OCD,' he said flatly. I ignored his statement. From day one I had felt an eeriness in his presence; the way he launched into conversation without the general formalities of a greeting first.

Steve had his hands in his pockets. He was the opposite of the type I would have gone for in the past. I had always gone for the big-built, tall men with strong hands that I had grown accustomed to being placed firmly on my waist and lifting me up over their shoulders. Hands that had once given me the security I had craved, but now I could only associate them with being wrapped tightly around my wrists, pulling me, dragging me.

I couldn't figure out what Karen saw in Steve. He was a short man with small hands that he perpetually kept in the pockets of any trousers he wore. Today, he was wearing jogging bottoms, his hands placed causally in the pockets as though he had been standing there for an age, perhaps observing me for longer than I would like to contemplate. His head was shaved very close to his scalp; he wore it this way as a homage to the army, which he was no longer a part of. Was it this resemblance to someone I didn't wish to remember that made me recoil whenever Steve was around?

Steve looked around the kitchen and not at me. I tried to follow his gaze to see what he was looking at.

'Karen about?' He sniffed. His voice was hollow and empty. For a moment, I considered if he cared at all if Karen was about.

It occurred to me that if Steve was here alone, then he had made his own way into the house. He could only have come through the front door, which would have meant using a key. Surely Karen wouldn't have handed out a key to her boyfriend of three weeks without discussing it with the rest of the house? I thought that a successful house share was about being respectful to your fellow house mates. This was the sort of scenario that I had envisioned would be worthy of a house meeting. My body gave an involuntary shudder as I considered the prospect of Steve having access to the house any time, day or night.

I should by now, at my age, have the emotional energy to approach Karen and raise the issue with her, but for some reason I could not imagine myself doing that. Instead, I began to imagine how things would be from here on in, having to sneak around my own home, always in fear of the prospect of bumping into Steve. The thoughts began tumbling through my mind before I could stop them and rapid ruminating led to catastrophising, as I imagined a drunken Steve arriving here after the pub and trying to find his way into my bedroom.

'I haven't seen her today,' I said breathlessly, and then finally, after what had felt like an age, I edged forward and began to make my way past Steve. We were both stood close to the pantry and the bins, leaving little space to manoeuvre, so as I passed him, he turned his body at the same time to walk past me, presumably to go to the garden to smoke a rolly. Suddenly, but only momentarily, we were almost nose to nose. All my senses heightened. Panic rose in my throat; it felt as though something was stuck there. I swallowed, but it felt forced and uncomfortable. He was so close to me I could smell his skin. Then casually, without uttering another word, he stepped to one side and let me past.

I felt as though my instincts were lagging, but then some might say that my instincts weren't properly sharpened beforehand, otherwise I would have foreseen the incident that changed my life forever.

* * *

With a dry mouth and a pounding heart I found my way into my bedroom, locked and unlocked the door six times, ending on a lock. Then I stripped the one-day-old sheet from the mattress and pulled out clean, white, starched sheets from the ottoman at the end of the bed. I set about pulling the flat sheet over the mattress protector and finished up with perfectly tight hospital corners; a learned skill that transported me back to sleeping in a single bed in a six-by-eight-foot room a mere few weeks ago.

After that experience, changing the sheets every day became an obsession. It evolved from when I was unable to sleep and would lie in bed feeling numb, thinking of things to do and jobs to keep my mind occupied. Anything to make me feel something. It had now become a compulsion, and if I didn't do it each night, I would lie in the sheets thinking about the amount of dirt or hair that could have contaminated them in the last twenty-four hours, and then I just couldn't rest; I knew something terrible was sure to happen if I slept in dirty sheets.

I threw on the duvet cover and pulled on four clean pillow-cases. Then I sat on the end of the newly made bed and thought about Mrs Clean's Instagram that I followed earlier and what tips there might be for bedrooms. Mine was okay, but I needed more tasks to do each day, simply making a bed every night wasn't time-consuming enough. Sure, I'd have a workload to contend with when the introductory course started on Monday, but that still left me with plenty of hours to fill each day with the other menial tasks.

I pulled out my phone from my back pocket and found my way back to Mrs Clean's page. As I entered her profile, I was presented with yet another new photo. It was an image of a kitchen, taken on an angle so it was lopsided; it was a technique I have seen done a few times already in just a few hours scrolling through different profiles.

I could see why her account was so popular: over one million followers. I looked again at the kitchen, and I saw some sort of resemblance to the size and shape of our kitchen downstairs, which made me feel as though something similar could be created to modernise it. Mrs Clean's kitchen was a mix of pastel-grey kitchen units and stark-white surfaces, gleaming and shining, with a deep, aluminium double sink.

Without thinking, I hit the heart button and liked the photo along with 32,135 other people. Would Mrs Clean see my like out of everyone else's?

I began scrolling through some more of her other posts.

I was drawn to an image of a hallway. The walls were bright white, the floor a light hardwood. On the wall were three large black-and-white prints in frames, but because the photo had been taken at an angle, I couldn't see them properly. I noticed that there were two small grey circles underneath the photo, so I swiped across and another photo was revealed. This one showed the three monochrome prints straight on. One was of a volcano erupting, one was of a wave crashing against a cluster of rocks, the third was a series of waterfalls. I looked at the image of the photos for a long time and imagined myself standing in her hallway as though I was standing in an art gallery.

I continued scrolling. I looked at the date of the first post and found it fascinating how one woman could go from having zero followers to having over one million within a year. I thought about the summerhouse and how I could make it my project, upload some photos to my Instagram site and take some inspiration from Mrs Clean. I could already feel the satisfaction within me growing, overtaking the numb feeling I had been stuck with for years. Just looking at the glorious organised symmetry stirred up something within me. Things I hadn't felt for a long time. And I wanted to feel more of them.

But just as I was starting to believe I could immerse myself amongst these tiny squares as a way to escape the horrors of the past, my phone rang. Across the screen was a mobile number I knew, and suddenly I was being dragged right back there.

5

We had been together for three months when he asked me to move in with him. I was ecstatic. We had done everything that couples in the movies did. He took me shopping, bought me clothes and jewellery, we sat at the back of the cinema throwing popcorn in each other's hair and drove to the seaside to ride the Ferris wheel and eat candyfloss.

Once we were living together, all I could think about was those films I had watched over and over with Mum. How those couples existed next to one another, cooking together, brushing and flossing their teeth next to each other in the bathroom, then taking it in turns getting the kids to football practice. Families sitting around a table, having too loud conversations, but no one minding because the love was so fierce.

I was scared to tell Mum I'd be moving out, then D encouraged me to just get it over with. I apologised profusely to her.

Her response was, 'You're fine. Go and do what you need to do – don't let me hold you back. God knows I let your father do enough of that to me.' She looked up towards the heavens, something she would do every time she spoke of my dad, even though she wasn't religious. I remember him, of course. I remember it all. But I choose to block it out. The only reminders were the episodes that Mum had. Too often for my liking. She said she could cope. I promised to visit every week.

We didn't move far. The flat we found was just on the outskirts of town, about a ten-minute drive from Mum's. There were no bus routes that went back that way, and I still hadn't learned to drive.

'You can walk to the shops from here,' he said. It was only later, my fifth time at the shops, that I realised I would always be making these trips alone.

I never knew exactly what it was he did. He told me he worked in construction and that he had an office in the next town. I tried on occasion to dig a little deeper; I wanted to understand his job better so when I was speaking with other people, I could explain it in great detail with admiration and pride.

'If I tell you, I'll have to kill you,' he joked. But by then I had not learned how quickly a joke could turn sour, so I laughed along as though it was the funniest thing anyone had ever said. It was fine, I thought. He works hard and supports us. I don't need to know the ins and outs. Only the pit of my stomach was protesting; didn't couples share everything? There weren't supposed to be lies and secrets. That's not how it played out on the screen in the hundreds of films I had watched growing up as a kid.

Sometimes he would come home from wherever he had been and look at me sat on the sofa as though I was a leech. 'You could have cleaned up.' There was a sourness to his tone that I was starting to hear more regularly, but which I attributed to tiredness.

The flat was spotless. I had nothing else to do with my days anyway. I had suggested I get a part-time job, but he had insisted that I didn't need to, that everything was taken care of and that all I needed to do was be here for when he came home.

'I need you, babes.' He would put those strong arms around me, the harsh words he had said moments ago already evaporated and forgotten. He would draw me close, I would feel him press himself against me and I knew I was worth something.

I thought about my mum often; I would call her from the flat when he was out. I don't know how that became a pattern, but it did. Somehow a phone call with my own mother became something I felt I needed to hide from him because after one month of living together, I still hadn't visited as I had promised. Whenever I mentioned her, he would wrinkle his nose and busy himself with anything to hand, a laptop or his phone usually. My suggestions of a day out and popping in to see my mum quickly evaporated around us.

I began to wonder why it was becoming more difficult to get him to do things for me.

'I could take a taxi?' I said to him one day. 'It would save me bothering you.' I felt a nervous lump form in my throat.

'But I like you bothering me.' He wrapped me up in his arms. I felt the lump melt away.

Then he pushed me back a couple of inches so I could see his face.

'Babes, you really want to go back to that life? What is there for you now? This is your life, here, with me. Things are really starting to take off – soon we can move out of this place into somewhere spectacular, and, you know' – he looked down and touched my stomach – 'maybe have a little family of our own one day.'

I felt my heart leap because I had already noticed that I was late. My cycles had been as regular as clockwork for over four years. So I knew. But something made me keep it a secret for a little while longer, perhaps the foresight that it was to be so short-lived.

I enjoyed those few short weeks of just me knowing about my baby, each of us simply existing, one within the other. I cherished having something so precious that was dependent on only me. Even then, not knowing how soon it would be gone, I loved it so hard, so fiercely. When I told him he would soon be a dad, although he laughed and spun me around, telling me what a clever girl I was, he went very quiet for days afterwards. It wasn't long after that something switched within him, as though he could sense there was a possibility I could love something or someone more than him.

Just eleven weeks into the pregnancy, as I lay there bleeding, the baby falling out of me, I played the films out in my mind. I had watched them a hundred times: *Dirty Dancing* and *When a Man Loves a Woman* were particular favourites and reminded me that I could still be saved.

It wasn't his fault, I told myself over and over. Next time I would remain sullen; less conceited. I still loved him.

Instagram post: 27th April 2019
Hello, my little cleaners, how are you all doing on this bright spring morning? I have been busy buying cushions. They are my absolute favourite thing to buy because they really are one of the main state-ment pieces to each room. I get a little obsessed. I like to match them to each season, so I am busy adding some yellows and greens and pinks to my sofas now. It's out with the winter accessories and in with some spring pieces. I hope you enjoy looking at my photos as much as I enjoy creating the looks for you all to enjoy.
Have a great day.

Mrs C x

#ilovespring #MrsClean #cleanstagrammer #cleaning

127,980 likes

mrsj.r You are such an inspiration, Mrs Clean. I love the mix of the spring colours.

carolineness17 I would never have put green and pink together like that, but it really works, doesn't it?

vinsta_gramma I'm getting these for my wife.

lucybest65 It must be thrilling to sit around all day with nothing to do but fluff your cushions.

vinsta_gramma I've been telling my wife that for years lol.

We were all sat in the lounge at the end of the weekend. There was a gardening programme on the TV that none of us were watching. Mini and Karen had been shooting a TikTok video, Sophie had a pile of crocheting material in her lap, halfway through a pink scarf that I had been eyeing up since she began.

I had sensed an atmosphere forming about fifteen minutes ago, but I was trying to ignore it. I caught the girls looking at one another as though they were trying to find the right moment to say something.

I had lots to do to prepare for my course that started the next day, and as I stood to leave, Sophia cleared her throat and spoke.

'Regi, we want to have a party next weekend for Mini's birthday. We hope you don't mind.'

I looked around the room at the sombre faces, and then I had to stifle a laugh.

'If it's a party surely you should all look a little a happier?'

Karen and Mini exchanged looks.

'The girls – not me might I add – thought that it could be too much for you,' Karen said impatiently, her eyes red from the hay fever, 'and because this is your home too, we didn't want to turf you out.'

'We're skint,' Mini piped up. 'And a house party is cheap and so much fun.'

I thought back to the house parties I had attended when I was a younger, funnier version of myself. When friends would pop over at the drop of a hat. When life felt like it meant something and everything was just beginning, like a flower blooming. Only to be cruelly crushed as soon as it blossomed.

'Well, of course, you do whatever suits,' I said as I felt my stomach tighten and my grip increase on my thumbs.

'So, you'll be here?' Karen asked. It sounded as though she didn't want me to be, and that going out would have been the better option.

'Of course,' I said breezily. I stood up and picked up my empty mug from the coffee table. 'I'm off to bed – big day tomorrow.'

'Yes, it is – good luck. Hope you find your way around the campus okay,' Sophia said with an empathetic smile.

There were no first-day-of-university jitters. It was simply something I had to do.

As I stood my phone began to ring. Its sound penetrated the whole room.

'Jeez, Regi!' Karen squeaked and covered her ears. 'Are you going deaf?'

'Sorry, sorry.' I went to grab the phone and in my haste I knocked it on the floor. The ringtone rang out loud and trill. 'Sorry.' I fell to my knees, picking it up from under the coffee table. By the time the phone was in my hand, the ringing had stopped. I looked at the missed call that had no name to it, but the number that I would never forget. I felt my gut lurch, the same way it had when it rang just yesterday.

'Sorry, I... I guess don't use the phone that often.' And I

didn't. I had bought a new phone when I moved to London. I had not given this number to anyone from my past. But, of course, there were some people who, no matter how hard I tried to hide, would always be able to find me. I knew it would only have been a matter of time. I only wished I could have had a little longer to enjoy starting over and building a new life for myself.

'Are you going to ring them back?' Mini said. 'It sounded urgent at that volume.' She laughed and looked around the room for encouragement.

'I'll check the settings.' I held the phone up like the alien object it was. 'It's newish – I need to just find the volume.'

'Here.' Karen stood up and brashly removed the phone from my hand, then she expertly navigated her way into the settings and found the volume control. She dragged it down with her finger.

'See, just like this. That's at a more acceptable level. Especially when you're on the train tomorrow.' Karen sounded slightly irked, a tone that had crept into some of her interactions with me, and I had yet to work out why.

'Okay,' I said, feeling the heat of the embarrassment creep up my neck. For the first time since I had been living here, I felt as though I were the older one trying to fit in with the young, cool kids. 'I'll be off to bed then.'

'Night,' they all called in unison, and I headed for the door. On the other side, I heard their voices drop to a whisper followed by the shrill sound of Mini laughing.

I felt the edginess creeping around my body, but comforted myself with the notion that soon I would be in bed with clean sheets, looking at what Mrs Clean had posted in the last couple of hours.

I walked into the small utility room off the hallway. I bent down and retrieved the clean sheets from the dryer. I took a moment to close my eyes and inhale the sweet, floral scent.

As I pulled the sheets away from my nose, I opened my eyes and stumbled backwards in horror as I saw the undisputed silhouette of a face close to the small window opposite me. I pulled the sheets back to my nose, shut my eyes and started breathing in the sweetness to calm myself. It's only my imagination, I repeated to myself. But I could still see the face in my mind's eye; the perpetual sardonic look, his lip curled at the corner, the laughter in his eyes that in the beginning I loved but by the end was as though he was laughing at me. I felt a tightening around my wrists, and I was wrestling with the blankets that had seemed to have become tangled around my arms and neck. It was no use, I couldn't stop the panic rising. I tried to focus on the scent on the sheets. Just breathe it in, Regi. You're okay.

Suddenly hands were on me, tight around my wrists and then tugging at the sheets as I pulled harder.

'Regi,' came Sophia's voice. The sheets were pulled down from my face and Sophia began unravelling them from around my arms.

I looked to the window. The face had gone, but I could still feel a fuzzy sensation on my wrists. Sophia was looking at me. She put her hand on my shaking arm. I instinctively jerked it away.

'What happened, Regi?' she said softly.

I dropped the sheets in the empty laundry basket and put my hand over my mouth, my other hand on my hip. I breathed through my hand and blew out a long breath. Then I removed my hand and placed it on my cheek. 'Do you know, it was the weirdest thing. The condensation on the window, it caught me off-guard. I thought it was a face.'

'Whose face, like Jesus's? You should have taken a photo and sent it into a magazine – they pay money for that.' Mini was trying to squeeze through the door and into the small space that was already overcrowded with two bodies.

'I don't think she meant that,' Sophia said sombrely. 'Did you?' There was a sense of pleading in her voice. I didn't want to drag these girls into everything so soon after moving in. They knew I was damaged goods. Did they need to know the rest?

I choked out a laugh. 'To be honest, it was more like Pope Gregory VII.'

'Our brains are hardwired to see faces in everything. It was just a hallucination.' Mini moved a little closer, and I pressed myself against the wall. 'In fact, everything we see is a hallucination – you'll never actually see reality because your brain—'

'Thanks, Mini, for the psychology lesson, which we really appreciate.' Sophia side-eyed me. 'I think Regi is perhaps a little overtired and jittery about starting a new course tomorrow.'

Mini threw her hands up in the air. 'Anytime, there's more where that came from.' And she retreated from the room.

Sophia offered me a strained smile. 'But you're okay though?'

'I think you're right, and I am just nervous about tomorrow,' I lied.

Sophia's face loosened. 'Well, that's normal. You have been through so much and tomorrow is a big deal. Starting a course later in life can be daunting.'

I thought about the importance of the next day as my first day at uni. But it was a more important day in another way; one I didn't wish to remember or draw attention to.

'Thanks, Sophia. I'm not that old.'

'I know, I'm sorry, I just meant that, you know, the majority of the class will be teenagers and in their early twenties, so that's all I meant. I'd be nervous.'

I picked up the duvet cover and began to fold it. 'It's okay, and

I know it will be fine.' I could feel my heart rate returning to normal.

'Okay, well, text me if you freak out in the day. I can always dash over from my campus to meet you for a coffee if you feel you need me to.'

I looked at Sophia. 'Thank you,' I said. I thought about how in another world, in another time, Sophia and I could have been proper friends, the kind who told each other everything and didn't hover on the border of the truth. Except I imagined it would be the other way around and I would be the mentor, the stronger of the two, and she would be taking advice from me.

* * *

The next morning, I arrived at uni, made my way to the main entrance and navigated to my first class without a hitch. At the door, I squeezed my way past a small crowd of three or four people, who were talking as if they had only just met one another but were going to hang on to one another no matter what. Another intruder at this stage would upset their dynamics, so I skirted past them into the chilly room and found myself a safe space at the back where I noted there was also a fire exit. The notion that I could throw myself through it at any given point was a small comfort, but what I wanted to do right then was open and close it several times before I was able to settle. I had brought along a fiddle toy cube that had six sides with things to touch and move, something to distract myself from the doors and windows. I pulled it out of my bag and began subtly clicking the three sliders back and forth. It didn't give me the same satisfaction, but it would get me through the first lesson.

A small, round woman of about sixty came into the room and stood at the front.

'Okay,' she called loudly. 'This is your first theory lesson of the week for your introductory textiles course. I'm Denise, this is Room D-12, let's get started.'

* * *

After an hour and a half with only ten minutes' break, I burst out of the room. I had made it through, but it had been the struggle I knew it would be. I thought about the seminar I had at 2 p.m. – a whole two and half hours away. I navigated my way through seas of ambling bodies, students of all ethnic groups, some huddled together laughing, others were laid about on the grass, just living in the moment. I felt a pang of envy for their simple lives.

I had to remind myself that it was a short course, an easy, introductory level of just a few months to take me through to the summer when I would be free until September when the real work began. But it was still a shock to the system to find myself in alien surroundings amongst hundreds of people, trying to find my way to rooms – I felt as though I was eleven years old again, and it was the first day at secondary school.

I was starting to feel deflated, as though all of this were for what? Who was I doing this for? I had suffered, I was suffering, did I need to prove to myself or anyone else that I could carry on? Was life really worth living when it was only you that you were living it for?

I found my way into the main campus building, rounded a corner and collided with another body. Male and heavy.

'I'm sorry, are you okay?' He rested both his hands on my shoulders and attentively checked me over. It was too much for me, the physical contact as he held me at arm's-length and looked me up and down. I shook myself out of his soft grip, then looked up and was relieved to see one of the nicest faces with the kindest eyes that I had seen in a long time. A face that was shrouded in a messy, short beard and set on a lean frame. At first glance I would have pinned him as mid- to late-thirties. He was wearing a thick denim jacket with a grey hood poking out of the top. He reminded me of an American lumberjack.

'God, I'm so sorry.'

I shook my head. 'I'm fine.'

'Okay, well, so sorry again. I'm racing around like a doofus. My mum always told me off about that as a kid. I'm Will.' He offered me his hand.

'Oh.' I wasn't prepared for an introduction. 'Regi.' I gave his hand a quick shake and tried not to wince at the intimacy.

'Oh, wow, is that short for Regina?'

'Yes, it is.'

'So your parents saw you as a queen, did they?'

'You know your name meanings,' I said swiftly, looking around at the bustle of the corridor.

'I dabbled in some onomastics prior to anthropology, sociology, and now I teach philosophy.'

'Oh wow, that's some resumé.' My interest had suddenly piqued.

Will acknowledged the compliment with a smile and tilt of his head. 'So, what do you teach?'

'Teach? Oh no, I'm here as a student. Textiles. I'm an artist of sorts.' I looked down at my feet.

'Wow, well done, that's great, a mature student – I mean, you don't look *mature* mature. I just thought as the average age here is twenty-one that you were a teacher, but student, that's cool. Really cool.'

I smiled at how he tripped over his words and half shrugged his shoulders, self-conscious of his words.

I smiled and shuffled my feet awkwardly and considered what

was happening here: a male and female roughly the same age bumping into one another in a college corridor. Was this a meet-cute? Whatever it was, I could not and would not allow myself to think anything of it.

'Anyway... Will, it was good to bump into you, but I've got some serious getting lost to do in this huge place, so if you would excuse me.'

'Of course, of course. Although if you do get lost and you can't find your way back to the main campus, you can usually find me in Room 4, just off the main hall. I could help you on your way again, or at least offer you some refreshments.'

'Room 4, main hall. Great.' I gave a small salute. As I walked away, I laid my hand on my chest to steady my quivering heart.

I found the library first, a great ornate section of the uni that looked as though it had been there for decades. I instantly felt calmer as I swept past the large oval reception and began to walk between the aisles of books; I felt safe amongst the words and paper.

At the end of an aisle there was a small chair, which I needed no encouragement to sit in. From here I could see people gliding past as they perused the shelves of books. I felt the weight of the day catch up on me as jittery bubbles leapt through my stomach. I had stepped into the toilet on the way to the library; once inside the cubicle I opened and locked the toilet door six times. The girl in the next cubicle asked whether I was stuck.

Now sat in the comfy chair in the library, I pulled out my notepad and pencil, hoping inspiration would flood through me after my first lesson and I could get some sketches down, but all I could feel was heaviness in my head as my eyes fluttered shut.

* * *

I jolted and sucked in a breath as my eyes opened and my heart raced. I didn't remember closing them and if I did, I had only meant to rest them, not fall asleep. I hadn't slept well last night, but I had presumed it had been because of the face in the utility window, but in hindsight perhaps I *had* been anxious about my first day. I sat there panting, trying to get to grips with my surroundings. I looked at my phone to see what time it was. I had been asleep for a matter of minutes. I looked back up, and my eyes caught sight of a black baseball cap at the end of the aisle. My mouth went dry and I grabbed my bag and coat and shot up out of the chair. I hurried to the end of the aisle where I saw the tall male in the baseball cap walking with intent towards the reception and then exit. I sped up and found I was inches away from the back of him but not knowing what I would say or do if he turned. I did not have the confidence to initiate a move. Was it him or was I doing what Mini had suggested and hallucinating? Suddenly, he stopped and bent down to pick something up. He spoke but I could barely hear his voice, but I could tell his words were aimed at a woman who had just walked past me and also past him. She stopped and turned, took two steps back and thanked him for whatever it was she had dropped. He turned towards me slightly and I could see some more of him. He had the same build and that trademark baseball cap, but immediately I could see that I was mistaken. I edged away, I didn't know this man. I skirted around them both to get to the door and headed out of the library into the fresh air, where I inhaled big gulps of oxygen.

* * *

Instagram post: 29th April 2019

Hello, my lovely cleaners. How are you all? I've been a bit busy getting into the spring-fever spirit. Does anyone else get spring fever? As soon as that cold spell ends, and I feel a waft of warmer air, I'm all over it. I start with the windows because as soon as I see that sun coming through, it shows up every smear. I have always used a very old-fashioned method for washing my windows – it was passed down my family generations that way. My method is one part distilled vinegar to ten parts warm water in a spray bottle. Always give the windows a wipe down with a microfibre cloth or paper towel first to get rid of any dust. Then you're good to go. I've done before-and-after shots so you can see just how good the technique is.

Happy spring cleaning!

Mrs C x

#springclean #lovinglife #mrsclean #cleaningwindows
164,458 likes

staffiemumjenni Could this woman's house get any better? Great window-cleaning tip.

caraway98 This woman is amazing. I love her style.

the_sunday_feeling Why can't I see her face?

@wisewoman45 Cos she wants to be anonymous. So people like you don't start slating her.

the_sunday_feeling Hey! I was only asking @wisewoman45. I would never slate someone on here.

escapetothebookshelf She's like the Banksy of Instagram.

underthe_sheets I think it's inspiring. I wish more people would focus on the art rather than the person.

lucybest65 I think it's weird.

7

I arrived home after my afternoon lecture and immediately raced to my room. I found all the pound coins I could and stacked them up in fours, then nudged them into a perfect line. I opened and closed the window, pulling the lock across, then unlocking it again, only to relock it a further six times. I ripped the sheets from the bed and found the dry ones that I had brought up that morning from the tumble dryer. I performed the meticulous task of making sure the flat sheet had perfect hospital corners.

I felt hot after the exertion and walked to the window, daring myself to unlock it and open it an inch. A cool breeze trickled through and I took a moment to allow the spring-afternoon air to cool my face. I even closed my eyes for a second.

Then I heard it. The undeniable sound of 'Mama'. I stumbled backwards. Was someone playing a trick on me?

I stood on the chair and peered through my window that looked out over the first four back gardens on the street, and I could just about make out a tiny frame under the arm of a woman with the flash of blonde hair. I was sure it was the same woman I had seen dragging the child inside the other day. Here she was again, heading back into the house with the child tucked under her arm like a rugby ball. The child, who I still couldn't make out if they were a boy or a girl because of their wild hair, was beating the back of the woman. I heard their back door slam and the tiny echoing protests of the child.

My heart was wrenching as I climbed down from the chair and stumbled away from the window, falling into another chair in the corner of the room. It was just a test. I could get through this. There were always going to be times when I was reminded too vividly of my past, but I wasn't prepared. I thought about the locks of hair that were so familiar, the pained cries that pelted through my body and filled me with the guilt I would never be rid of.

Moving to this house had been the best decision yet. For the first time in a long time, I felt as though I had come up for air, but, now, I was being plunged back into the icy depths of water again.

There was a knock at my door. I jumped from the chair and stumbled forwards. I opened and closed the lock five times before opening it on the sixth, no longer caring that I probably appeared to be a crazy person to everyone in this house. I had the urge, the compulsion; the monster had reared itself and I had to feed it. Thankfully, it was Sophia on the other side.

She looked at me sympathetically. I hated that look on anyone, and I wished more than anything it wasn't Sophia wearing it.

'Just checking how your first day was?' She tried to hide what she was thinking, but I could see the concern in her eyes. I knew she didn't mean anything by it. I stepped back and allowed her to come into the room. 'It's looking nice in here now.' Sophia looked around and I tried to see the extreme neatness of the room through her eyes.

'It was fine, I guess.' Trying to remember the day but only seeing an image of Will in my mind's eye.

I looked towards the window.

'The neighbours, I...' I stopped myself.

'What is it, Regi?' Sophia headed to the window. 'Are they being too noisy?'

'No, I... I just heard something. It was nothing.'

I couldn't talk to Sophia, or anyone, about this because I hadn't disclosed my past. Without that information, I was just a crazy thirty-something woman ranting about hearing and seeing a child.

'Are you sure you're okay?' Sophia sidled closer to me. I stepped backwards as I felt the edge of fear creep over me. I could trust Sophia, right?

'What is it you're worried about, Regi?'

Was that concern in Sophia's voice, or sympathy?

'You don't have to tell me, but we have the party this weekend, so maybe you can let your hair down a bit. Enjoy yourself?' Sophia folded her arms across her chest and shrugged her shoulders up and down.

'I guess... I guess I'm just tired.' I glanced back at the window, the cries of the child ringing in my ears. Sophia was right; I needed to make room for enjoyment in my world that had been so crammed full of other emotions that my soul had been clouded in darkness.

'Yes,' I said. 'Yes, I'll look forward to the party.'

* * *

After Sophia left, I sat down in my immaculate room and pulled out my phone and plunged straight into Mrs Clean's Instagram account. How I longed to have a kitchen like hers, with so much symmetry and surfaces that gleamed. I knew that my life could never again be filled with the joyous rapture of children's laughter, so I would need to fill the void somehow. Here, in this shared accommodation, would be a good place to practise. I had the summerhouse I could work on, and the kitchen was the hub of the house; I could make that into something using all these ideas that Mrs Clean was handing out for free.

I noticed Mrs Clean had posted a new photo of the inside of her fridge. The image showed clear glass containers with lids, labelled with whatever was inside. She had boxed up ingredients for a fish pie: potatoes mashed in one container, the raw fish in another and the sauce in another. We had a large enough fridge, where we each commandeered a shelf, so I imagined I would be able to replicate this system pretty easily. She had added a name of the website so I could navigate my way straight to the place that sold the containers. I bought six. I wouldn't be able to plan for the whole week with only one shelf to myself, but I could organise a couple of days in advance.

The very thought brought a bubble of excitement to my gut, and I was thankful when it wasn't replaced with the fear that had shrouded my body for so many years now. This was what I needed all along: a bigger focus, an actual purpose. I could hear voices from my past reminding me I was allowed to feel joy in certain things. I didn't need to remain a prisoner in my mind forever.

I found myself back on the Instagram home page and along the top was a small round circle with Mrs Clean's profile picture on it. I remembered these were the stories that Mini was telling me about, so I clicked on one and found myself watching a fifteen-second video of Mrs Clean mopping her floor. There was an ad hashtag and something which read, *Swipe up to buy*. When the video had ended, I went back and watched it again. The camera was obviously on some sort of tripod as it captured the whole of the kitchen and Mrs Clean mopping. She had her back to the camera. There was a song accompanying the video: Dolly Parton's '9 to 5'. Mrs Clean was swaying to the beat as she mopped. It was fun and I found myself smiling as I watched. So far, I had not seen any images of her face, although I knew she used a filter occasionally to hide her identity. She had been crafty and arty with her shots. An arm holding a spray gun, a leg up on a footstool. In this video, she had on a pink bandana, which covered most of her hair except for a swish of blonde which crept through the bottom. She was wearing pink Marigolds, black leggings and blue slippers, and a pink apron was tied around her waist. And having looked through most of her Instagram posts by now, I was beginning to realise this woman wished to keep her face away from the camera and that air of anonymity made her even more appealing to me.

I went downstairs and thought about preparing my dinner. The kitchen was empty. I looked around and saw the potential again, how this kitchen had such a similar layout to Mrs Clean's kitchen and how I would like to replicate the exact same fittings. If the house were mine, of course. But for now, I was sure I could find great comfort in testing out a few of Mrs Clean's ideas. I walked to the fridge and opened it. It really was a mess and having seen the cleanliness of Mrs Clean's fridge, I felt an overwhelming urge to get stuck in right away. I pulled out a tray of half-eaten lasagne with the foil all scrunched up. I placed it on the counter and as I turned back to the fridge, I physically jumped. The fridge door had closed and in its place was Steve.

He looked at me and blinked.

'Jeez, Steve,' I said and opened the fridge again. He turned and walked around the door, so he was half behind me, half to my other side.

'You're making dinner?' he asked tediously.

I continued to remove items from the fridge and lay them on the side.

'I was, but now I'm cleaning.' I spoke into the fridge.

'Good. Therapeutic,' he said, extenuating the word.

Karen walked in, sneezing into a tissue. She paused by the fridge.

'Hey, babe,' she said to Steve and I was reminded that I hadn't had a word with her yet about her boyfriend letting himself in without anyone's consent.

'You ready?'

'Sure am,' he said.

'Have fun,' Karen said with what could only have been sarcasm in her voice. I guessed if I was a young girl sharing digs in my early twenties, I would have been offended. But Karen didn't know the joy that could be gained from a clean and organised fridge space.

Karen walked out of the door, but Steve stood still for a second longer. 'Bye, Regi.' He sounded very restrained. I looked over my shoulder at him as I crouched back down in the fridge. He was looking directly at me, as though he might say something more. And even though his expression was neutral, I felt all the joy within me wash away. It felt difficult to swallow and there was a pain in my chest. I turned my attention back to the fridge as a ripple of uncertainty flared up within me, a flash of a memory, a face from the past and the nothing look Steve gave me before he turned to leave. I shook my head and tried to make the thoughts fall away. You are safe, Regi. All is well.

I looked back at the doorway and seeing that he had gone, I blew out a long breath.

Fifteen minutes later I had wiped down all the shelves and sides of the fridge with a spray gun of antibacterial cleaner and the cleanest cloth I could find. I decanted oven trays of food into smaller containers and labelled them, then I wiped all the bottoms of the jars of jams, marmalades and pickles and put them all into the side compartment of the fridge, freeing up another shelf. I stood back and admired my work. It was as good as Mrs Clean's posts, so I pulled out my camera and snapped an image of the inside of the fridge, wishing I had done one of the damn tap-to-tidy photos that Mini had told me about. I posted it on my own Instagram wall and tagged Mrs Clean. Maybe she would see it, maybe she would reply.

I looked at the time. It was getting on for six and I needed to eat. I warmed up a can of soup and sat down at the table. The sound of the doorbell trilling through the hallway made me jump out of my skin. I walked to the kitchen doorway and waited to see if anyone else would answer it. But Karen and Steve were out, and I could hear the sound of the shower from the bathroom and music playing from Mini's room. I edged closer to the door, knowing I would have to answer it if no one else would. I felt an unease unfurling within me, and so I prepared myself to open and close the lock six times. I worked as fast as I could, not knowing who was behind the other side or what their reaction would be to my behaviour. I took a deep breath and pulled it open.

A man in a fluorescent jacket was standing there. Behind him, his white van chugged away on the road.

He handed me the package, then held out a device for me to sign with my fingers. I shakily gave my signature and looked at the package, which I could see was addressed to me. Intrigue swept through me, but the fear was stronger. I didn't remember ordering anything other than the storage tubs Mrs Clean recommended, that wouldn't arrive for a couple of days, and no one knew my address. I carried the box to the kitchen table where I examined it. Footsteps at the doorway made me spin around to see Sophia standing there in her towel.

'Did I hear the door?' She edged closer. 'Cool, Amazon, what you been buying?'

'I... an alarm clock,' I say quickly, thinking on my feet.

'Nice.' Sophia went to the fridge and opened it. 'Oh my... wow!' she turned to me. 'Is this your work, Regi?'

I felt a sudden flutter of pride. 'Yes, it is.'

'Good job. Now I can actually see what the hell is in this fridge. I always look at it and think I must do it but, you know, I never do. Obvs.'

'I've been getting some inspiration from some cleanstagrammers.'

'Cleanstagrammers. Hey, getting down with this Instagram thing, then?' Sophia pulled out a jar of pickles and picked one straight out of the brine with her fingers. I looked on slightly appalled, glad that pickles were not my bag.

'Maybe I'll have to check her out. I'm glad you have found something to, you know, to ease your mind a little.'

I cleared my throat and nodded. I wished I could speak, say the words to her. Tell her how I became this strange creature that stood before her. I would have loved her to have known me in my former life.

Once Sophia had retreated to her bedroom, I darted to my own room to open the package. Once inside I locked and unlocked the door six times, then tore open the box. Inside was a white box, and on the front it read, *Non-stick hamburger press.*

I dropped the package on the bed and took a few steps backwards. I had always been a woman of simplistic needs, never requiring materialistic things to make me happy. The memory began to filter back. I had been standing in front of the TV watching as a chef made burgers with this simple device. I remember saying out loud, what a fab gadget it was and maybe it could go on my birthday present list. I received a sneer in return. 'I can get you more than a piece of cheap plastic for your birthday, babes,' and it was never spoken about again. Only now here it was, sitting on my bed in a house I was absolutely certain no one else could have known about.

Some people will keep on hunting relentlessly until they find what they want. He was one of those people. I looked at the package on my bed. And today, on the day I turned thirty-six, I knew his small birthday gift was also another of way of telling me he had found me.

8

THEN

'Found you,' he whispered in my ear. His breathing was ragged, and his speech was slurred. His breath was laced with the sweet tang of yesterday's drinking and the sharp scent of the shots of brandy he had been on since lunchtime. It was now 3 p.m. He had been calling for me. I had thought to hide, never wishing to be around him when he had been drinking, I had hoped he would eventually tire and fall asleep on the sofa. But he searched the house until he found me in the airing cupboard. I quickly turned it into a game. 'You found me!' I said with a tight smile and threw my arms around him. He pulled me out of the small space and lay me on the floor on the landing.

He was bearing down on me, holding me firmly by both wrists. His legs straddled my waist and even his heels dug into my sides as extra force to hold me still. But I knew he was drunk, and he would soon tire.

'Were you... trying... to... hide... from... me?' he slurred. I wished for something to distract him, and to my relief the door-bell rang. He clumsily fell off me and staggered to the door. The package the post lady handed him kept him busy and away from me until he eventually passed out on the floor next to the sofa.

When he woke several hours later, I had prepared a simple meal of mince, potatoes and carrots. He didn't thank me but later, as I passed him in the lounge to tidy up a few bits, he pulled me into his lap and there we stayed as the TV blared out repeat episodes of a British sitcom we had both seen a hundred times before.

'This is living,' he whispered lazily into my ear. I suppressed a shudder and looked past the television and gazed at a small, dark splatter on the wall. I made myself believe this moment would pave the way for more moments like this until we found our way to a place that felt relatively normal. It was only when I had been staring at the patch on the wall for five minutes or so that I realised I was staring at my own blood. A vivid reminder of his last rage.

I wriggled myself out of D's lap and excused myself to go to the toilet.

'Don't be long,' he called after me and winked at me suggestively.

When I returned after an unnecessarily long toilet trip, he was asleep.

I fell to my knees next to him and examined the softness of his skin, the light smattering of stubble and the way his lips were parted slightly as he softly snored. As I knelt there, I tried to will an unconditional love that would carry me through this, shield me from the brutality. My body could withstand the beatings, but my heart and my soul were slowly dying. All the dreams I had of a family life were shattering. I knew now that this was who he was, and I could and would never change him. But that wasn't what terrified me the most. What scared me more than anything was that I knew I would never leave him. That no matter how much pain he caused me physically or how many times I cried myself to sleep at night, leaving was something I knew I couldn't do. And I had no explanation for it. It was simply a feeling that I could neither get rid of or change, no matter how much I tried. I was trapped and no one was going to save me.

9

I walked through the college corridor on Friday and I saw him. There was no escape. He was coming straight at me. I shoved my chin down into my scarf, dipping my head, but it was too late.

'Regi!'

I looked up in mock surprise. 'Will!'

We stopped in front of one another. I gave an awkward smile. There was no denying he was an attractive man and that he was clearly interested in me. I couldn't help but be reminded of what it was to be attracted to someone and how good it felt.

'Have you had a good first week?' He leant against the lockers to his left and clutched a red folder to his chest. A small smile played across his lips; his dark eyes were looking at me so intently that I began to feel a prickling sensation under my armpits. I didn't know where to look, so I looked down at my Converse trainers.

'Yes, thanks.' I scuffed my feet on the floor.

'Found your way around okay?'

'No problems.' I looked back up to find Will's bright eyes

looking intently at me and I was surprised to feel heat rising up my neck and into my cheeks.

He snorted a small laugh from his nose.

'What?' I shook my head.

'Ahh, I kinda half expected – hoped for – a knock on my door and to see you looking lost, that was all.' Will's face broke out into a smile, the skin around his eyes crinkled at the edges.

'There's a few of us old ones hitting the pub after class. It's the Fiddlers Inn, just outside the college. A few of the students find their way in, but overall, it's refreshing to get away from it all. Fancy it?' Will said, widening his eyes in anticipation.

I stood there, thinking about what to say. I had nothing to give to a relationship right now, and dragging this out was only going to make it worse for both of us.

I thought about home and what waited for me. Opening and closing doors countless times, changing my bedsheets, a meal for one and maybe some TV with one of the girls. It was nothing to rush back for, but I knew that taking him up on his offer would escalate the relationship further and I wasn't ready to share the little scraps of what was left of me and my life with anyone.

'I, um, can't tonight. I have a...' I suddenly I remembered it was the party tomorrow night, '... there's a party at my house tomorrow, one of my much younger millennial house mates is celebrating their birthday – I said I'd help get things organised.' That last part was a lie. I had no intention of playing any part in event organising for a twenty-first-birthday party.

'A party, wow.' Will raised his eyebrows in interest. 'Sounds fun.'

And now I had insinuated that I was looking for a date? Why was all this such a minefield? I remembered when talking to a guy was the easiest thing on Earth to do.

'So, well, yeah, that's what I need to be doing, but have fun in the pub.' I began walking away, my chin pushed back into my scarf.

'Hey, Regi,' Will called, and I stopped and slowly turned around. He stood facing me, one hand raised. 'Have a good weekend.'

Regret raged like a flood within me. Threatening angry tears, I turned and walked away. I stared straight ahead of me and saw myself in a parallel universe, one where I hadn't made any mistakes. One where I didn't have to hide anything about myself and one where I could accept Will's offer.

I felt the gloomy sensation that something terrible was about to happen, and I needed to do something to ease it. I had the journey home to get through and so once I was on the train, I opened up Instagram to see what Mrs Clean had been doing. It no longer felt like a want, but more like a need as I took in the seamlessness of her grid; I felt the dismal sensation melt away and a calmness fell over me. Within these boxes, I had begun to feel a strange sort of safety, as though I were in an alternative world.

Mrs Clean had posted again, and this time she was running a competition in association with a cleaning brand to win some top-of-the-range cleaning gadgets and equipment. The image accompanying the words was of her hallway again. I could see those three black-and-white prints on the wall on the left, and the floor was gleaming. Right at the end of the hallway was an image of the products she was giving away and a mop and bucket. All I could think was that it was a little sad, that a woman would be staying in on a Friday night and I felt a little sorry for her. I wondered how old she was. In my mind, she was my age. For a moment I imagined a world where I would go to her house on a Friday night and we would have a drink and compare cleaning tips. I thought about what I had planned for the evening. Drying my sheets, tidying my room.

I had more in common with Mrs Clean than I thought.

I just love it, were her signing off words.

'I just love it.' I mouthed the words to myself to see if I could conjure up any more love associated with cleaning. I was certainly enjoying it, but did I love it?

* * *

Back at the house there didn't seem to be any sense of urgency over a party that was happening tomorrow night, and, by the evening, everyone had gathered to hang out in the lounge, including Steve. Bowls of nuts and crisps were out on the coffee table alongside glasses of wine and bottles of beer; there was word of ordering a Mexican takeaway. I joined them as I did most evenings for a little while, mainly as the nights by myself in my bedroom were too long to be alone with my own thoughts.

I took the chair opposite the sofa where Mini and Karen were sprawled out at opposite ends. The conversations were easy to listen to, never really wavering from magazine or TV topics: who wore what to the Oscars, would there be another series of *Friends*, what were the best night creams currently on the market? Steve had arrived about half an hour ago. He now sat contentedly in a tub chair in the corner of the room, listening, nodding in the appropriate places. I couldn't help seeing someone else whenever I looked at him, and my body would occasionally give an involuntary shudder like it did now.

'You okay, Regi?' Sophia asked. Her curly hair was piled high in a bun and she was wearing her glasses. She peered over them and looked at me.

'Just felt a slight chill.' I tried to shake off Sophia's concern, but she was already pulling the throw from the back of the chair and holding it out for me. I gave an insipid smile, sat forward and gingerly pulled it over my legs, trying not to think about the last time it had seen a wash.

'So, I'm thinking balloons, confetti, candles, the lot tomorrow. I'll pop over to that party shop in the morning and grab some stuff.' Mini chatted away.

'You're not supposed to go and buy your own decorations for your party,' Karen said.

'No, you're thinking of not seeing the bride before the wedding,' Mini said deadpan, and Sophia and Karen exchanged a look and a smirk.

'No, I just don't think it's fair that you should be the one to put your own decorations out on your birthday,' Karen said, dabbing her nose with one hand and smoothing the stray hairs across her head with the other.

'Oh right, so you're gonna do it then? You don't drive for a start,' Mini said, grabbing a handful of nuts from the table and putting them in her mouth.

'I'll drive you, babes,' Steve said from across the room.

I felt my eyes half close as I looked across at Steve. His delivery of the word *babe* had seemed somewhat disingenuous.

'Oh, thank you, darlin'.' Karen blew him a kiss.

I saw Sophia raise her head and flash a look over towards Steve, who looked up at her with a neutral expression at the same time. I wondered if Sophia felt the same way about Steve as I did. I made a mental note to ask her when we were alone.

'Right, I'll order the takeaway.' Sophia began tapping away at her phone. Everyone, including me, started shouting their orders at her. Steve and Karen got up and left the room.

I saw Sophia glance over at them as they left. She then caught my eye and quickly stuck two fingers in her mouth. I smiled.

Half an hour later, when the doorbell went, Sophia looked at me.

'Would you mind? The money's there.' She pointed at the table and leant back over Mini's phone where they were scrolling through Pinterest, getting party ideas. I grabbed the kitty from the table as I felt the monster building up inside me. I took long, slow breaths as I walked to the front door. No, Regi, you don't need to open and close the door six times before you greet the Deliveroo man. You could just be a normal member of society and open the door and then sit down and enjoy the meal with everyone else. But I couldn't. I knew I first needed to feed the monster, and then I could feed myself.

I performed my ritual and I was greeted by the young delivery guy. He didn't bat an eyelid at the disjointed sounds of me trying to open the door. I could have been drunk out of my mind for all he knew. I thanked him, paid with the kitty and took the delivery back into the lounge.

Karen and Steve appeared, looking a little ruffled. When I got back into the lounge, I could see Karen was diving straight into the takeaway, but Steve seemed to linger in the doorway as I was trying to edge my way through.

'Need any help?' He held out his hand to relieve me of the plates and cutlery.

'Nope. I'm fine,' I said as I tried to edge my way past. I was sure I felt his foot reach out and touch mine. 'Right, you animals, let's have a little civilisation here, everyone grab a plate,' I called to the room. Steve suddenly shot me another one of his neutral looks and to me it felt as if it was carrying some kind of warning.

* * *

Instagram post: 4th May 2019

Good morning, my lovely cleaners. I hope you're all having a wonderful day. Nothing beats the smell of freshly washed and line-dried linen on a bed. I love the feeling of those 'just washed' sheets when I get into bed at night. These sheets were gifted to me by the lovely @fredalinen and I love how white they come up every time I wash them. I use a brand called @fresh. Not gifted, I just absolutely adore the fragrance of their products. Next thing will be to redesign this bedroom altogether and get some fitted wardrobes, but for now, I am enjoying the sunshine. Hope you are too.

Mrs Clean x

#spring #linen #fabric #Lovinglife #MrsClean #Cleansheets #instaclean

256,673 likes

forgetmenots This is bloody gorgeous as it is. Fitted wardrobes would ruin the authentic look you've got going on there.

Poole4030 @mrsclean your posts keep me sane.

beckybooloopa Love Love Love.

lucybest65 How do you keep your house so clean? Obviously, no kids.

anthonyr.smith Defo no kids. No one can keep their house that tidy and have kids.

lucybest65 And you say 'not gifted' but let's see how long it takes before she's collaborating with Fresh. It's like you only have to mention them once and boom, sponsorship.

everythingispink You sound jealous @lucybest65

lucybest65 Not jealous, just annoyed at how easy these Instagrammers have it these days.

10

NOW

I woke up on the morning of the party with a raging headache. I needed to find pain relief straightaway.

I opened and closed the window six times, even though I craved a slight breeze. I looked out through the window to the empty courtyard next door, with the small stretch of grass beyond. No child today.

I thought back to the days I knew and loved best; when a child that age would want to be outside in this weather, running, discovering, so full of curiosities. To witness it was like sunshine flooding my soul. Nothing made me happier.

I opened and closed my door six times, counted the steps down to the kitchen where I knew there was some ibuprofen in a drawer.

I had promised to get the summerhouse finished before the party, but I needed to take my usual trip to the coffee shop first before the furniture would arrive later. I was sure, as much as I didn't care to, it would appear rude if I shirked away from decorating the lounge once Karen and Steve got back from the party shop. I took two ibuprofens from the packet and swallowed them down with water.

Back up in my bedroom, I couldn't rest. I found I was pacing the room and wringing my hands. I grabbed my phone from the bedside table and went into Mrs Clean's most recent Instagram post. It seemed her followers were arguing over her using the names of brands. I looked again at a post she had put up yesterday. It was just a shot of a pile of freshly washed sheets and her feet up on a footstool in a pair of pink fluffy slippers. Amongst the wording accompanying the post she had written, *Even clean queens need a break – feet-up time.*

She had used the hashtag *#fridayyvibes*. Everything in the background was out of focus. It now had 167,546 likes and endless comments.

I felt a wave of relief wash over me, my stomach no longer felt tense. I was happy in this little world. I had come to feel safe in smaller spaces, having spent a year confined to just one small area.

I found myself scrolling through a few of yesterday's comments. The majority of them were positive responses, wishing her a happy day and to not overdo it, or that they were doing something similar themselves. I felt an overwhelming urge to comment, to be a part of this community, but I would not know what to say. A few of the really negative comments stood out amongst the sea of positivity and love for Mrs Clean.

lucybest65 I'm sure a rest is just what you need after all that 'self-promotion' #itsallrightforsome

Underneath that were a stream of responses to lucybest65 and her negativity.

singstheword What's your problem?

milofortune43 Who rattled yours?

ifieverask Give the woman a break. She's having a cup of tea for five minutes.

Lucybest65 hadn't responded to any of them. I grew up in an era when trolls didn't exist because we used to talk face to face. It amazed me how people found it so easy to post something so negative just because they weren't looking the person in the eye? I had begun to feel some sort of affiliation with Mrs Clean; I found her posts soothing and inspiring all at once, and now I knew I would be keeping my eye on lucybest65's comments.

I could see Heather the moment I walked through the door of the coffee shop and so already I felt as though this day was going to be okay. It was reasonably quiet for a Saturday morning. I had even beat the Boden mums and dads, and I couldn't hear any child sounds.

A thought occurred to me. What would happen if I swapped drinking out for drinking in? I asked Heather if that would be possible.

'Of course it is. But I'll put it in a takeaway cup, just in case you change your mind.' She gave me a knowing look, and I wasn't sure whether I should have felt embarrassed or thankful.

I chose a seat next to the window, where I could appreciate the view of the mews with its curtains of trees framing the street like a little stage.

I took a sip of my coffee from the takeaway cup, thankful the ibuprofen had done its job of numbing my headache. I gazed around the mews, trying to relax into the moment; to normalise this novel sensation of just being. I fiddled with a napkin, folding it and unfolding it several times until the seams met just perfectly. There was a general hum of the coffee machine behind me as milk was frothed and beans were blended. I found it almost melodic and momentarily closed my eyes.

I opened them slowly.

My eyeline was automatically drawn to the huge oak tree in the centre of the mews, opposite where I was sat.

I almost didn't see him.

He blended into the tree at first, in his khaki trousers and green bomber jacket. But it was the black baseball cap that caught my eye and held my gaze. His head was cast downwards, a mobile phone in his hand. I felt the familiar pang of panic, but it was quickly replaced by a surge of anger that coursed through my body. I still wasn't ready to face him. I stood up quickly and my chair scraped backwards. A few diners turned to look at the commotion I had caused. I turned to the counter, aware of the ruckus and saw Heather look up from behind the counter.

I mouthed, 'Sorry,' and headed for the door. If he was engaged in something on his phone, then I might manage to get out without being noticed.

I yanked the door and stepped out into the street. A family of four kids and three dogs walked past me, blocking any view in front of me. When they had passed, I could see the oak tree again. The space where he had stood was now empty.

I looked around the mews, trying to catch a glimpse of the baseball cap. But it was as if he was never there.

* * *

I arrived back at the house just as everyone was getting up. Karen and Steve were in the lounge writing up a list of what to buy. I bypassed them and went straight upstairs, where I locked and unlocked the door six times. I went over to the window and repeated the same there. Visions of his face were still fresh in my mind. His stance, his posture. The very essence of his being was not something I would forget in a hurry. Instinctively, I touched my wrists. I could hear the voices of the house rising up the stairway and filtering into the bedroom. The excitement for the evening was building. I should have been downstairs, revelling in excitement and offering my services on Mini's ever-growing to-do list. The loud trill of the doorbell made me jump and my heart skipped. Then I blew out a long breath and remembered that the chairs were arriving today and that it was probably the delivery guys with the furniture for the summerhouse. I opened and closed the door six times before finally letting myself out and down the stairs.

Karen had already opened the front door and the delivery team were at their van unloading a sofa and chair.

'It's probably best to bring them round the back.' I gestured to them with my hand.

I walked back through the house and unlocked the side gate. I looked around and as no one was about I opened and shut it several more times, I'm not sure how many I was up to when the gate began to move and one of two of the two delivery guys was pushing his way through. He shot me a frustrated look and so I stepped back and allowed him through. He was carrying just the bucket chair. I skipped ahead of him and opened the door to the summerhouse.

'Just chuck it anywhere.' I motioned to the empty space.

'Chuck it? You'll be suing us for all we got.'

'Well, then... Place it just here.' I pointed to a corner I had prepped with a large green sprouting pot plant. I had seen a small table in a retro preloved store a few streets away, and I thought the combo of the three would look smart and classy in the corner. The sofa would sit bang in the middle of the larger window with a long coffee table in front. I felt a hint of pride that I had been able to do something for the house and the girls, as well as putting my stamp on a small area of the vast house we shared. They had all offered to give me something towards it, but I felt I wanted to contribute something to compensate for what I lacked in house mate skills; to make up for my odd and erratic behaviour.

Whilst the delivery guy headed back to the front to bring through the sofa, I took a moment to stand in the garden. The sun had been out all morning, but only now could I feel a little warmth spreading across the garden, and I took a moment to bask in it. Suddenly, my ears were alerted to a commotion, raised voices fuelled with heightened tension. A style of conversation I was so familiar with it was almost as though I was listening to my past, except this conversation was happening in another language. I moved closer to the fence; I was already certain I knew where it was coming from. The stepladder was still perched next to the fence and I took a moment to decide if I fancied venturing up there, but the temptation was too much and the desire to put faces to voices was bordering on obsession.

I quickly scooted up the ladder and crouched down on the third step, so only my head was peeking above the fence. I couldn't see anyone, but the back door leading onto the patio was wide open. A gruff male voice spurted words in his native language. The voice became raised and agitated until it was punctuated by the high-pitched protests of a female. They were both talking very fast. Suddenly, a man stepped out of the door with his right hand on the door handle to pull it closed. As he stepped out, he looked upwards and made direct eye contact with me. Just before I ducked my head down, I was met with a scowl as he muttered something else in his language and slammed the door. I stepped down the ladder, shrouded in guilt. I was familiar with rows that attracted the attention of others, but those arguments had been drenched in emotions too raw, too painful, so it never sat well with me when I heard the screams of others.

I looked down the garden as the delivery guys were bringing the sofa through. It looked so much better than it did online. It had a soft linen grey cover. I had bought a selection of cushions in greys, yellows and greens, some with geometric designs to stand boldly against the plain sofa fabric.

I spent the rest of the morning organising the summerhouse, removing the cellophane from the chair, putting down a couple of rugs, bringing in a portable heater and adding some of the knick-knacks I had bought. I would head down to the preloved store later to collect the table.

Then I decided the time had come to take a photo and post it on Instagram. I tried out the diagonal angle from the doorway, managing to get in two chairs and the plant pot, and it seemed to work.

I posted it with the words, *Summerhouse renovation complete.* I tagged Mrs Clean in it and then felt a flutter of panic. My profile name and picture didn't give anything away about who I was, so I wasn't worried about anyone tracking me down and finding me. But I was still putting something of mine out into the world, and it made me feel slightly exposed. Yet wasn't this the norm now? People posting their entire lives online?

I found my way back into the house around lunchtime. I was feeling the beginnings of hunger. Only Mini was about.

'Where's everyone else?' I asked her.

'Karen and Steve got "stuck in town" – translation, stopped for a pub lunch. Sophia has gone to Oxford Street to buy an outfit. What will you wear tonight, Regi?' Mini was pulling salad items from the newly organised fridge, which I was surprised to see still remained fairly clean and tidy, although secretly I was already looking forward to cleaning it again. I considered Mini's question of outfits, then it suddenly struck me that recently my social schedule hadn't warranted any clothes that went beyond one choice. These days I had unconsciously begun wearing a uniform of sorts: jeans, floaty shirt, Converse trainers or Doc Martens and my trademark tie-dye scarf to push my face into when I didn't fancy eye contact.

'I don't really have anything,' I said ashamedly as I looked at Mini who was dressed in tight blue skinny jeans, black bodysuit and a silk wrap cardigan. What she was wearing for a casual afternoon around the house was the kind of thing I would have worn for a night out.

'There's a really cool clothes shop just down the high street, it's near to the preloved shop? Do you know it?' Mini said.

I did know the shop she was talking about, but the thought of having to spend any more time perusing shops today after the events of the morning down at the mews was not eliciting any excitement. I had intended to rush out, grab the table and come back. But Mini's comment suggested I should make an effort. It was her birthday party after all.

As I pulled on my boots and hat, it occurred to me that this was the first time in years that I had participated in any kind of celebration. I hadn't even acknowledged my own birthdays and had let this year's one slip by without any of the girls knowing. The only person who had reached out to me, I wished that they hadn't. Maybe I would go down to the shop as Mini had suggested and pick out an outfit. But the thought of treating myself, doing something to make myself feel and look better, wasn't sitting right with me, as usual. As much as I tried to focus on the fact that I was also doing this for Mini, to help her celebrate her birthday, my mind was working on overdrive. This time I was trusting what it was telling me: you don't deserve any of this.

11

You don't deserve any of this. His words rang loudly in my ear, long after he had left the flat, and I was alone with only my feelings. I was trying to unpick his words that were echoing around the empty rooms I wandered through, making me rethink every sentence I had uttered before his anger surfaced.

I looked at the grey velour sofas and crystal chandeliers, the furniture he had ordered and had delivered without me having any say. I thought about the strange foreign spicy foods and bottles of lager in the fridge that he insisted I order. I heard his words again.

You don't deserve this.

I wondered if I should have written down everything I had said. Perhaps I should have started recording our conversations when I could sense his anger rising. Maybe then I could work out where I kept slipping up. Surely, after all this time, I just needed to know him a little better, dance around his outbursts, try to meet his needs a little better.

Maybe it was me? My period was due. I could feel it coming,

and I was frustrated because I didn't want it; I wanted to be pregnant again.

His words rang loud and true. I didn't deserve anything he gave me. He provided for both of us, and I was acting selfishly.

He had come home from work and I had been feeling sorry for myself all day. I was tired and hormonal.

It had been hot in the flat all day and he had started restricting the times and hours I went out. So I drew the curtains to keep the heat away, and I must have fallen asleep. I woke to the sound of the front door slamming.

I sat bolt upright and looked around at the mess I had intended to clear up, and I thought about the dinner on the side I had intended to cook.

After he had shown me how upset he was with his fists, I lay on the floor as I always did after he had left the flat. I lay there thinking that it would all come together in time. Time was all we needed. We hadn't been together very long; we were still learning about each other. I was young; I hadn't been in a relationship before. He was older than me by ten years. He understood women, as he told me regularly.

Later that evening, still alone in the house, I picked out my favourite film, *Maid in Manhattan,* and curled up on the sofa. I looked at the bruises on my arms. I was already anticipating the burst of a rainbow-hued bouquet that came after the violent purple. I found beauty in the colours, knowing they were already fading.

The bruises would come and go. But my soul was broken beyond repair.

* * *

Instagram post: 4th May 2019

Hello, my cleaning crew, I hope you don't mind me popping on here again today. I just have so much cleaning stuff going on right now. I just remembered I have my cleaning caddy all lined up ready to go which is packed to the brim with all my favourite sprays and room spritzers. I am going to start by stripping my sofa cushions, then I'm moving on to the skirting boards and radiators. No corner will escape me this month. By next month, the place will be well and truly gleaming. I have been in hibernation for far too long and now it's time to wake up and start smelling the sweet scent of air fresheners and upholstery cleaners. Do I hear a hell yeah? Send me your pics on stories and hashtag it #springmrsclean

Mrs C x

#springclean #mrsclean #spring #cleaning #cleanstagrammer
134,989 likes

maybebaby You've just reminded me I need to strip my cushions too. Thanks, Mrs Clean.

barbellsandbooks I have zero energy to do any cleaning today so I'll enjoy watching the results of your labour.

jcaraballo09 Hell yeah!

lucybest65 I just don't understand how anyone can get a thrill out of cleaning their radiators. Surely she's a young woman – I know we don't get to see her and she prefers a certain amount of anonymity, but come on! Hasn't she got something else she'd rather be doing? Wiping down your radiators on a Saturday?

dreadlockginger Whatever floats your boat, innit?

12

NOW

I dragged myself out to the shops. Knowing that I only had to go as far as the next high street was some sort of comfort. Shopping had never been my idea of entertainment. I used to be an organic fun kind of girl: reading, long walks in the woods, conversations by the campfire at night. What was I now except a shell of that woman? I missed her from time to time and the pure rapture I would gain from such simple activities.

The clothes store that Mini had mentioned was easy to find and right next door to the preloved shop, and so I decided to have a quick browse and collect the table from next door on my way home. I had noticed the clothes shop plenty of times, but the thought of going in and trying on clothes, perusing the rails and racks filled me with an unbridled sense of doom.

The bell pinged as I let myself in through the front door. The woman behind the counter wore a bright-pink piece of cloth as a bandana. Her cheeks were rosy, as though she spent a healthy amount of time outdoors. She looked slightly older than me, maybe early forties, and she greeted me with a hello and smile that made me feel we could have been friends in another life.

'Just let me know if you need any help,' she spoke softly with a slight husk.

'Okay, thanks.' I tried to match her soft tone.

The shop was a bit of a mixed bag from incredibly unique and independent labels to a selection of Boden pieces in the corner.

I picked up a shirt that looked like it could be my size, then I looked at the rack of shoes that were next to the window. I was just picking up a flat red shoe in a six when I was startled by banging on the window. I looked up and was surprised to see that Will from uni was standing outside, waving like a lunatic. He did a funny thing with his hand, indicating that should he come in, or I should go out, then before I knew it, the bell pinged and he was in the shop. I felt a wave of embarrassment at us meeting under such intimate conditions. I considered the claustrophobic surroundings, the one exit where Will was standing, blocking it, then the red shoe in my hand and the shirt flung over my arm. He was now assessing my potential purchases, things I hadn't even decided if I liked yet. I felt a furious fluttering in my stomach that rose into my chest, constricting my breathing.

'Regi,' he sounded out of breath even though he had only been standing outside, 'how are you?'

I quickly looked down at my white Converse trainer boots, which looked more than 'a little' scuffed.

'I'm good.' I managed to look back up at him. 'Do you, er, live around here?' I tried not to sound suspicious at our meeting here.

'Marlon Street, two roads down from here. You?'

'Yeah, a few roads down, the other way.' I feebly pointed to my right. I had no intention of telling him the name of my road.

'I saw you walk in. Sorry, hope you don't mind me bashing the window like that – hope I didn't scare you.' Will was rushing his words. He was wearing his trademark denim jacket with a hood. 'How's it going? Spot of shopping?' He pointed to the shirt draped over my arm. 'It's nice. Suits you.' He raised his eyebrows really quickly and flashed a smile.

I sniffed out a laugh. 'I haven't even tried it on.'

'Well, I can tell. You'd suit anything.' He smiled.

I heard the shop assistant clicking her pen on and off and occasionally typing something on the keyboard in front of her. I stole a glance at her, wondering what she was making of this awkward meeting.

'So what brings you... here?' I asked.

'Just a few errands. How about you?'

'I'm picking up a table from the shop next door. And obviously, a party outfit,' I said, looking at the shirt. 'Although now I'm not so sure...' I trailed off.

'Oh no, you should give it a go. Why not try it on? I have an eye for women's fashion.'

I looked at him questioningly.

'I mean, I have three sisters, so girls' clothes, it's kinda all I've ever known.' He pointed to the shirt. 'What have you got to lose?'

I looked at the price tag. 'Thirty-nine quid?'

The shop assistant cleared her throat.

'What's the occasion again?'

'My house mate is turning twenty-one.'

'Oh yes, the student house party, that's right. Twenty-one, my God. I can barely remember what I was doing then. Something highly illegal probably.' He laughed, and I smiled at the infectiousness of it. I briefly cast my mind back to when I was twenty-one. I knew I was dealing with things that were way above what a girl my age should have been dealing with.

We stood looking at one another for a moment.

'The changing rooms are just over there.' The voice of the shop assistant reached us.

'Okay, I'll just...' I walked past her and she gave me a knowing smile before I disappeared into the changing room. I pulled the curtain to and adjusted it so no cracks were showing. I pulled off the top I was wearing and carefully folded it and put it on the bench. I could hear Will approach the till and begin to make small talk with the shop assistant. He was asking her how long the shop had been there.

I pulled the shirt over my head and assessed myself in the mirror. It was a good fit. I tried to conjure up some excitement so that when I appeared on the other side of the curtain I might look a little happier than I actually felt.

I tentatively pulled back the curtain. Will jumped up from where he had been leaning against the till, his eyes open wide with intrigue.

He nodded approvingly.

'Stunning. I reckon that's the one.'

'How about a woman's prerogative to try on fifteen more tops and then buy the first one she tries on?' I tried to disguise the smile that was creeping its way across my lips. It had been a long time since I had heard a compliment like that from a man.

'I mean I can happily hang around all day if you need to try on more,' Will said with a glint in his eye.

I narrowed my eyes at him as a small smile played across my own lips.

'I like your style. Luckily for you, I don't do shopping.' I looked at the assistant who was looking on with interest. 'I'll take it.'

At the desk I handed over my card and the assistant put the shirt in a brown paper bag. Will was trying to feign interest in some of the clothes rails. I looked over to where he was standing and that was when I saw it. How I hadn't seen it before was beyond me. The boldness of the design was so eye-catching, I knew it was forever embedded in my brain. But for some reason, today, my mind had chosen not to see it. I had, in fact, walked straight past it on my way to the changing room. But now, it was there, staring me in the face and dragging me back to that fateful day.

I felt my legs go first, I grabbed for the counter but missed and dropped my purse, coins and cards scattered everywhere. Everything seemed to slow down. Then, as my body absorbed the shock, I went into protective mode. Will was speaking, but I couldn't hear him. He was next to me and he reached out his hand to grab me. That was the last thing I saw before I fell.

* * *

Will had gone home and fetched his car and driven me the two blocks home, even though I had told him over and over that I was fine to walk. As we drove, sadness consumed me. Will had seen a part of me I had been hoping he wouldn't.

He parked the car and ran around and opened my door just as I was about to do it for myself. The gesture surprised me, and I had to stop myself from looking at him oddly. Once outside the car, he took my hand and straightaway I was floored by the touch, realising how long it had been since I had had such close physical contact with anyone.

We reached the front door, and I pulled my front door key out of my bag. I looked up at Will, who stood hesitantly.

'I would invite you in, but it's carnage.'

'Hey, no, I understand. I just hope you're okay.'

'I'll be fine, like I said. I just forgot to eat properly before I left.'

'Well, make sure you eat something now.' Will looked at me with concern 'Eggs. They say eggs are good.'

'Protein.'

'Yes, protein.' Will cleared his throat. '... Protein is good.'

'Okay, I'll crack on then.'

'Ha, you made a joke.' Will laughed.

'Unintentional, I assure you.' I felt the pull of the house and turned towards the door, to where there would be warmth, the security of my things around me, where I could open and shut doors and windows until the pain that was bubbling in my chest subsided.

'You get yourself inside then,' Will said perceptively.

I pushed the key in the door. Will walked backwards away from the front door, his hands were pushed into his pockets, he side-stepped a woman on the pavement – he was doing the two-step – then called, 'Take care of yourself, Regi!' and opened his car door, slid in and drove away.

I pushed my way into the house and made a dash to my bedroom before I came into contact with anyone. I opened and closed the door six times, ending on a lock. Then I stood in the middle of the room, fell to my knees and cried silent, heavy tears.

13

NOW

I opened my eyes, which felt thick and heavy. I had somehow made it to my bed and fallen asleep. I had forgotten just how much crying took it out of me. The first thing I thought was why did I not see it? It was the most prominent child's sweatshirt in the shop. It was a rainbow motive, for goodness' sake. How could I have missed it? Mostly, why had I not seen it before Will arrived? He was intrigued by me before, and now his interest in me would have definitely piqued. I wasn't sure whether in a good way.

I hadn't meant to nap, but the shock had taken it out of me. I could hear plenty of commotion in the house, and I knew I too should be getting up and helping out with the preparations.

I pulled myself out of bed and took myself over to the window. I glanced over at next door and tried to see if I could catch a glimpse of the mother and child. The child who bore so many familiarities... But there was nothing. Even though the sun was now shining brightly, there was no sign of life.

Suddenly there was a banging on the door. I went over and

unlocked and relocked it six times. When I finally opened it, I was greeted by a breathless Mini.

'Sorry to disturb you, Regi, but we need a third opinion on a few things. Sophia is still out and well, you've a good artistic eye.'

I forced my face into a smile.

'Sure, gimme a minute.'

* * *

Downstairs, I found Mini, Karen and Steve all looking rather lost, standing around the coffee table, which was laden with banners and bunting and balloons.

'How should we set it all out, Regi? The last time any of us had a party, we were kids and well...'

Mini stopped short and looked at Karen and then me. 'We just thought, you know, you might have some idea.'

'Oh, I see.' Suddenly I could see exactly what it was they were trying to imply. That I was the obvious choice, the mother hen of the group and that I would have had the experience of this kind of thing.

Well, they were right. I had. But like everything else, I had forced myself to forget about it. I couldn't remember the last time I had to think about a birthday party. I tentatively walked over to the paraphernalia and pulled out some bunting.

'You need to hang these centrally.' I walked over to the large mirror. 'Maybe here in the middle.' I demonstrated by holding up the bunting. 'Then the same with those banners, maybe across the doorways. I used to...' I stopped myself, but not before three faces were locked on me with raw interest. 'What I would probably do,' I righted myself, 'is stick some of these on the walls, at an angle.' I grabbed some of the smaller happy birthday signs and held one diagonally against the wall.

'With the balloons.' I turned round to face them. 'Bunches of threes scooped into corners, make sure there's a good wad of balloons at the front door and on the side gate. People like that.'

'Brilliant. Thanks, Regi. Karen bought so much, I just felt overwhelmed once she got it back,' Mini said, and she came and stood next to me and gave my arm a small squeeze. I looked at Mini and smiled, remembering what these kind gestures meant from a friend and how I had always been the one to throw my arms around everyone. I found myself reaching over with my other hand and placing it momentarily on Mini's.

'Well, you sound like you know what you're talking about anyway,' Steve said, and I heard a brightness to his tone that I hadn't heard before. I locked eyes with him for a second, trying to gauge his intent. Why did he remind me so much of someone I was trying so hard to forget?

I turned to go to the kitchen, but took a step back and grabbed a bag of balloons and a banner.

'I'll stick some of these in the summerhouse.'

I opened the door to the summerhouse and found the warm afternoon had turned it into a sauna as I was greeted by a waft of hot air. I stood and looked around at what I had created, and I felt a swell of pride. The same swell of pride I had felt when all three girls had oohed and ahhed at how beautiful it looked and what an eye for interiors I had. Even Karen, who had become so awkward around me.

I blew up three balloons and stuck them to the front door. I Blu-Tacked a banner above it, then stood back to admire my handy work. I looked once again inside the summerhouse and I realised with all the commotion in the clothes store I had forgotten to pick up the table. I looked at the time on my phone and saw that it was getting on for five o'clock. It was too late to rush back for it now.

I was drawn back into the warmth of the summerhouse, and I sunk into the new chair and drank in the warm afternoon sun. I found myself thinking about Will, wondering if I should have invited him. Perhaps having him here would give me some support? He had shown interest when I had mentioned the party. But then I thought about the horrors of the clothes shop that afternoon, and I shuddered at the memory. I would get through this. I needed to do it, to thrust myself amongst people and try to start leading a normal life, one that wasn't filled with dread and fear.

* * *

People started arriving from 6 p.m. I was upstairs getting ready, which these days didn't involve a lot of effort. I changed into the new shirt, which now already held bad memories of the store where I bought it, but I tried to push that image from my head. I opened and shut the window six times, brushed my teeth for a full thirty-four seconds, then I ripped off yesterday's sheets and threw them in the corner. I had already brought up the fresh sheets, and so I went about making the flat sheet as taut as possible with nice, neat hospital corners. I then went about lining the pillows up so that they sat perfectly and placed two cushions neatly next to one another. I could hear voices travelling up the stairs and into my room. Finally, when I knew I couldn't stay in the bedroom any more, I went to the door, unlocked and locked it six times, then I headed downstairs.

* * *

There was a crowd forming in the kitchen, and music was playing from a docking station. A few people I had never met before were standing next to the fridge. Mini was standing in her pink figure-hugging mini dress, pouring orangey-looking drinks from a dispenser. She looked up as I entered.

'Oh, Regi, come and try some of my punch. I probably over did it on the rum – let me know what you think?' She giggled and handed me a glass. 'You look lovely. Cute shirt.'

I took a drink and thanked her. Yes, she had overdone it on the rum, but luckily rum was... had been... one of my favourite spirits.

I was thrust back to a happy time, with someone I thought I loved, who I thought loved me, by my side. I took another long sip and tried to drown the memories as I could feel the strength of the alcohol do its thing. I thought about putting the glass down; I could just pretend for the rest of the evening, fill my glass with lemonade and let people think I was drinking vodka. I knew that was the sensible choice to make because although the swell of the alcohol in my body was giving me the lift I needed right now, tomorrow would be a different story. But Mini filled my glass up again, and somehow it kept finding its way to my lips as I stood in the kitchen trying to wash away the uncomfortable sensation of mixing with strangers.

Mini moved us all into the lounge to show off her handy work and there were a few whoops of glee from her young friends who were clearly taken with her artistic skills. She threw me a coy glance and I sent her a wink back. She had managed to do a great job with the decorations. Big, thick streamers hung from each side of the large mirror whilst bunting adorned the centre. Balloons sat in threes, as I suggested, on lampshades, over the doorway, on coffee-table legs and against chair legs whilst the small, shiny happy birthday banners were splattered diagonally.

In the corner, someone had set up a strip of disco lights and a plug-in disco ball. There was a fold-up table with a set of decks on it. I realised things hadn't changed very much since I was this age. Young people of every generation have generally done things the same. A party is a party so long as there are lights, decorations, booze and guests.

By 9 p.m., the house was heaving. I had no idea that between them, Sophia, Mini and Karen had so many friends. I guessed I was looking at friends of friends, acquaintances, bums-on-seats, anything to fill the house and make it feel like a real party. Which it did. I had moved between rooms for what had felt like hours, always finding myself with a drink in hand, occasionally engaging in stunted conversations only for them to be drowned out by the booming music or a rowdy guest. I seemed to lose all sense of what was going on. It suddenly felt so late. I was standing in the hallway when I realised I was more drunk than I had intended to get. I looked at the doorway to the lounge and began to sway along to the music. It was a song I recognised. I slowly staggered into the room, where it was packed from wall to wall with bodies drinking, laughing, dancing. I accidentally fell against a body and looked up and saw a young guy. I apologised profusely, only to see a snarl on the face of the girl I presumed was his girlfriend. I held my hands up in surrender and carried on past them. I managed to do one lap of the lounge, then found myself back in the hallway, where people were huddled or gathered on the stairs. I headed through into the kitchen; every counter and space was filled with bottles and cans and open packets of crisps and dips. I noticed how no one had bothered to even place anything in a bowl.

'How uncouth,' I muttered to myself.

I took down a couple of ramekins from the cupboard above my head and filled one with some roasted peanuts and the other with salty pretzel-type things. I then put the empty packets in the bin even though the whole kitchen was a write-off. I wondered who would take on the brunt of the cleaning the next day and I already suspected it would be me. But it was fine, I would need the distraction. I found a plastic cup and filled it with water from the tap. I pushed my way past a few huddled bodies and found my way to the back door and headed to the summerhouse. A group of gaggling girls and one lad had already found their way out here. I noticed one of them was smoking. I looked at my newly purchased furniture.

'I'm afraid there's no smoking in here,' I said before I had a chance to prepare which tone of voice I was going to use. Judging by the looks on their faces, I realised I must have used my least warming voice. One girl gave me such a foul look then stood up and pushed past me whilst the other muttered something about me sounding like her school headmaster. The lad took a moment longer to leave, but before he did, he flashed me an embarrassed smile.

I fell onto the sofa and laid my head against the fabric.

'Enjoying a moment of solitude?' A voice arrived in the room. For a moment I thought it was the lad who had just left, but when I opened my eyes, I saw Steve standing in front of me. I squinted a little as I tried to get him to come into focus.

'I see you've had a couple of drinks. It's nice to see you enjoying yourself.' Through my drunkenness, his voice bore even more of a repellent quality, and I wondered what exactly it was that Karen saw in him. He sat down on the chair. I laid my head back against the sofa again, but I kept my eyes open. We sat in silence for what felt like hours but could only have been minutes, or even seconds.

'Are you enjoying the party, Regi?' came Steve's voice again after I had hoped more than anything that he was just going to disappear from the room and leave me to enjoy some sanctuary. I imagined myself falling asleep in here. I sat up and looked at Steve. His short hair looked even shorter today, as though he might have had it cut just for the occasion. He was wearing a tight black T-shirt, even though he was not very well built at all. I would even go as far as to say he was bordering on skinny, a look that perhaps hadn't served him well in the army.

I knew Steve was drunk too. I could feel the air between us was charged.

'How long have you and Karen been together now, Steve?' I slurred.

He shook his head as he tried to think. 'I'd say just over a month now. But I'm not very good at keeping count. That's more you girls' jobs, isn't it?'

'That's a rather sexist comment to make.' My voice came out small and rough, but not as offensive as I had anticipated.

'Well, you think about that kind of stuff more than us. I'm sure Karen has put it in her diary or something. I don't know. What about you, Regi, no man on the scene?'

I shook my head and leant back against the sofa again. 'I'm very happy on my own, thank you.'

'It's good that you have made that decision and you are comfortable with it. There's nothing worse than being with someone and knowing they aren't quite for you.'

I glanced across at Steve, wondering why his words sounded weighted with sadness.

Steve caught my glance and held it. 'It's probably best to wait for the right one. Cos when you know, you just know, don't you?'

It wasn't even a question; it was a statement. I couldn't gauge the connotation. I was too drunk and too tired. I suddenly felt exposed and vulnerable, half lying back on the sofa. I realised this was the longest conversation I had had with Steve without anyone else in the room.

'Hey,' came a voice from the doorway and we looked away from one another and towards the door, to see Karen standing there sounding and looking breathless as she looked from Steve to me and back to Steve again. 'Why are you two skulking around in here?' I couldn't deny there was a hint of paranoia to her tone.

I looked over at Steve and went to say that it was he who had followed me in here. Perhaps it was our brief conversation, or the sour look on Karen's face, but something stopped me from saying anything.

As Karen moved closer she began interrogating Steve as to where he had been. My senses rose above Karen's interrogation and past the open door, where I heard the distinct raised voices of the couple next door again. I stood and left the summerhouse, past the heightening tones of Karen's voice and into the cooling night air. I edged my way towards the back of the garden, hoping to take a look over the fence, despite the man catching me earlier. The back fence only ran halfway along the garden until it was replaced by hedge. As I began to set up the stepladder, I saw a small gap in the foliage, as if an animal, a fox, perhaps, had made its way between the gardens. Did it lead through to next door? The alcohol still swirling through my veins gave me a little confidence to creep closer, to see where it would take me and if indeed that could be through to next door's garden.

I crouched down and realised I could fit through it. Just. I peered to the right and I could see enough of a clearing, a small portal, to suggest it would indeed take me through to next door. Suddenly, I felt like Lucy in *The Lion, the Witch and the Wardrobe*, and I had found this secret gateway to take me into another world.

'Regi.' Karen's voice was loud and sharp behind me. 'What are you doing?' I quickly stood up and brushed the mud and grass from my jeans.

'Are you being sick?' she asked.

'No, I...' I stopped myself. Of course I wouldn't say what I thought I had heard coming from next door. 'I thought I saw a fox.'

She narrowed her eyes at me. 'Are you sure you are feeling well?'

'I think I'm going to, erm, go to bed.' I turned to head back into the house.

'It's not even 10 p.m. yet?' Karen said. 'The party will be going on until dawn. I hope you have sleeping tablets?' she called after me as I walked away.

'I can sleep through anything,' I said. I took a final glance backwards and saw Steve looking my way as Karen turned back to him to continue her ranting.

I made my way through the house and towards the stairs. I stumbled past bodies lounging on the steps and found my way into my bedroom. I locked and unlocked the door six times, ending on a lock. Then I stood listening to a low hum of chatter woven through the pounding sound of the bass from the DJ.

I fell onto the bed, glad that I had changed the sheets already. The alcohol had done its job; I could feel tiredness engulfing me. I hadn't thought about Mrs Clean for a few hours but now I was alone with my own thoughts, she had crept into my mind again. I wondered what she was up to, how she had spent her Saturday evening. I had just about enough strength left in me to take a quick peek before I fell asleep. I opened the Instagram app. Along the top of my home page, I could see the small icon where her stories were. It was the same image Mrs Clean used for her profile; a photo of her hand in a pink Marigold. I clicked on it and found my way to an image of a perfectly made bed. The sheets were stretched to perfection, just the way I like to keep them.

After a few seconds, it disappeared. I clicked it again and examined the same image. I looked at how neatly she had made the bed, at how the cushions sat perfectly symmetrical, all six together, in two rows of three. It was very satisfying to look at. Then it was gone again. I pressed the icon again, this time I held my finger on the image, searching more quickly for moments of symmetry; the way she had taken the photo so the whole room was at an angle, a black-and-white photo on the wall just above the bed. My finger tired and slipped and the image disappeared.

I impatiently stabbed my finger at the screen again, and this time I took a moment to look at the texture of the wallpaper. It was a geometric abstract pattern. I looked at the image for a minute, trying to see a pattern emerge in the hexagons. Then there was something else, something that didn't fit with the black and white and greyness of the room. My eyes were drawn to another colour in the corner of the image. A flash of red. I was sure of it. In my drunken state, my finger tired and I had to bring the image up again as the timer had run out. I clicked and this time I used the time to look straight at the corner of the photo where I could see something peeping out from the bottom of the bed. I leant into the photo and could just about make out a tiny red shoe.

Eventually, tiredness overtook and my hand dropped to the side, still gripping my phone. I closed my eyes and dreamt about hundreds of tiny pairs of shoes, all dancing to the beat that rose from beneath me.

14

NOW

I woke up with a start; my was mouth dry, my phone was next to my hand. Why had I been dreaming so vividly of babies' shoes? Then I remembered what I saw before I fell asleep. I tried to switch on my phone, but it was dead. I hadn't put it on to charge, which was also part of my perfect evening routine, which I had managed to sabotage by drinking too much last night – something I had not meant to do.

I was glad I had managed to miss most of the evening's events. I wondered, with dread, what the house would look like when I opened my bedroom door. I stood up and walked round to the bedside table, plugged in my phone and pressed the on button. I waited as the icon showed and the phone began to fire back to life. My home screen was back. I took myself straight to Instagram. Did I dream that image last night? I couldn't have done. I specifically remember watching the same story over and over again, looking at the neatness of the room, feeling a sense of connection to Mrs Clean and to her house. It was because of that that I had noticed the shoes. There was definitely something that I had seen. But the story was gone.

I slumped to my door and opened and shut it six times to feed the monster that was growing rapidly this morning. Once in the corridor, I could see and smell the carnage of last night's activities. I stepped over a beer can, then made my way slowly down the stairs past crisp packets, food debris and puddles of liquid, which I hoped was just alcohol and not where someone hadn't made it to a bathroom in time. I headed straight to Mini's room and knocked tentatively. She was the one who had introduced me to Instagram; she could tell me where to find the story I had been looking at last night.

There was no answer after my second knock. I was about to walk away when I heard Mini croak, 'Yes...'

I opened the door and the smell of stale alcohol hit me. I could see Mini lying on her side on the bed, and there was a body on the other side of her, male, tall and gangly with a wiry-haired chest. Light from the hallway spilled across the bed and onto Mini's face. She stirred, then slowly opened one eye. I stood holding my breath. As Mini registered my presence, she opened her other eye, sat up and squinted at me. She looked sheepishly across at the other side of the bed and then back at me.

'Are you okay?' she said in a loud whisper.

'I... I'm sorry. I didn't mean to disturb, I thought you'd be up. It's just I wanted to know how to find the stories on Instagram. You know, when someone posts one, I watched one last night and well this morning it's gone.'

Mini shook her head a little. 'I don't know, they only last twenty-four hours, unless the host saved them in their highlights.'

'Where would that be?' I whispered back as the body next to her let out a loud snore and shifted in the bed. Mini looked over at him and then back at me. She picked her phone up from the bedside table and rubbed her face.

'It's seven fifteen, Regi.'

'I know, sorry. I thought it was later, I fell asleep pretty early,' I said and began to back out of the room.

'Don't worry, it's fine. Look, just along the top here.' Mini pointed at her phone and I took a few tentative steps towards the bed and stretched to look so I wasn't too close to either of them. I could see where Mini was pointing to; just under the personal information on the personal page of the Instagram host was a row of circles, all with different titles underneath them.

'Okay, great, thanks. Sorry to disturb.' I took a few long steps backwards and shut the door. I heard the muffled sounds of Mini's bed guest saying something and her soothing voice saying something back. I headed back to my room where my phone was charging still. I opened Mrs Clean's Instagram page and looked under the personal information where Mini had shown me. There were a selection of Mrs Clean's highlighted stories, all under different headings. I sat and watched through all thirty-six stories in the different categories, but not one of them was the story I had seen last night.

What had I seen last night? My memory of it was already fading. Many of Mrs Clean's followers talked about how she didn't have any children. How she presented herself as a single woman living in a house. I had always seen her house as the baby she couldn't have. Perhaps she had guests round and someone had left a toddler-sized shoe under her bed. That had to be the only explanation. But I felt a new growing interest forming inside me. I wanted, no, *needed* to know more. I wanted to know her story; who she was, whether she had children but perhaps chose not to photograph them? An Instagram photo was only a moment in time; it didn't represent someone's entire persona or their whole life. And it was for this reason that I wanted to know more. The snippets were simply not enough for me.

I went into one of the newest photos on her feed. It was an

old-fashioned radiator painted white, and a pink-Marigold-cladded hand with a cloth wiping it down. Underneath she had written about her weekend being full of spring cleaning. I started looking through the comments, to see if anyone had mentioned anything about seeing a red shoe in an Instagram story last night. There were so many – thirty thousand or so. But as I scrolled through, I began to see the odd few negative messages and the one from lucybest65 stood out.

I quickly sped through as many comments as I could and saw nothing. No one else had noticed. I remembered how I had fallen asleep clutching my phone, which could only have meant that I was looking at the story right up until I fell asleep. I must have studied it pretty hard. I doubt anyone else looked as intricately as I did, and it was only because I had looked at it so many times that I spotted it. If I wasn't looking as much as I was, I certainly would have missed it.

Who was she? Was she a liar? A fraud? Maybe she didn't even clean her own house and paid someone to do it for her? I was beginning to wish I hadn't touched a drop of alcohol last night as my intrigue grew. I had been given a snapshot into someone's life and then not been given anything else. It was addictive. It made me want to keep coming back, to find out what other pieces of this woman's life I was slowly putting together. The 'Banksy of Instagram' as one of her followers had referred to her.

I found myself sitting in my lecture on Monday and Mrs Clean drifted into my thoughts as she was doing more and more often these days. The vanishing red shoe was all I could think about. I kept going back to her profile and searching each photo on her grid for other clues about her life. I needed to know more about this woman, how she got to live in this house, the house I had dreamt about, so full of symmetry and so aesthetically pleasing. The house I had seen myself living in with my family. What exactly did it take to become an influencer? How did it work? I had been so removed from the world of social media for so long – I had been living my life purely on autopilot, it seemed. Now I was re-engaged in society, I had so many questions. So many thoughts, specifically about Mrs Clean, this woman who was living a fabulous life of luxury and cleanliness. She had begun to drip-feed me tiny snippets of her life every day. The more she posted, the more I wanted to see, but it still felt like it was never enough.

I was scrolling through another post of Mrs Clean's and hadn't heard the tutor call my name. Suddenly, I felt eyes on me and it was like I was fourteen again and in secondary school as I felt the heat rush to my neck and cheeks. I looked up at Sheila, the lecturer, and only then could I hear the echo of her question lingering.

I put my mobile down on the table, face down.

'Sorry, I missed that – I was researching a pattern technique,' I said, feeling more guilty at my lie.

Sheila gave me a knowing look and turned back to the board and continued with the lecture. Thirty-six years old and I could still be made to feel like an incompetent child. Wow. The shame gripped me and then slowly it began to morph into something else; a desire to run, to do anything other than sit still. I managed to hold on until the lesson had ended, and then I rushed across the courtyard to the ladies' on the far side of the college where it was always quiet. I knew I could open and close a door a few times and not be spotted by anyone. I emerged from the toilet a few minutes later and began my walk back across the courtyard. I turned left to a patch of grass and found a spot away from people.

I sat down and pulled out my lunch box; a salad and a smoothie. Once I had helped with the clearing up of the party, I prepared my lunches for the next few days as part of my weekly meal planning that Mrs Clean had demonstrated on her feed. I pulled open the lid on the Tupperware just as a shadow fell over me. I looked up and saw Will.

'Hey, Regi, how are you? How was the party?'

I strained to look up at him, his height towering above me.

'Hey, Will.'

'May I?' he pointed to the patch of grass next to me.

'Sure.' I nodded. I felt a mixture of embarrassment for the last time I had seen him and my episode in the clothes shop. But then I also felt something else, something which felt like relief, that I was no longer sat on this vast patch of grass alone.

'How was the party?' Will sat with his knees pulled up to his chest. I was grateful he had chosen to ask me about the party and not the incident over the weekend. Although I still felt the topic hovering over us, as though it needed to be spoken about. I wasn't sure if I should have thanked him for his kindness and understanding or skate over it, pretend it hadn't happened.

'It was good.' I picked at my salad with the fork I had packed. I looked at Will. 'To be honest, I didn't see much of it – I drank too much and was in bed by ten.'

Will scoffed. 'That's brilliant. Nice one. A girl after my own heart.'

I shifted a glance at Will, my look filled with questioning. It had been too long since I had had to assess a man's intentions. Will seemed keen to be around me, and he had asked me out for a drink; I should be confidently translating that into 'he likes me'. But though I felt something simmering in my gut whenever I saw him, how could I reciprocate, how could I fulfil my role as a partner in a relationship? Up until now, the thought had never crossed my mind. I was in a place that was too dark, that even the light that came from the feeling of a new relationship couldn't touch it. I still had the echoes of accusations that had been screamed so close to my face, followed so suddenly by the empty silence that was just as palpable.

'I dig an early night,' Will said, gauging my look. I looked back down into my salad. He cleared his throat. 'But you rocked your top though, I hope?'

I nodded. Trying to arrange some semblance of words. 'Right through until morning,' I said brightly.

'You slept in your clothes? Now I'm impressed.' Will gave a quick raise of his eyebrows.

'Bit of a lightweight these days,' I said, allowing a small smile to edge its way across my lips.

Will smiled with his eyes, then looked up towards the sky and closed them, showing his appreciation for the warm midday sun. He opened them again and brought his attention to me. I had to quickly look away so that he wouldn't catch me staring.

'Sorry you didn't get to have much of a time at the party. Maybe I should have hung around, taken you out for a drink instead.'

The way he said 'taken me out' as opposed to 'us' going for a drink, I understood the connotations behind the sentiment. And I found it strange to think that someone would be interested in this version of me, this version that I had no comprehension of. I had lost my self-actualisation. I no longer had any understanding of who I was or what I projected into the world. Sometimes, I had an overwhelming desire to get back to my past. I'd imagine myself opening a door and walking into my life from ten years ago and just picking up from where things were, when everything was so easy and simple. Even though I didn't know it at the time. Of course, I would have returned to those blissful years with hindsight and steered my life away from the danger and sadness.

Will was looking at me, maybe waiting for a response. But what should I say: 'No thanks, I'm socially inept with OCD compulsions that stem from a trauma I'll never get over, so I'm kind of staying away from the dating scene, for, oh, say... forever.'

I smiled weakly and picked some more at my salad.

'So, tell me what your kids have been learning from you today?' I just couldn't get into a conversation about having a drink alone with this man. His perception of me was based purely on what he could see. Once he lifted the veil, I was sure I would be nothing more than a disappointment.

Will smiled knowingly as I bypassed his reference to a drink. 'Oh, not a lot, I'm sure. They all seem to drift off – no one seems to have an attention span any more. Everyone has their head in their phones.'

I thought about my own obsession with Instagram and wondered how many hours I had lost to my phone recently. Even thinking about it made me want to take my phone out and check in with Mrs Clean.

'I'm sure most of them are here because they have nothing better to be doing. There are a few who are totally into it though. But they're the rare ones.'

'So were you a boffin at school then? Always concentrating and handing in your assignments on time?'

'Well, mostly.' Will looked sheepish. 'I knew how to have a good time as well though. That's what the noughties were for.'

I cast my memory back to those carefree days, which for me didn't last long enough. I was bogged down with life's worries way too early when I should have been off doing what my house mates were doing now: partying until the early hours, with no care or worry. Maybe this was why I unconsciously chose to live with girls over a decade younger than me; maybe I was reminding myself what my life could have been like if I had made a different choice.

'So what do you like to get up to outside of college, Regi?' I thought about the way Will let my name roll off his tongue. I had always enjoyed listening to people when they inserted my name into the sentence.

'I, er, I don't hang out with my house mates. They just tolerate me.' I gave a small, hollow laugh.

'I'm sure you have something to offer. Wisdom? The moral high ground? Been there, got the T-shirt?'

I shook my head. 'I wouldn't know how to offer any of those things.'

'Oh, come on now, you're a woman of the world. I reckon you've seen a few things, done a few things.'

I froze at his words. The memories of the past would never fade. I had done plenty of things. So many of them I was not proud of.

'Have you put your name down for the exhibition?' Will was looking at the sky again. 'I mean, I've not seen your work, but I guess it's good enough for you to get on this course, so you should consider it. It will help with your grade at the end.'

'Exhibition?' I asked. I had come here with no real intentions of doing any extracurricular activities. This was a short course to get me through into the first year. I hadn't thought about doing any more than I actually had to do.

'The art exhibition. Anyone from an introductory course or the first year of a degree course can exhibit. It's not happening until mid-July, so you have a couple of months to prepare for it. I thought that might be your sort of thing.'

I really wished I knew what my sort of thing was. Right now, I felt as though it was Mrs Clean. But I didn't talk about that. She was my secret passion.

'I bet you were quite the little joiner in your day?' Will continued.

I shrugged. 'Maybe, a long time ago,' I said wistfully, remembering all the groups and clubs I was a member of. Then instantly I regretted my tone as Will looked at me with a wonder in his eye.

'So, you gonna sign up for it?'

'I guess,' I said quickly.

Will looked at his watch and wrinkled his nose.

'That's me then. No rest for the wicked.' Will stood up and brushed his trousers down. I eyed him subtly from the corner of my eye.

'Hey, let me know if you ever want that drink, you know.' Will threw a backpack over his shoulder and looked down. I looked up and squinted.

'Thanks. I will.'

'You will go for a drink or will let me know?' Will said tentatively.

I let out a small laugh. I couldn't fault him for trying.

'I'll let you know,' I said. Will lifted his hand to wave.

'Okay, Regina, I'll see ya.'

I felt sorry for Will then, the way he pronounced the name *Regina* with such veracity and passion. It was a wonderful name and had it been the name I had been blessed with at birth, I would have felt a connection to it. But it wasn't my real name. Like so many other things about me, it was a lie.

15

I was pregnant again. I had just turned nineteen. D had been working away more and more, and I was beginning to enjoy the freedom. I felt a growing maternal instinct, and I often felt long episodes of relaxation, yet I was equally terrified of what would come when he returned. He was usually in high spirits for the first few days, but then things would start to grind on him. Like the flat.

'I'm sick of it in here. It's too cramped.' He paced up and down the lengthy kitchen that I had always found to be more than adequate.

'Well, can't we think about moving out somewhere soon?' I thought of the tiny foetus growing inside me. He stopped his pacing and looked at me with a hard glare. I felt my gut tighten and my mouth went dry. I looked at how close I was to the door. Could I make a run for it? But before I had time to consider it properly, he was by my side. His arms slipped around my waist as he yanked me forcefully towards him and locked me there.

'You don't need to worry about that. I have it all sorted. That's what I do, isn't it? I have a job I need to do to secure us a nice little house. Don't you think I want that for you, my queen? I was only discussing it with someone this morning.' He spoke so softly that anyone who overheard him would think me the luckiest woman in the world.

'Really?' I said, surprised. The flat was fine for the two of us, even three or four of us. I had made it nice over the last few months, ordered some extra bits of furniture when D was having a 'generous day'. And now I was meticulous. I made sure it was tidy beyond anyone's expectations, every single day. D had spoken of us moving occasionally, but now it sounded as though it would actually happen soon.

'Yep.' He bent his legs and arched his back a little so I was curved into him, my head almost at his height.

I felt the intensity of the closeness between us.

'You know how you said that maybe one day you imagined us as a little family?'

He gave a mere nod.

I swallowed again. 'Well, I think that that time might be here very soon. I'm pregnant.'

He let go of me so quickly I thought I would fall backwards. I braced myself, ready for a fist or a kick. His hands were running through his short hair, an action he often did when he was riled.

'You mean, I'm going to be a dad?' I looked at him and I could see his eyes glimmering with tears. It was a side of him I had never seen. I nodded.

'Fuck me. I'm not sure I'm ready for this. I mean, look at me – I still feel like a kid myself. But, heck, I'm nearly thirty – if not now, then when?' He pulled me back towards him again. He was whispering things into my ear, promising me all sorts of things.

I knew I should have felt the ecstatic feelings, like they did in the films, as he pulled me into his arms. I felt as though I should have closed my eyes and inhaled him in whilst I imagined my future. I tried to focus on the positive, the new life inside me, but all I could think of was how I had already been here once before, and how he had reacted as if the last one meant nothing. I hadn't forgotten his reaction that day when he came home and found me bleeding the first time I was pregnant. I made no accusations – he was never made to feel responsible – but I had expected a little empathy. It was his child as well. He simply told me to 'clean up the mess and stop overreacting – it happens all the time'. That baby may only have been mine for a few months, but I would never forget it. I would never forget the way he treated me.

I made a promise to myself that when this new baby arrived, I would protect it with my life.

* * *

Instagram post: 6th May 2019

Hi guys, me again! I can't believe how lucky we are with the weather right now. I feel so blessed to have my little bit of space outside to play around with. I've been pottering around in the garden. I have a little pop-up greenhouse, which was gifted to me by @growyourown after I showed my green-fingered side during the summer months last year, but sadly I was a bit too late to start growing anything really substantial. This year, however, I have got ahead of myself, and I've started courgettes, tomatoes, cabbage, broccoli, lettuce and rocket. These are all things I absolutely love to eat myself. If this weather keeps up, I'll be happy out here until the end of summer. Now all I need is a lovely glass of wine.

Mrs C x

#vegetables #growyourown #mrsclean

78,899 likes

kelly.winkler What an inspiration you are. I'll be following suit once I get home from work.

wonderstuff I planted spuds first time this year. Can't wait to see them in a few months. #thegreatoutdoors.

lucybest65 Doesn't anyone else think it's sad that this woman is all alone in her garden with only her plants to talk to?

F16kb3 Why are you always giving her a hard time? Just let the woman be.

lucybest65 I'm just pointing out that it's not normal.

bornfree It's perfectly normal to talk to your plants.

16

NOW

I had finished college early and had come back to an empty house. I sat at the kitchen table, taking a well-earned rest from cleaning out the kitchen cupboards. I had surprised myself when I began the task willingly, as opposed to through compulsion. I got stuck in and settled into a flow and eventually found myself drifting off and thinking about other things. Things that weren't the past; the stuff that haunted my thoughts most days and drove my compulsive behaviours.

Eventually I picked up my phone again and I automatically navigated my way to Mrs Clean's account, where I looked at her most recent post. It was an image of a perfect patch of artificial grass with a small neat path next to it that I presumed led back to the house. Just to the right was a shot of the pop-up greenhouse she had been gifted. It was fairly extravagant and almost the size of a full greenhouse. I pressed the tag of the company who had gifted it to her, and it took me through to their profile page. On their personal info was their website. I hit the link and found myself navigating my way to their pop-up greenhouses. There was quite a range, but I soon found the one that Mrs Clean had been gifted, which was almost a hundred pounds; a luxury for many. A memory drifted through of growing seedlings on my windowsills as a child. The look of pure joy on my mother's face when I showed her the first sprouts of life that were bursting through the soil. As an only child, I never had to fight for her attention.

I had been pushing these sorts of images away, but just recently, something had begun to shift, I had begun to allow myself to ponder over a few memories. In the same way I had begun to assess myself and my feelings whenever Will was around.

I scrolled through the comments on the post and I saw another comment from lucybest65. There she was, moaning again about something that Mrs Clean was doing. I didn't understand why people followed an influencer, only to criticise them constantly.

Knowing that we could be kindred spirits was one of the reasons I looked forward to seeing Mrs Clean's posts. I felt a flutter of excitement whenever I saw she had posted something new, and this was something I had not felt for so long, but Lucy's comments were marring the whole experience.

I thought once more about leaving a comment, something nice. Maybe she would notice it and comment back, but I didn't bother. I thought again about us as friends. Perhaps if I privately messaged her, told her how inspired I was by her work, she might message me back and we could strike up a rapport. But she had over one million followers. Why would she possibly answer my message? I stood up and went back to my work. I stooped down and began placing all the pans back into the clean, freshly wiped cupboard. They had been filthy, covered in crumbs and grease with pans and pots falling over one another. Once I had them all back in, there was so much more room. I stood back to admire my work.

'You did a good job there.' I swung round with force, my heart suddenly beating in my mouth as my body so easily defaulted into flight-or-fight mode.

Steve was leaning against the door frame.

'How long have you been there?' Panic rose in my throat as I thought back to how I had spent the last few hours, where I had presumed I was alone.

'Not long.' He stretched and yawned. He was wearing a white vest and it rose up a little, revealing a little flurry of hair around his navel. I averted my eyes immediately. 'I just woke up.'

So he had been in the house for some time. I paid what some might consider to be an extortionate amount of rent every month to live here, and I couldn't even feel relaxed in my own surroundings.

'Fancy a cuppa?' Steve walked over to the kettle, stopped and looked down at me crouched by the pan cupboard. 'Crouching tiger, hidden dragon.' He put his hands out and stood statue still. Then he broke into a laugh; it was the first time I had seen him make a joke with me when the others weren't around. He had a short, hollow laugh. I stood up and headed over to the table to retrieve my phone.

'Regi, I—' Steve began to speak, but the panic was raging through my body.

'Enjoy your tea,' I cut him off as I left the room.

Upstairs, I threw my phone on the bed and locked and unlocked the door, then ended on a lock. I paced the room for a few minutes, knowing I needed to confront Karen, but thinking about the way she looked at me the night of the party when Steve sought me out in the summerhouse, I wasn't so sure there would be a good time. I was drunk that night, but one of the last things I remember, even through the darkness of the garden, was her penetrating stare.

I stripped my bed and remade it with the clean sheets in a pile by my drawers. Still, the strain in my chest wouldn't shift, so I opened my phone and navigated my way to Instagram. It was a relief to see that Mrs Clean had posted a story since I had looked a moment ago downstairs. The calm washed over me.

It was a video of her ragdoll cat. She was stroking it with a brush that she wore on her hand like a mitt. The cat was purring loudly. But underneath that I could hear her breath, small and shallow, just out of sync with the cat.

To hear her breath made me feel her realness and humanness even more. But I couldn't just reach through the screen and touch her or talk to her. The injustice of this app was infuriating.

We could be friends, I was sure of it.

I was thrust away from my thoughts and scrolling by a knock on my bedroom door. After my series of unlocking, I found Karen on the other side, unable to conceal her annoyance.

'Hi.' The tension was fierce in her throat. I stood back to let her in, but she remained in the doorway. 'I just wanted to check everything was okay, you know,' Karen said, 'because I just asked Steve who was in the house and he said you. And well, after the party, I felt things were a little weird.'

I shook my head in bewilderment.

'I didn't think things were weird, but what is weird is that Steve comes and goes in this house as though he owns it. I pay a lot of money to live here and I feel... some of the time, uncomfortable. He seems to just show up, turn up out of nowhere, like today. I presumed the house I pay top London prices to live in was empty. Then suddenly, Steve is behind me in the kitchen. I would like to feel safe and secure in this house. I chose to live with you and Sophia and Mini. Females. Not males. Not Steve.'

Karen was shifting uncomfortably from foot to foot and staring straight at me. There was a wildness in her eyes.

'Fine.' She crossed her arms. I imagined this was not something she was fine about at all. 'It's probably something else anyway.'

I shook my head, not understanding.

'I mean, he's always there when you are. So maybe it's you and not him!'

'Come again?'

'He's been acting weird, You obviously have a little crush on him, which is fine.' Karen threw her hands up in the air dramatically. 'It always happens to me. I get a boyfriend and someone else manages to get their claws into them. Steve is mine. Just so you know and so there isn't any confusion here.' She circled her finger in front of her, turned on her heel and clomped off down the hall. I shook my head in disbelief. To think that I would fancy Steve? He reminded me too much of someone I was trying to forget.

* * *

Later that evening, we were all sat eating together. It was a takeaway curry for Meat-Free Monday, one of the quirky things the girls had established to distinguish between days of the week: Taco Tuesday, Whatever Wednesday, Thirsty Thursday and Fajita Fridays. It was all new to me yet slightly endearing how they all liked to come together each evening and how they also included me. However, this evening as we sat, I could sense Karen's anger and, from the odd looks that Mini was throwing my way, I presumed others could sense it too.

We were all clearing away the takeaway and stacking our

plates into the dishwasher, when we all turned to hear a loud vibration coming from the kitchen table.

'Erm, I think that's your phone, Regi,' Mini said. I looked to the tabletop where I could see my phone creeping towards the edge with each vibration. I strode over, glanced at the screen and shoved the phone in my pocket where it continued to vibrate for several more uncomfortable seconds. I had set it to silent but didn't realise it was on a vibrate setting as well. I took in a deep breath through my nose and blew it out through my mouth as subtly as I could. I supposed I could block the number. But it wouldn't make any difference. He would find me.

'I don't think I have ever seen you answer a call,' Karen said, and I know she was only saying what the others were thinking. I had, of course, answered calls, just not very many.

'Maybe, Regi prefers texts,' Mini said as she stacked her plate in at an awkward angle and put her cutlery in the wrong way.

'Or Instagram,' Sophia said, and even though she hadn't meant to be malicious, my fists clenched as I felt a surge of heat across my cheeks.

I closed the dishwasher with too much force as Sophia edged over to me. 'It is where you've been getting all your cleaning-hack ideas from, isn't it?'

Mini looked over from the other side of the kitchen. 'I told Regi about all the cleanstagrammers. I said she should do some tap-to-tidy posts on her own Instagram site.'

'Well, you certainly have the bug.' Sophia looked around the kitchen, which was now clutter-free and organised. 'And the house is a lot tidier. I found horseradish in the fridge the other day – I didn't know we had horseradish.' Sophia laughed.

'Well, I think Regi should get out more,' came the sharp tone of Karen's voice and both Mini and Sophia shot her a look then looked at one another.

'Well, that's just rude. What do you mean by that, Karen?' Sophia looked at me, bewildered. Karen ignored Sophia and carried on putting things away too loudly. Sophia put a hand on my shoulder. 'I think you're doing a great job around here. I'm just sorry we're not as keen to go all out as you are. You must think us terribly messy.'

'Have you ever thought about online dating, Regi?' Karen said offhandedly.

'Never,' I retorted.

'Well, I think it would do you the world of good. You like being on your phone a lot, clearly you have bags of time and you're single.' Karen put way too much emphasis on the word *single*.

'It's not a bad idea,' Mini said. 'Dating is so different now, I mean to when you did it last. Maybe.'

I had never dated. I had met and fallen in the love when I was young. Maybe too young. Until then it was the odd snog and unsuccessful episode in bed with someone I neither really liked nor fancied, but I felt as though I should have been going along with it because that's what girls my age did.

Sophia shrugged. 'Yeah, but you've got to want to do it in the first place. You can't just put yourself out there if you're not really fussed.'

'Well, it's the only way to meet people nowadays, isn't it?' Karen said, her voice a little too high. 'I mean you do want to meet someone, don't you, Regi? Unless, you know, you have someone, a secret boyfriend you're not telling us about.'

'No secret boyfriend,' I said flatly, narrowing my eyes at Karen. I felt a flicker of rage. I wondered how much longer I would tolerate her mouth. Pretty soon I would need to do something about it.

'You should go for it, Regi. You really are very pretty – you should definitely do it,' Mini said sweetly.

'Yes, and do come home and tell us your dating stories,' Sophia said.

'I can get you set up on the app – it's dead simple,' Mini said. 'If you can master Instagram, you will definitely be able to master a dating app. It can become quite addictive.'

I was intrigued.

'I just say go for it, Regi. I don't think it's healthy just sitting around the house when you're not at uni. I know you've been doing the cleaning, and that's great, but you're not our mother,' Karen said with a catch in her voice.

I raised an eyebrow at this comment and Sophia stepped in.

'What she means is' – Sophia gave Karen the eyes – 'is that you're fabulous and gorgeous, and you should be out there finding someone like-minded, having some fun.'

I suddenly remembered what it felt like to receive a compliment like that. The thought of someone saying that to me filled me with uncertainty. But Sophia was right about finding someone like-minded. The girls were good for everyday company, and Sophia was beginning to feel more like a friend to me than the other two, but occasionally I considered what it would be like to meet someone who was my age and shared similar interests.

'I'm sure you can find someone with similar traits to you, you know if it's the OCD stuff that's bothering you. I'm sure there're loads of blokes who have compulsions,' Karen said matter-of-factly.

'My God, who's rattled your cage today, Karen?' Sophia said firmly, and Karen looked visibly shocked at the outburst.

'Er, no one,' she said eventually. 'I just hate seeing Regi moping about the place, becoming obsessed with cleanstagrammers.'

'Hey, I'm not obsessed,' I said sharply.

'So why is that the fifth time today I've seen you pick up your phone and check out what's-her-face's profile?'

'It just automatically falls on that one. I don't follow enough people yet,' I said, not understanding why I felt the need to justify myself.

'Oh, just get her set up on Tinder already, Mini,' Karen called from the hallway as she walked out of the kitchen and stomped upstairs. The sound of her bedroom door slamming made all of our bodies jerk.

'What the hell has got into her?' Sophia sat down at the table.

'She thinks I'm trying to steal Steve,' I said with one hand in the air in disbelief.

'Oh my God, really?' Mini scoffed. Sophia's mouth opened to say something, but Mini carried on. 'She's paranoid. Granted, it's happened twice before with two separate boyfriends. She must be desperate to match you up with someone if she doesn't want you to steal Steve.' Mini stifled a giggle. Sophia gave a weak smile.

'Hey, I'm happy to get the app and for you to show me how it works, but I'm not promising anything,' I said.

Mini squealed and clapped her hands together. 'Really? Oh, brilliant. Oh, Regi, this is so fab. I really think you are going to find your true love.'

I smiled at her enthusiasm, neglecting to tell her that I had stopped believing in true love a long time ago.

Despite my reservations about finding companionship via the internet, I watched as Mini eagerly installed the app on my phone, and before I knew it, I was posing awkwardly on the sofa for my profile shot. My phone was new. It had a handful of numbers in the contact list, one or two apps and no photos of me from my past. I did not need the constant reminders of seeing the old me, the one who didn't carry any of the burdens I carried today.

It was only when she had finished and my account was complete that I realised my face was now out there online, and I had no idea who could be looking at it.

17

The next morning I awoke to the sound of the house coming to life. The pipes creaked as someone ran the shower, I heard the clink-clank of crockery as it hit the countertops in the kitchen; someone clomped down the stairs and along the corridor. It was probably Karen. She was still harbouring some anger, and whilst she was generally moody with all of us, she seemed to be directing most of her anger towards me.

My phone rang. It was him. These calls were coming through more often. It wouldn't be long until he turned up here. Would I be ready for him? Or would I run away like I had been doing for too long?

I dressed lightly in denim shorts and a white T-shirt. I stripped my bed, unlocked and locked my window six times before I left the room and walked down the stairs as Karen was coming back up the stairs. I looked at her boots; she was, indeed, the clomper.

'Morning,' I said confidently. Karen grunted something back, but I was already halfway down the stairs and I was going to be late for my seminar if I didn't hurry. I grabbed a muesli bar, an apple and a bottle of water from my cupboard in the kitchen and stepped out of the house, thoughts of the morning's missed call on my phone still playing on my mind as I looked at the ground and tried to walk within the cracks of the pavement.

I walked along the avenue lined with trees on either side and wished more than anything that I had given myself a spare few minutes to grab my favourite coffee for the journey. I found a seat on the train easily and sat down and opened my muesli bar and water. I put the bar to my mouth and that was when I caught a glimpse of a black baseball cap through the gap in the chair in front of me. I edged to the right to try to get a better look and dropped my bar. I bent to pick it up. Once I was sat back up again, I looked through the gap and could now see a black beanie hat. No baseball cap in sight. My mouth was dry and I no longer felt hungry.

I walked the two blocks from the station to the university. Flashes of the black baseball cap kept appearing in front of my eyes, and I had to physically shake my head to shift them. I needed more distractions. Karen, through her subtle micro-aggression, was absolutely right; I needed to get out, even if it was just for my own sanity. I didn't need to look at anything long-term, but I needed to start finding my way back to some sort of normality, not just painting by numbers and pretending that I was a normal person just because I paid rent and bought a fancy, overpriced coffee every now and again. I needed to do it, not just to show those around me that I was okay, but to prove to myself that I could. I needed him to know I had moved on; once he could see that, maybe he would leave me alone.

I knew what I would start with, and the conversation I had

with Will the other day reverberated in my ears. I would sign up for the exhibition. I needed to fill my days and hours with as much as I possibly could.

I went to the main art block and found there was a little desk with a piece of paper taped to it. I wrote down my name, student number and a rough outline of what my exhibition would be.

From the images I had been collecting on my phone, I had been subconsciously building towards a project. Now I had a reason to create it.

I headed to my first lesson of the day. It was a practical, and I knew I could lose myself in the colours and textures. I had been making some preliminary sketches, and I felt a wave of enthusiasm that it might turn into something good.

At lunchtime, I found myself in the spot where Will and I had sat and chatted a few days ago. I didn't want to sit and imagine Will showing up, taking a seat and distracting me with his shiny eyes and easy conversation, so I pulled out my phone and checked in on Mrs Clean. She had posted, in her stories; this time a photo of a toilet taken on an angle. There was some sort of hanging plant spidering its way from a basket that was attached to the wall. There was a candle on the windowsill and I realised it was an ad for this particular candle brand. It said, *Swipe up to buy.* So I did, and found myself on a website that sold purely organic candles. Without too much thought, I ordered a lavender, basil and lemon one. I had never heard of that combination, but I was pretty sure that was the one Mrs Clean had on her windowsill.

I looked up from my phone, half expecting to see Will, but I didn't. I felt something in the pit of my stomach; regret at not taking him up on his offer for a drink. I thought about the dating app that Mini had installed for me and talked me through. I hadn't looked at it since we uploaded my information yesterday.

Mini had asked why I didn't have any photos of myself on my phone. I hadn't taken a photo of myself in years, I told her.

It was hard not to think about when I was a different person, and I did, all the time. I felt truly robbed of everything, not just the loss of the life I knew and loved, but I had totally lost who I was. I looked back on images or texts from days before it happened and thought to myself, how could I have ever been so happy? How can I now feel so different to that person who was bantering on text messages and taking selfies with a perfect streak of lens flare across her face? It was me, but it wasn't me any more. That me was gone, and I didn't think she would ever return.

I looked at the dating app and I could see there were profiles of suitable men in front of me, and I was now supposed to what? Check them out, decide if liked them? 'Swipe right to say you like them, left if you don't,' was what Mini said. I looked at the first profile. It was a tall man in a police uniform. I immediately swiped left. I was presented with another potential suitor: Darren, stocky, muscles, clean-shaven, likes going to the gym and socialising. I swiped left.

Next, a preppy-looking guy with neat, dark hair, wearing a corduroy jacket and jeans. Solicitor, enjoys walks, meals out and books. Okay, I thought, this sounds as though it could be something I could possibly endure for an hour or two. I took a deep breath and swiped right, then quickly shoved my phone away. If he decided he liked me too, then it was going to be okay, I reminded myself. It was just two people having a conversation, but I would have to make sure we only went for a drink; eating food in front of strangers was out of the question. I had just about managed to train myself to eat with my house mates, and I did that as little as possible.

But it was going to be okay. Because much worse things had happened.

* * *

By the time I had arrived home from college, I had received a match. He, Calvin, had decided he liked the look of me and had messaged me, suggesting meeting for a drink at the weekend. For that I was grateful. I couldn't handle anything more than that.

I went into the house and was relieved to find I was alone after I hollered a couple of hellos and poked my head around Karen's door to make sure there was no sign of Steve. I made a herbal tea and went out to the summerhouse. I sat and closed my eyes, my tea cradled in my hands. The sounds came floating through, the same sounds I had been hearing for weeks: the pained cries of a child. My body flooded with the same fear I had been plagued with for years. I stood up and put my mug down on the table and went to the doorway. The child's cries were strong and persistent. I couldn't look over the fence again. I remembered the hedge at the end of our garden. Although I had yet to explore it further, I was sure that it could take me through to their garden. I left the summerhouse and headed towards the hedge. I shot a look back at the house to make sure that no one was watching me from the window and got down on all fours. Edging forwards, I clambered to my right, through the undergrowth until I could feel I was pushing my way into their garden. The hedge opened up again into a small clearing.

Finally, I could see the child. It was a little boy. My heart pounded and tears sprung into my eyes. He was almost exactly like... No, it couldn't be. The long, unruly hair, the size and age of him, it was all so familiar. He was standing just inside the house next to an open patio door. Alone. I took a chance and shifted myself forwards into the clearing. I was still surrounded by shrubbery with a wide view of the patio and a small patch of grass in front of me. As though he could sense me there, the little boy looked up at me with his big eyes in alarm. He was standing quietly, no longer crying, but I put my finger to my lips and a small 'shhh' escaped them. He edged forward so his feet were balancing on the patio-door ledge. He looked uncertainly behind him, then placed one foot on the patio. He took another precautionary glance over his shoulder, then placed the other foot on the patio. My heart was filling up with maternal love as I imagined him breaking into a sprint and running into my arms that had been so empty for so long. But he just stood there. I looked around the garden and noticed how there were no toys, no sandpit, no push bike, scooter or football. Nothing. The garden was perfectly clear and exceptionally well pruned. There was shout, a name was being called.

'Raff... Raff,' came a woman's voice, the same woman I had seen and heard before. The boy looked panicked and rooted to the spot.

'Raff! Raff!' she was screeching in the European accent I still couldn't place. Then she continued to shout in a language I didn't recognise. Raff, who was still frozen to the spot, let out a high-pitched wail. I shuffled backwards as I heard the woman arriving at the doorway and turned my body into the shrubbery. The screams continued and then faded as the patio doors were slammed shut. I shuffled back, but I was still looking at the spot where he had been standing where there was now a small puddle.

* * *

I felt sick as I went back into the house. I paced around the kitchen, looking for something to do to relieve the panic that was building through my body. I raced upstairs, wringing my hands, an act that I only did when things were spiralling out of control. I opened and closed my window six times, making sure the latch was firmly across on the final lock. Then I paced my room, desperately thinking of ways to feed the monster who had reared his ugly head. I went back downstairs and began pacing the kitchen again.

Suddenly, I heard the front door close and I stopped dead. I couldn't see anyone like this. I went to the kitchen door to make my way back upstairs again, but Sophia was already there before I could make my escape.

'Hey, how are...' She trailed off. 'Regi, are you okay? Do you want to sit?'

She dropped her bag on the floor and strode over to the cupboard, took a glass down and filled it with water. She guided me to the table and I sat, shaking; I couldn't keep my legs still. She sat next to me and I placed a hand on my quivering leg.

'Regi, what is it?'

I looked at her. 'The boy, the boy next door, I...'

Sophia looked quizzical. 'What boy?'

'There's a child, a boy, long hair, and his mother...'

I stopped.

The mother; her face and her voice were suddenly so familiar to me. I had met her before.

'Who is his mother?' Sophia stroked my hand lightly.

An image from a few weeks ago sprung into my mind. 'I remember, I saw her, she was in the shop. She couldn't afford a kid's bottle of paracetamol. So I bought it for her.'

Sophia tightened her grip on my hand. 'Oh, Regi, that was such a nice thing to do. Good for you.' Sophia tilted her head to one side. 'And the boy?'

I looked down at Sophia's hand on mine. I now felt embarrassed for what I had done, sneaking into someone's garden that way.

Sophia was still looking at me intently, waiting for a reply, and even though I had been trying for so long to hold it all in, the words were out of my mouth before I could stop them.

'He reminded me of my son.'

18

THEN

A baby boy arrived late summer shortly after my twentieth birthday. I called Mum and told her, saying I would try to get over to see her. But I never did. I wasn't surprised when there was no offer of a visit from her either. I had stopped expecting one. I wondered if she knew how things were between D and I? If there were any telltale signs during our phone conversations that she then likened to her own relationship with my father?

But, deep down, I knew I overthought things when it came to my mum. She was no longer capable of real emotions. I could hear it in the hollowness of her voice.

D hadn't laid a finger on me since he found out I was pregnant again. We had moved into a four-bedroom detached house on the outskirts of a village so with that and the baby arriving, life held a novel aspect to it. I had come to recognise that boredom often brought on bouts of anger, which I would be at the receiving end of.

I still hadn't learnt to drive. D said it was too dangerous for me to learn when I was pregnant. And once he had made it abundantly clear that my life was at home with the baby, I couldn't imagine asking him to sit with his son whilst I booked in a few lessons. The only way for me to get anywhere was if D took me or if I called for a taxi. We were now miles away from my mum. We were miles away from anything or anywhere, and I didn't know anyone.

D appeared to be pleased with the baby. He kept spinning him around and lifting him up too high over his head. I would touch his arm and ask him to be careful – he was still delicate, I reminded him. He would look at me with a hardened expression and continue his spinning game. I could take whatever he did to me, but not what he might do to my baby. Not again.

I couldn't think of a suitable name for him, and D's lists of complicated names from past uncles and second and third cousins did not suit him at all. D referred to him as the baby; to me he became Baby Boy. I would keep thinking of names. I watched the credits at the end of every film, trying to spot a name that I liked and that I thought would suit him.

He had a set of lungs on him, and I became more tense with him when D was around. I needed to walk and to be out of the house so I could calm him and that worked for all of us. D would have his headspace back and be able to 'hold a bloody thought in his brain' and me and Baby Boy would get some time together alone.

I had a growing sense of unease, and I was sure that was what fuelled Baby Boy's crying; it was as though he could sense my worry. D may have kept his distance during my pregnancy, but he began changing again; the same signs were back: the look of disdain, the stressed tone, the unnecessary requests for me to perform menial tasks at times that were inconvenient to me, such as when I was feeding the baby or cooking dinner. Times that he knew I might protest or if I asked a simple question or made a suggestion. I knew better than to push things any further. I knew when to stay back and when to be quiet.

I stayed inside the house a lot. I lived my life on a knife edge, always looking and waiting and expecting. There were times when his love was completely wholesome, when he would look me in the eye, tilt my head up so I was looking at him too, and say exactly the right thing. He would tell me that I was everything that he ever needed. And that would be enough to push the thoughts away, and I would once again feel that all-consuming sense of hope, that this was it, and things could only get better.

* * *

I woke one morning to yet another searing hot day. It felt tropical as though a thunderstorm was needed to clear the sweltering heat. The atmosphere felt too close and had made D's mood palpable.

Baby boy was loving the warmth and slept deeply all morning in only a nappy with a muslin draped over him; his tiny arms spread upwards, his little legs slightly curled inwards. He'd not been quite so content in the night. D had groaned and rolled over, muttering something about shutting him up. Eventually I had retreated with Baby Boy in my arms to the spare double bed where we both dozed until late into the morning.

It had been such a long time since he had done anything to physically hurt me that I had become lackadaisical. The house-work had got on top of me; clothes hanging for days and yesterday's dishes were still sat stacked next to the sink. The heat was pressing down on my skull, making me feel weary from only a few full hours sleep. Baby Boy was just two weeks old and I had read that it was best to get a nap in when the baby slept.

I had just laid him down for his afternoon sleep in his basinet in the spare room, hoping I could get just half an hour's shut-eye, then I'd strap the baby to my chest and tackle the housework.

D had been out and I jumped at the sound of the front door slamming. I could smell the alcohol on his breath when he got into the house, but I knew he had driven. I didn't dare comment.

He reached out to grab my arm to pull me to him. I knew what he wanted from me, but I was exhausted and still postpartum. I must have jerked my arm away – an instinctual action in my weary state. I had forgotten how to be alert.

I watched his face change colour. A deep red crept from his neck and flooded his cheeks as he spat the insults at me; a prelude before the main act.

Fear gripped me, effervescent bubbles of terror frothed in my throat. The beautiful bond that had been forming between me and Baby Boy had filled me with so much love that I had forgotten what it was like to be perpetually terrified.

He didn't hold back this time. The kicks and the punches found their way to every part of my body. I held an image of Baby Boy's face in my head, knowing I had to survive this for him.

Afterwards, as I lay in the corner of the lounge, I made up excuses for him in my head: he was drunk, he was tired, he was stressed. It was a slight blip. Tomorrow, I would try harder and we would be okay.

After he had left that night and I knew he wouldn't be back until morning, I went to put the night latch on the door. Half an hour later, in my tired and bruised state, I could not remember doing it, so I returned to the door, checked the lock and, to be certain, I unlocked and locked it again.

Just before I went to bed, I checked it once more.

19

Sophia closed the door softly behind her and left me alone in my bedroom. She had brought me a vodka, neat, and I managed to swallow it down through my gulps of tears. She knew she wouldn't get much out of me, and so she had kindly walked me to my room and laid me down on my bed, with the vodka doing its work. There was a part of my brain that was willing me to get up and start doing something in the bedroom, strip the bed, straighten something out, but the more prominent side had been lulled by the alcohol and didn't want to do anything but lie still until the thoughts had disappeared. The niggling thought, the one that was willing me to perform a compulsion, was that I had stupidly brought up the subject of my son with Sophia. It was a natural thing to do, of course, but I had stopped sharing my true feelings such a long time ago. It was the child; he had brought all the feelings to the surface. He reminded me so much of what I once had. I felt like a failure, that everything I had been trying to hold on to was suddenly out of my grip. I had tried to keep it hidden for so long from everyone.

* * *

I woke up fully clothed. The room was pitch-black. My throat was dry and scratchy and I knew I had been sleeping with my mouth open, probably snoring. I grabbed my phone from my bedside table and saw there was a missed call from *the* number. He had called only a few hours ago. It was now 2 a.m. I wondered how much longer I would be able to get away with ignoring him. Not much longer. It wouldn't be long before I would find myself face to face with him, and the thought of that made my gut twist with terror.

I had been asleep for almost ten hours. Apart from a slight dull buzz in my head, I felt wide awake. I knew getting back to sleep any time soon was going to be tricky. It was alarming to be suddenly awake at 2 a.m. when the world felt so empty; it was easy to feel all alone.

There was a pair of clean pyjamas folded neatly over the end of the bed, so I removed the clothes I had been wearing at college that day and pulled them on. I decided a hot drink would help me get back to sleep.

The house was so silent as I opened my bedroom door that I felt my heart thumping in my ears.

I stole down the stairs, careful not to tread on the parts of the steps that I knew would groan back at me. I found my way into the kitchen with the torch from my phone and turned on one of the lights to make myself a cup of herbal tea and sat down at the kitchen table. I could hear the creaking of the house as the central heating came on, the temperature in the house had dropped and even though warmer days were here, we were still feeling the cold in the night, especially as the house was so old. I opened my phone and looked for Mrs Clean, to see what I had missed whilst I had been asleep, and just as I had thought, she had posted on Instagram stories and a new post. The woman was busy. I was becoming accustomed to seeing which posts were ads, and I noticed that the main post on her Instagram account was just that. It was an image of a geometric abstract rug, grey and yellow. It was unusual to see a flash of colour in her shots as everything was usually black and white and grey. The photo was taken on an angle again, and I was somewhat taken with the design and colour. I looked at it for a long time, longer than any rug I had ever looked at before. Then I went down to the comments section and scrolled through until I found the ones I was looking for. The ones filled with outrage and hatred.

marvingayandgetiton Who does she think she is? That's two ads back to back. You need to rein it in, love. We don't come on here to see you flaunting your money.

mrsdownside I don't mind the odd ad but come on, two in a row, not to mention one last week.

deux_enfants Is it me or is this woman posting more and more ads? What is it with these female Instagrammers? It's all about the money.

lucybest65 I think she is pretending to be someone she isn't. It's so obvious.

I stopped on the comment from lucybest65. Her name seemed to be on every post from Mrs Clean. I didn't know why I hadn't clicked on her profile before, but now, as I found my way into her account, I could see it was pretty sparse: a few badly taken images of the dinner she had cooked last night (*Beans on toast – pimped*, read the caption), a too close-up shot of a flower just in bloom and a shot of something she had watched on TV – a police documentary. Her own profile picture was an image of Velma Dinkley from *Scooby Doo*.

It seemed odd that she would follow someone like Mrs Clean,

and then mouth off at her for trying to make a living. It felt as though lucybest65 was only out to spread the hatred. Lucybest65 was a troll; someone who followed successful people's lives in order to cause disruption. I noticed that her comments came in regularly and they attracted a fair few likes and comments themselves. I decided from here on in, I would keep an eye on her. For some unfathomable reason, I felt a need to protect Mrs Clean.

A loud bang came from just outside and I froze. I looked down at my phone and thought about the missed call that had come through at midnight, just a few hours ago.

I got to my feet and made my way to the front door and peered through the spyhole. I couldn't see anything. Then I heard it again, the noise; like plastic on tarmac. I began to unlock the door as dread tugged at my insides. To curb some of the fear, I shut the lock five more times, but it still gripped me like a vice as I slowly pulled the door open, not knowing what or whom I would find on the other side. It was deadly quiet on the street and I was surprised to be greeted by a clear, starry night with a moon that was full and bright. I shivered in just my pyjamas and stepped outside. I could immediately see our main bin had been thrown over and the contents had been ransacked by an animal of some kind. Probably a fox. I wasn't going to be falling back asleep any time soon, so I headed back to the kitchen to grab a pair of Marigolds and a few bin liners.

Outside the house, I slapped them on and I lifted up the wheelie bin and then picked up the bag that had been ripped open. I started sifting through the rubbish and placing things in the new bag when my fingers met with a hard, plastic object. I recognised it immediately as a pregnancy test. I turned it over and saw the word *Pregnant* and then *3–4 weeks*. I supposed that someone from the street could have thrown it in the bin on their way past, but it was too embedded in the rubbish, as though someone had stuffed it right in amongst everything else to hide it. I just hadn't imagined that any of the girls would be getting themselves pregnant at their age. I presumed everyone had it all figured out; there were certainly enough options available for them.

I immediately started wondering who it could be. I thought of Karen first; she was the one who seemed the most settled. Then there was Mini in bed with her young man after the party, but those dates didn't add up; although she could, of course, be seeing other people. I was sure it wasn't Sophia as she hadn't been in a relationship for over a year; she was apparently taking time away from blokes and I'd never seen anyone come by the house.

I was reminded of the time I held a test like this in my hand. It was just blue lines, not a fancy digital version like this. We had gone for the cheaper option. What I remember most was being told I didn't need to buy the cheaper options, that we had plenty of money. And I suppose we did. We had. But I had been brought up to be frugal, which was why I got into textiles. Creating things from nothing was always what I was good at. I shivered as I felt the cool night air filter through my pyjamas. I quickly finished stuffing the rest of the rubbish into the new bag, including the pregnancy test, threw the new bag into the bin and shut the lid down tightly.

I took one last cautious look around and went back into the house.

I locked and unlocked the front door six times, ending on a lock, then removed the Marigolds, washed my hands and took my tea and phone back up the stairs.

I locked and unlocked my door six times, then I fell into bed.

* * *

At the breakfast table the next morning, I stole intermittent glances between Mini and Karen, trying to work out which one of them was pregnant. I tried to look for any signs of nausea or tiredness, but both of them seemed their usual selves. Mini was making light chit-chat and Karen was still trying her best to ignore me.

'I got a match,' I said to swerve the conversation to something I knew they would both be interested in.

'Oh my God, that's amazing.' Mini almost choked on her tea. 'What's he like?'

'Well, I don't know, I'll find out this weekend. We're going for a drink.'

Mini screwed her face up in confusion. 'So you mean you haven't actually even like chatted or anything?'

I shook my head. 'No. He asked if I wanted to meet for a drink and I said yes.'

Karen shook her head, and I was sure I heard a small snigger escape her lips.

'It's just, well, usually, you sort of chat via your messages first, get to know more about them,' Mini said informatively.

'But surely that's what meeting them face to face does? You forget, Mini, I'm old school. When I was your age, there were none of these apps – it was plain and simple. He looks nice enough and shares similar interests, so I am sure we'll have plenty to talk about.'

'So when do you go on this date then?' Karen asked without looking up at me.

'Friday night.'

'Nice,' said Mini.

'Do you think it's too soon?' I said, suddenly worried I had made the wrong decision to meet him so soon. Perhaps I should have continued to chat to him for a few days, as Mini had suggested.

'No, no, it's fine, you obviously think it's okay. I mean, I personally would be all flirty-flirty for a few days, but that's mainly for entertainment purposes.' Mini wrinkled her nose.

'Okay, well, I'm going to meet him and simply hope he's not an axe-murderer. I'm sure he will be fine.'

'Why do people always use that reference? Axe-murderer? It's so retro,' Karen said.

I smiled. 'I suppose it is. In my day, there were a lot of films with women running away from men with big weapons.'

Mini raised her eyebrows and sniggered.

'Now it's all cyborgs and dystopian mania,' I said.

'Well, I'm sure you oldies will have a lovely time remembering your favourite slasher movies,' Karen said, shovelling a mouthful of All-Bran into her mouth.

'Ahh. It's going to be great, isn't it, Karen?' Mini shoved Karen slightly harder than she had meant to and Karen sloped to one side, shot Mini a look and then rested her gaze on me.

The date was just two days away and I contemplated cancelling about a hundred times, opening the app, setting out a message to him before deleting it again. I kept reminding myself that I had to do this for my sanity. I needed to just get out there, have a few dates, and behave like everyone else. Not someone who checks the locks on windows six times and crawls on their hands and knees into their neighbour's garden. This was not me; I was better than this.

Eventually, Friday arrived. We had arranged to meet at a pub in

Waterloo at 7 p.m. I arrived outside the pub five minutes before our scheduled date. I stalled for a few seconds and was just contemplating heading back home again when I heard, 'Regi?' I spun around and saw a real-life version of the man from the photo on my dating app. It was surreal, to say the least. His features were more prominent than his photo showed. His hair was now a lot longer, set high on his head and swept stylishly to one side. His shirtsleeves were rolled up and a light-green jacket was slung over his arm.

'How are you?' he asked, a slightly posh cut to his voice. 'Good journey, I hope?'

'Yes, it was great,' I replied on autopilot, realising afterwards I was talking like a robot. It hadn't been great; I had been anxious and scared the entire way and, anyway, who ever has a 'great' journey into central London?

'Good, good.' He nodded and I stood very still, suddenly unable to speak or move.

He blew out a loud breath. 'So shall we...?' He gestured to the door to the pub.

'Yes, oh, yes, let's,' I said as he held it open for me.

The atmosphere hit me like a wall as I entered the pub. I began my breathing techniques immediately, hoping that it didn't look too obvious. It was hot, busy and unfamiliar. I hadn't frequented anywhere like this for such a long time.

'What do you say we find a quiet corner?' Calvin's voice was suddenly loud and in my ear, and I jumped at the closeness of him.

I followed Calvin as he navigated us through the crowds and to a corner at the back of the pub that was quieter and calmer. I immediately looked for the sign for the toilets and also a fire exit. Both of which were within visible distance.

'I'm just going to...' I said as he went to sit, then he righted himself and nodded.

'Oh, yes, sure, absolutely. Hopefully you're not doing a runner through the toilet window,' he said deadpan, and then his face broke into a smile.

I looked confused, then I managed a smile. 'God, no. Of course not.' I scooted off towards the toilet.

Inside the cubicle, I unlocked and locked the door six times. At the sink, I lathered my hands for thirty-four seconds, counting in my head as I did. I looked at myself in the mirror, wondering who the stranger was staring back at me. Eventually I mouthed, 'You can do this.'

I found my way back to Calvin, who was perusing the drinks menu and not on his phone, which I found refreshing. I had already checked my phone on the way here on the train to see what Mrs Clean had been posting. In fact, I had been checking several times a day, always on the lookout for the newest post and always checking in with lucybest65, the troll, to see what she had been posting.

And lucybest65 just wouldn't let up. She was there commenting on every post, making her opinion known and not very kindly as per usual. I thought how strange it was that the best part of my day was when I could look in on the cyber lives of two women I had never even met. But here I was, and I needed to live in the moment, this crazy moment of... what was I doing? I supposed it was a blind date of sorts, even though I had seen his face in a photo. And there he was in the flesh, looking at me with a small smile, maybe as nervous as I was about the date.

'You came back then,' he said as I slid into a seat at a right angle to him.

'I did. I contemplated slipping out the window, but these pins aren't as nimble as they once were.' I looked around as I spoke and rubbed my hands on my knees. They felt sweaty. My mouth felt dry. I wondered who would get the drinks.

He smiled graciously at my attempt at banter. 'Well, now you're staying, for a while at least, what can I get you to drink?'

'Okay, I'll take a vodka and tonic, with a splash of lime, please,' I said.

'Good stuff.' He stood up and edged his way past my chair, which I had to nudge in a bit to let him past. As soon as I saw he was out of sight, I pulled out my phone to see what I had missed since I had last looked, which was just over half an hour ago.

Mrs Clean hadn't posted any new stories or posts since this afternoon, but there were more comments. I had to scroll down for a good few minutes to find what lucybest65 had been saying.

Just four words stood out.

The woman needs help.

When did the world become so confrontational, why were people constantly looking for the bad in everything and everyone? The connection I felt with Mrs Clean was constantly being marred by this unnecessary unkindness. Yet I couldn't stop myself from searching for lucybest65's comments whenever there was a new post. I slammed the phone down. My foot tapped manically under the table as I balled my hands into fists.

'Everything okay?' Calvin set my drink down next to me.

I looked up. 'Oh, yes, yes. Thank you.' I unclenched my fists and calmed my tapping as I looked at the glass with welcome eyes and even before he had sat himself back down I had taken a long drink.

I subtly wiped my mouth with my hand and watched as he took a sip of his pint of Guinness. He pressed his lips together as he swallowed.

'Well, thanks for coming. It's Richmond you live in, you say?'

'Yes, that's right.'

'Very nice. There's some lovely houses round there, and the parks.'

'I share a house. With three girls.'

'Sounds busy. Is the house nice?'

'Yes, it is actually. It's pretty old, as you can imagine. Creaky pipes, clunky floorboards. But so much character.' I could feel the warmth of the vodka penetrating my body. Calvin was nodding.

'I love old houses, they have so much personality. I love a novel with an old house.'

'Like *Rebecca*?' I offered.

'Like *Rebecca*.'

'*Turn of the Screw*?'

'Urgh.'

'Yep, hated it too.' I took another long drink of my vodka and Calvin followed suit with his Guinness.

'*The Haunting of Hill House*?' Calvin set down his Guinness.

'Ooh, creepy.'

'Ooh, how about *The Lion, the Witch and the Wardrobe*?'

'Of course!' I said.

'*The Suspicions of Mr Whicher*?'

'I reckon we've covered them all,' I said with a small smile.

'No, never – there are hundreds, I know there are. Maybe we could make it our challenge to read a selection? Our own little book club.'

'How very quaint.' I pushed a stray hair behind my ear and Calvin watched me over his pint glass. 'I've never been in a book club before.' I knew it was the sort of thing that women my age did. If I was doing school runs and meeting other mums, I supposed I would probably be the founding member of one by now.

'Well, I think now is the time. I declare this the first meeting of the Old House's Book Club. You pick the first title.' Calvin finished his beer with a final gulp. I was surprised at how easily he had finished, but then when I went to pick my own glass up I could see it was empty.

'Another? Maybe you could think of the first book whilst I am at the bar?'

I smiled and handed him my glass.

I fidgeted in my seat for a moment and then pulled out my phone. I couldn't keep ignoring these comments from Lucy. I went straight to Instagram and found the most recent comment that she had left. I quickly started typing a reply.

Regitex @lucybest65 Why do you have to keep having a go? Mrs Clean seems to be doing a fab job as far as I can see, and she has to make some money somehow, so a few ads here and there makes sense. I believe what you are is jealous.

I hit the send button before I could change my mind. It was the alcohol; I certainly wouldn't have made a statement like that to someone I didn't know without it. Somehow, with the swell of the alcohol inside me I felt I had the right to comment. Now I was as bad as the rest of them. I felt a wave of shame and regret wash over me as I placed my phone down. Calvin appeared next to me with another vodka and tonic and lime.

'Thanks, you'll have to let me get the next ones,' I said.

'Everything all right?' He gestured to my phone.

I looked down at my mobile on the table and then quickly picked it up and shoved it in my handbag.

'Oh, yes, yes, it's fine, I was, I just had to do something.'

'You're not "needed"?' he said and used his fingers as quotation marks.

I looked down at my bag and then at him. 'Oh, you mean... Oh right, I get it, God no. I'm a terrible liar – if someone was on the other end pretending to have an emergency, I'm not sure I could keep a straight face.'

Calvin smiled, sat down and took a sip of his Guinness.

'Besides, you should think a little more of yourself. That's twice now you've presumed I'm doing a runner and we're only on our second drink. Has that, you know, ever happened before?'

Calvin cleared his throat and looked down at his pint.

'Once,' he said coyly.

'Oh no!' I said, trying to suppress the laughter. 'What happened?'

'Exactly that, her phone rang just after she came back from the loo and she started this over the top dialogue, all "Oh my God, are you okay?" and then said she had to go as her friend had just had a car accident. I mean, it was a bit dramatic.'

'So how did you know that she was lying?'

'Apart from the amateur performance? Well, when I went outside for a fag – that was when I smoked; I gave up two years ago – I saw her, on the other side of the road, laughing into her phone and clearly in no rush to get to a phantom car crash.'

I stretched my mouth out. 'My God, that's terrible. Sorry. Your ego must have been severely damaged.'

'That was the hardest part to recover from, I must admit. But still, life goes on and here I am. Having a drink with you – two drinks so far – and you haven't tried to leg it.'

'Not yet. But if you switch to drinking Cinzano and lemonade and try to drag me to a karaoke bar, I may make a swift exit.'

Calvin laughed. 'No chance of that.'

We carried on drinking and laughing, and by about midnight I was well and truly hammered. Although I hadn't realised it until I tried to stand, and Calvin had to reach his hand out to stop me from falling.

We made it outside and I leant against the wall to catch my breath.

'Oh sorry, you must... think... me... such... a lie way...'

Calvin leaned against the wall next to me. 'Absolutely not, I think you rivalled me with your drinking. I'm sure you overtook me at one point.'

'Shhhhor–ly not.'

Calvin stood up and pulled me towards him. 'I should call you a cab.'

He touched my chin gently and began to slowly move towards me with his lips parted. I shot a glance over his shoulder and there he was, just behind Calvin, standing and staring at me with his black baseball cap pulled just enough over his eyes so I couldn't see them. I jerked away from Calvin's kiss and stumbled to the side, searching behind him for the figure, but there was no one there.

I slouched down against the wall. I could feel a hand around my wrist, the pain seared through my body, and as the panic set in and gripped my body I froze. It was how I had always remembered it, the hold around my wrist, pulling me until eventually I stopped all movement, closed my eyes and waited until I could open them again, to be told it was all a dream. But, of course, that never happened. It was never a dream. It was all so very real.

'Sorry, it was too much – I'm sorry, you're drunk, I'm drunk. I should know better at my age, for goodness' sake. Please accept my apology, I'm going to call you that cab.' Calvin started rooting about in his pocket for his phone.

'No, it's not you,' I said, although I still wasn't entirely sure if I could have gone through with a kiss.

'I need to—'

'Go? Yes, I know.' Calvin was tapping away on his phone, then he put his phone in his pocket. 'They'll be here in a minute.

Listen, Regi, I'm really sorry. I really like you and I shouldn't have done that. It was really stupid.'

'No, it's fine, I... I...' I looked around, trying to see where the figure had gone, he was just there. And so vividly. 'I had a nice time, Calvin. I want you to know that.' I spoke as slowly as I could so I could get the words out.

'It's fine, honestly. I don't need you to say anything.' He crouched down to my level. 'You have my number, and if, you know, you ever do manage to think of that book-club choice, let me know – we can have a read-along.'

I tried to snort out a laugh, but it just came out like a painful cry.

'Hey, look, your cab's here.' Calvin stood up and offered me his hand. I took it and he pulled me up to his level, our faces precariously close again, but whatever that had nearly been was gone. He pushed some notes into my hand. 'Put it towards the fare.'

I looked at the kindness in his eyes, but then all I could see was the face of the person who was behind the black baseball cap, who seemed to be everywhere. Never letting me be. Never letting me forget.

Instagram post: 10th May 2019

Hi guys, I know some of you have been having a moan about me posting ads, and, well, I counted up the ads out of all the posts I have done and it works out at roughly two a month. Which I think is just fine. In my opinion, a few people need to think about the positives in life. I just wanted to clear that up.

And so on with the positive vibes.

We are almost into summer now, so I wanted to talk you through some of my favourite products that I have discovered recently. These are all super kind to the environment, so I think you will love them as much as I do.

There they are all lined up in the photo and I have tagged the company who makes them as well so you can head straight to their webpage and discover them all for yourselves.

Keep up the cleaning and enjoy this lovely weather.

Mrs C x

#summersnearlyhere #adsarenotbad #cleaning #mrsclean

89,445 likes

ninetoone Enjoy your day as well, Mrs C. Love your work.

empalmer09 Can we see some pictures of you please? What do you look like?

lucybest65 Some people want to remain anonymous cos they are obviously hiding something.

ktdonners It wouldn't matter if she revealed every aspect of her life. You lot would still have something nasty to say. She can't win either way, can she?

lucybest65 Maybe she should have thought about that before she started this whole thing.

20

My hangover still hadn't shifted by lunchtime the next day. So on top of a raging headache, I also felt empty after the date. Calvin was a nice guy and we had had fun. But in hindsight, there was no attraction there, and I was sure the feelings were mutual on his part as well. I had enjoyed feeling normal for those few hours until we got outside and then I can't recall exactly what happened. Was I just too drunk and imagined who I saw behind Calvin? I couldn't shake the hollow feeling, as though the whole experience had been a little pointless. I knew I wasn't looking for love, and yet I went anyway. To appease others – Karen, in particular – but also so I looked as though I were a normal person, just getting on with my life.

I lay in bed and opened up Instagram to try to soothe my racing thoughts. I had not had any reply to my comment from lucybest65 on Mrs Clean's account. I wasn't sure what annoyed me more: her initial comment or not replying to mine.

It had been so long since I had been caught up with real emotions involving people, that I was shocked at my own responses. I had begun to feel things from opposite ends of the spectrum. Right now, I felt anger. Angry at lucybest65.

* * *

Calvin had kindly texted me early Saturday morning to check I was okay, and by Monday morning as I was getting myself ready for my first lecture of the day, I felt ready to reply to his text.

I'm sorry, I'm just not ready.

I had thought I was going to be fine, But I had to get rip-roaring drunk to navigate my way through the date. And that was no way to start a relationship.

His reply came in swiftly afterwards.

It's okay, I understand. It was just good to meet you. Perhaps we can still do our book club, but online?

Then he gave me his Twitter and Facebook handles and signed off with 'take care' and a kiss.

I smiled at the sincerity, and I knew it was all probably for the best. A relationship was not what I needed. I was perfectly happy with Instagram. It seemed to give me exactly what I needed in terms of reward systems for my brain.

The room was beginning to feel hot, so I opened the window just an inch to let in some air.

But as soon as I did, I could hear it, the pained sobs of the little boy next door, and my heart immediately began to tug; the sound of his cries were a physical pain in my stomach. I needed to scoop him up and I felt an overwhelming maternal instinct kicking in. I sat with my head in my hands. I decided enough was enough. The poor little helpless child next door was obviously being abused or neglected in some way.

I would do what I knew I needed to do.

I stripped and re-made my bed with clean sheets, locked and unlocked the window six times and lined up four loose pound coins in a row in perfect symmetry. Then I padded downstairs quietly so as not to wake anyone else.

As I approached the bottom of the stairs, I heard two hushed voices; Steve's and someone else's. I crept quietly towards the kitchen and stopped suddenly as I heard the hushed tones become strained, as though an argument was erupting, but they didn't wish to be heard. I edged a little closer, but it was no use, I couldn't hear anything of what was being said. I didn't have any time to waste, so I walked into the kitchen to see Sophia and Steve who were stood near to one another in the corner near the pantry. Sophia was still in her nightgown and silk dressing gown. Steve was in a T-shirt and joggers. He had obviously slept here last night. Karen, although she was clearly still angry with me, had made a conscious effort to not let Steve let himself in when she wasn't here. Steve took a wide step backwards and looked sheepishly over at me. Sophia was now busying herself with taking out a jar of jam from the pantry. I cleared my throat and went to the fridge to take out some oat milk.

'Morning, all,' I said casually.

'Hiya,' Sophia said. She pulled her dressing gown tighter around her, readjusting the tie around her waist.

Steve skirted past me, and Sophia called after him.

'I'll keep thinking of ideas – hopefully we can come up with a good birthday present between us.'

Steve gave me a quick look before he made it to the door and left.

'Birthday?' I said to Sophia as I filled the kettle.

'Yep, Karen's.' Sophia sat down at the table. 'Stick enough in there for me.'

I filled the kettle to just under halfway.

'When is it her birthday?' I took two mugs down from the cupboard.

'August.'

'August? Planning early then?'

'Well, not really, things get booked up really quickly, plus this is Karen we're talking about here, she's... like a sister to me.' Sophia's voice caught and I thought I saw tears well up in her eyes.

'Right,' I said and leant against the counter. 'Efficiency.'

'Is there enough in there for me?' Karen walked into the kitchen and pointed at the kettle. 'Hey, Soph, I haven't seen you all weekend. Is everything okay?'

Sophia fell into a chair and looked up. Her eyes were pooled with tears, and she quickly brushed one away that had escaped.

'God yeah, I'm fine. It's just this year, it's hard. I just popped back to Mum and Dad's on Friday, just for a change of scenery. Sometimes I get sick of looking at the same four walls. How was your weekend?' Then Sophia looked at me. 'Oh shit, Regi, your date, how did it go?'

Karen took my hot water, poured her tea, gave Sophia's shoulder a quick squeeze and headed upstairs. I was slightly perturbed that Karen wasn't staying to listen, as she was the one who was so keen to get me off to market in the first place.

I watched Karen leave. I took out a bowl and some bran flakes, then I sat down at the table. 'I, er, got a bit drunk.' I tried to force a smile, but all I could see was the figure in the baseball cap lurking behind Calvin as he bent to kiss me. 'He was nice, but, I dunno, as a friend maybe.'

'Well done, you – you did it, you went out and met someone new. That's great. It doesn't matter if you didn't hit it off, it was your first date. I mean, no one really hits it off on a first date...' Sophia trailed off and looked out of the window. 'Only a select few at least. I think I'll...' She stood up. I looked at her away with her own thoughts. 'I'm just going to get dressed.' She stopped and rested her hand on my shoulder. 'I'll skip that tea. Everything okay with you, though?'

'Yes, all good. Except...'

'What?'

'Well, I've got these concerns about the neighbour's child. I think they are mistreating him.'

Sophia looked appalled. 'Oh God, really, how?'

'Well, I don't know exactly. I just know he cries, like all the time.'

'Really? I never hear it?'

'I don't know, maybe my ears are predisposed to it, so there's the crying and I've noticed that they don't let him outside, ever, and the couple argue loads, and I have seen the mum being a bit too physical with him, you know, grabbing him and pulling him back inside. I don't know, something about it just doesn't feel right.'

Sophia nodded. 'Sure. I get it. What do you want to do?'

'Well, I'm going to call social services this morning. Get someone to go over there and check it out.'

I saw a small frown form across Sophia's forehead. She swallowed. 'Social services, wow, okay. Well, if you think that's best. Let me know how you get on.' She patted my shoulder and left the room, I couldn't help noticing with a slight hunch.

* * *

I left the house half an hour early so I could get to the café in the mews and order my favourite coffee.

It had been a while since I had been in there, and when I entered I couldn't see any sign of Heather. I approached the counter and a young man with dark hair asked me if he could help me.

'Erm, is er, Heather here?'

'Umm.' He looked confused for a second. 'Oh, dark hair?'

'Yes.' I nodded at his vague description.

'Oh, she left.'

'What, for good?'

'Yep, she left last week, gone home to...' He scratched his head. 'I dunno, somewhere.'

'Oh.' I felt myself deflate at the prospect at having to describe my exact coffee to this young man who wasn't showing much promise at retaining information.

'I'll just take a bottle of water and a chocolate twist,' I said glumly, already mourning the lost coffee.

I left the coffee house and collided with someone.

'Oh God, I'm so sorry...' I trailed off. 'I...'

Instantly, I recognised the woman as my neighbour. The very woman I was about to contact social services over.

She stopped and looked at me, and there was a flash of recognition in her eyes. She opened her mouth to speak, but then she walked on.

For a second afterward, I wanted to run after her and ask her if everything was okay, but I stopped myself. I had seen and heard too much already. Even the nicest-looking people could be abusive, and I knew I couldn't take any chances.

* * *

I arrived at college just after 9 a.m. for my seminar at ten. I knew I needed to make the call, and so I took my phone out of my bag and hit the phone icon from the website and waited to be connected.

I sat on the grass ten minutes later feeling slightly bereft and wondering if I had done the right thing.

'Hello, Regi, fancy seeing you here.' Will stood over me, and I shaded my eyes from the sun. I realised as I looked around, I was in the spot we had first sat in together.

'How are you?'

I felt a simmering in my gut, I couldn't stop thinking about the phone call I had just made to social services. It felt like a huge thing, and I needed time to process that. And now Will had arrived, looking rugged with his shiny, bright eyes.

He got himself settled just to the right of me; not directly in my eyeline, nor directly beside me.

'I've got no lessons to teach until eleven, so I thought I'd come in and get ahead of myself. How about you?'

'I... I...' I was thinking about my breath and how I needed to calm myself down. I settled for, 'Me too.'

'It's a gorgeous day, isn't it? We've been really lucky with the weather.' The sun was behind me and Will smiled at me with a slight squint. I wondered if I should move. 'Did you manage to sign up for the exhibition?'

'Yes, I did.' I felt the tightness in my chest evaporate slightly. 'I signed up the other day – I'm really looking forward to it.' I thought about the photos on my phone and the notebook I had been filling with ideas and I realised I really was looking forward to getting stuck into a project.

'Great, you can stay behind after hours if you like – they are keeping the art rooms open until ten from now onwards.'

'Oh right.' I thought about all that space and time to create, away from the hustle and bustle of normal college hours. It sounded idyllic. 'That would be great, actually. I could start tomorrow.'

'Yeah, do it – make the most of the space and time.'

'Yeah, I think I might.'

'Hey, listen, I'm going to shoot because I was going to give myself a bit of extra time to prepare for this lesson.' Will stood up. 'Take care, Regi, and I'll see you soon, yeah?' He lifted his hand in a small wave.

I was expecting him to talk about a drink again, but he didn't. I wondered why he didn't. But then I thought it didn't matter because all the while Will had been talking, I hadn't thought about breathing. My chest felt lighter, and for a few glorious minutes, everything had felt... normal.

21

Back at the house that evening I began to sense an atmosphere, more so than just Karen giving me the evil eye. We were all gathered in the garden, taking in the last of the afternoon sun. Sophia was stretched out on a reclining deck chair, huge sunglasses engulfed her face. Mini was perched on a chair she'd dragged out of the summerhouse and was trying to get music from her phone to come through a mini boom box. Karen was fiddling with a stray piece of thread on her summer dress, which she had put on as the weather had suddenly become so warm.

Sophia had now become quieter and more sullen and always with a faraway look in her eye. Karen was making occasional small talk, aimed at no one in particular, and Mini was her usual self, if not a little more restrained, I thought, or maybe I was imagining it. I had thought about the pregnancy test a lot over the last few days and after I had seen Steve and Sophia in the kitchen together, I wondered if he had confided in Sophia and it was indeed Karen who was pregnant. It would certainly explain her mood swings.

Sophia sat up and took her glasses off. 'Hey, how did the call go?' and even though she had said it quietly, Karen's ears pricked up.

'What call?' she asked and I felt a surge of annoyance at Sophia for bringing up our conversation.

Sophia sat up and pushed her sunglasses onto the top of her head. 'Regi has spotted some unusual behaviour next door, and so she phoned social services,' Sophia whispered.

'What do you mean, "unusual"?' Mini sat forward, picking up the whispering vibes and following suit.

I shifted uncomfortably in my seat, silently scolding Sophia who was usually more discreet with things I had told her.

'Well,' I began, 'I have heard a lot of crying recently and I witnessed some quite abrupt behaviour from the mother to the boy,' I said, keeping my voice low.

'I've never heard any crying – I didn't even know there was a kid next door,' Mini said.

'That's what I mean. He is never allowed outside, he just hovers on the perimeter of the doorway and his mum drags him inside with such force.'

'How do you know? How can you see?' Mini asked.

My heart quickened. I couldn't tell them I had slipped through the hedge into their garden. 'I have a pretty good view of their patio from my room. I saw the kid's feet and the mum shouting and then the door was slammed.'

'Well, the little brat probably deserved it,' Karen said, sneezing into a wad of tissue. 'Bloody kids. I'm never having any. The world is overpopulated as it is.'

I sat up, shocked by what Karen had said. I had been convinced she was pregnant. I had presumed it was all hormones. Clearly, I was wrong and she really did have it in for me. Unless she was playing a game with herself, perhaps some sort of denial. Or maybe she had got rid of it already?

'Well, let us know when you hear back,' Sophia said, putting her glasses back on and settling back in her chair.

I felt an unease growing. Everything felt out of sync because of what Sophia had made me share with the other girls. Why had she been so insensitive?

'Right.' I stood up, receiving a fluttering of interest. 'I'm going to cook – I'm going to go to the supermarket and make us all some dinner. Is everyone okay with a stir fry? Meat free obviously,' I said, paying my homage to their days-of-the-week food schedule.

'As long as you get prawn crackers and make egg fried rice.' Karen's voice still had an edge to it.

'Well, I'm sure I can manage that,' I said amiably.

As all the girls were in the garden, I took advantage of the privacy of the hall to open and close the door six times before I left. I had been feeling the effects of the conversation I hadn't wanted to have with all three girls about the boy next door. I needed the walk to try to alleviate some of the stress and fear.

I trotted down the steps and onto the path. The sun was beating down still, even though it was after five. I started running through a mental shopping list, trying to tally it up with things that I knew I had in the fridge and cupboard. Would I need to buy ginger? There was a nugget at the bottom of the fridge, but was it good enough or was it probably covered in mould by now? I knew I was really trying to distract myself from the thoughts that had started to build up in my mind that I no longer knew where to store. I could feel the past hurtling back towards me like a runaway train I knew I would never be able to stop. It would simply run me over. I was powerless.

Suddenly, as though I had willed it, I was knocked from my feet. I was stumbling to my left, unable to right my footing. As I tumbled to the ground, I could hear voices all around me. Then I felt the force of a hand on my wrist, then another hand grabbed my shoulder. I could smell the aftershave, the scent that was still so familiar after all these years. I opened my eyes for a second and saw the peak of a baseball cap and bare arms in a white T-shirt, exposing firm biceps. I tried to break free but it was no good, the grip was firm this time, the pain searing through my arms into my shoulder.

I could hear a voice, but it was soft. They were asking me something – I could hear the tone, even if I couldn't quite hear the words, which sounded very far away as though they were coming from another dimension, or a dream.

'Just leave me alone.' I heard the words, but I wasn't sure they were coming from me. Then the vice-like grip was released and my weight fell to one side. I looked up to see a blurry figure in front of me. I slowed my heart rate with long slow breaths – this time, in for four and out for seven, the way I had practised so many times before. It was part of my daily mantra, something I managed to do in private and in silence, when no one could tell what I was doing. Finally, when I looked up, I saw a man in front of me, his phone pressed to his ear.

'Hang on,' he said into the phone. 'Love, are you okay? You've been nonresponsive for over a minute, I'm just on the phone to the emergency services.'

'I...' I looked around me in the street where a couple of people had stopped and gathered. I looked again in front of me. A tall, well-built man in shorts and black T-shirt, with a blue bandana covering thick dark hair and thin white headphones hung around his neck, was talking on his mobile.

Then it all began to click into place.

'I fell,' I said quietly, suddenly more aware of the small crowd forming.

'Well, technically I knocked you over. I tripped on something and stumbled into you. I knocked you over. I'm terribly sorry. Is there anything I can do, are you okay? I have the emergency services right here?' He pointed to his phone. 'Shall I get someone to come out to you?'

I shook my head firmly.

'No, no, I'm absolutely fine, I promise. Just a little shaken.'

* * *

After many more minutes of reassuring the man, who introduced himself as Marcus, that I was okay, I walked the few hundred yards back to the house.

I pushed open the front door and saw Karen, who had been heading upstairs, turn and look at me.

'Oh, you're back. Did you forget your purse?'

I stood in the middle of the hallway, unable to say anything.

There was a flash of concern across Karen's face.

'Hold on, I'll get Soph.' She turned round and went back down the stairs and through towards the garden.

I was still standing rooted to the spot when Sophia arrived and took my arm and gently escorted me into the lounge and onto a chair.

'Can you get her some water?' she said to Karen. I could hear Mini's voice in the background.

'What's happened? Were you mugged? Was she mugged?'

Sophia was looking me up and down. 'You've a small scrape on your left arm here.'

Karen came back with the water and gave it to Sophia, who handed it to me as she sunk into the sofa next to me.

'I guess this means no dinner,' Karen grumbled. Just as she left the room I heard, 'She really does need to get some therapy, you know.'

'Ignore her,' Sophia said.

'Maybe she's right.' I spoke for the first time, my words sounding croaky and hoarse. I told her about the knock I had received. It was an accident, a jogger stumbling on a crack in the pavement, yet I had felt threat. I had felt danger. I explained what had happened to Sophia, omitting the part where I was back in my past, where angry hands were pulling at my wrists.

'Well, as long as you've not injured yourself too much. But I have been worried about you. I wondered if perhaps, you know, the whole thing with the neighbour's kid was some kind of, I dunno... I'm no therapist. It's just after you said he reminded you of your child, I wondered if that was a psychological thing, that you are pushing your maternal instincts onto that kid, because of the resemblance.'

I shook my head; I didn't know any more. I just knew my nights were haunted by crying and that there was a child next door that no one else had seen or heard except me.

I thanked Sophia for the water and excused myself to go to my room.

My bedroom was stifling hot, so I inched open the window just enough to bring a bit of light relief into the air. Along with the air came a flurry of voices. It was different to what I had heard of late. I peered out of the window and over into next door's garden to see a woman dressed in a black trouser suit with wild blonde curly hair. She was smiling and heading back into the house. Was that the social worker? They had said that someone would be looking into it for me and they had thanked me for my concern, but I hadn't expected them to be there so fast. Looking at the expression on her face, she wasn't showing any concern.

I pulled out my phone and went to Instagram. On my profile page there was something I had never seen before. A small red triangle – it looked like a paper plane – was in the corner. I clicked on it and it took me through to a single message. I gasped when I saw that the name on the message was from lucybest65.

I hesitated for some time, too scared to click it open. I was intrigued to know why she had sent me a direct message rather than reply to my comment on the post, which made me even more nervous. She could be saying something really mean and I wasn't sure I was in the right mindset to hear something unkind. I finally gave in to temptation. Took a deep breath and clicked on the message.

Now I have your attention. You need to be a bit wiser.

What? I had no idea what she meant by that. Was that a threat? Should I respond with a comeback or ask for more clarification? Was she trying to get me on her side?

I came out of the message only to be notified of more matches on the dating app. I had a quick flick through and began to feel physically sick at the prospect of meeting people and dating. What I needed was to be around someone who made me feel safe and secure. Who made me forget that I had to breathe in and out. I had a vision of Will in my mind's eye and realised that whenever he was around, I felt an inkling of happiness and what was bordering on contentment; I was curious to test the theory again.

22

NOW

The next morning, just after nine, I made another call to social services. I couldn't stop thinking about the woman who was in the garden next door; I was still worried about the boy.

A lady answered the phone and I told her my name and address and that I had put in a report for a child's welfare yesterday.

'Yes, yes, I have your name here. But I'm afraid we are unable to disclose any information.'

'But, what? I put the call in? I live next door. I need to know if he is going to be okay.'

'I'm sorry, but I am unable to give you more information at this time as all cases are strictly confidential.'

'Right. I understand,' I said glumly, even though I didn't. I needed to know more. I couldn't just carry on living next door not knowing what was going on or if the child would be okay.

I hung up the phone and placed it on the table. I was about to stand and go to the kettle when Steve walked into the kitchen.

'Oh, um, morning. I didn't know you were here,' he said

sheepishly. Things had begun to change since I mentioned my concerns to Karen. Steve seemed to dip his head down when he entered a room, as if trying to make himself invisible.

'Listen, it's fine, Steve. Come in, make your tea or whatever you're doing.' The conversation with the lady from social services was still rattling around in my head.

I stood up and went to the kettle and shook it. 'You having one?'

'Er, yeah, I was going to make one for me and Karen.'

'Right. I'll fill it up then.'

I stood against the side and listened to the kettle boiling. Steve leant against the wall on the opposite side of the kitchen, doing something with his phone.

Sophia came in and rescued me from the icy silence.

'Morning.' She walked into the kitchen in her slippers and dressing gown.

Steve cleared his throat. 'Morning.'

'How's things?' she asked me, quietly this time with more subtlety.

'I'm fine,' I said. 'Really, I had a blip. I need to focus on stuff. I'm doing the exhibition. I'm staying late tonight at college to utilise the after-hours facility. I find it difficult to get stuff done during the day when there are so many people about.'

'I know, right? Fucking people,' Sophia said, which made me laugh because Sophia rarely swore.

'I know, so many of them, right?' I said with sarcasm.

'I wish we had the place to ourselves,' Sophia said thoughtfully.

'That would be great, wouldn't it?' and I truly would love that. Which was why working at the uni in the evenings was going to suit me perfectly.

* * *

I was still reeling in shock from my phone call with social services as I got ready in my bedroom. I had a seminar after lunch, and I would stay on and work on my exhibition piece into the evening. I was still thinking about it all the way to the train station, and the ache in my gut tightened more when I bypassed my favourite haunt because Heather was no longer working there. I was lucky to have found Heather, who understood me, and, as ludicrous as I knew it was, the thought of using the café without her there brought the fear on. Something bad would happen. I would have to find somewhere new.

* * *

Once the train started moving, I called social services again. This time it was a different woman, slightly older, who answered the phone.

'I made the call yesterday,' I said as the cries of the child rang in my ears. 'I just need to know he is okay. I hear him every day, crying, I... just need...' I stopped because I knew I was going to start to sound silly. I took a deep breath. 'It's okay,' I said. 'I understand it's confidential and you can't tell me anything.'

'Listen, I don't know much about this particular case.' The woman spoke softly. 'I've been away for a couple of weeks, but I will speak with my colleague when she gets back in this afternoon and I will call you back and hopefully we can put your mind at ease.'

'Great, that's great, thank you.' I hung up and felt a slight sense of relief. Come on, Regi, I said to myself, today is going to be a good day. I was going to stay late at college where I would have the run of the art rooms; I could get into the zone making my art and just stop worrying about everything. It was exactly what I needed.

* * *

I found my way to the art room at about four. Just as I had expected, it was empty. I would relish this time, this quiet, to do exactly what I needed to get done. I pulled out my sketchbook that was already thick with 3D pages where I had stuck on material, paper and even hair from a wig onto pages to create the various themes when I first signed up for the course. This one I was working on had an autumnal theme: reds and oranges, streaks of black and yellow as well. I imagined it would be a coat design, but I hadn't decided on that for definite; it was just a work-in-progress. But I did not have to rush through it and make any decisions right now, instead I just allowed the art to flow organically.

I started getting into design years ago when I was practically still a child myself, flicking through magazine after magazine. Most girls I knew would flick straight past the adverts to get to the features, but I was always drawn to them and would stay looking at them. I would tear pages out, keep them in a folder that I kept hidden in a cupboard, away from prying eyes. It was my secret only; I was making a plan for my future. For the future of my little family. But life took a detour and it was only now, fifteen years later, that I was finally doing the thing that I had been drawn to so long ago.

I laid my scrapbook out on the desk and went and found myself a mannequin.

'Hello,' I said quietly to her as I arranged her to the side of my desk. Then I went to the drawers at the back of the room and began riffling through until I found the colours that matched the scrapbook design.

I had just set the material down on the counter when I heard my phone ringing. It was a local number, not an unrecognised mobile. I remembered that the lady from social services had said she would call and I hoped it was her.

'Hello,' I answered.

'Is that Regi?'

'Hi, yes.'

'It's Carol from the children's services at Richmond Council. I believe you have called twice asking about a referral?'

'I... I had some concerns over a boy who lives next door to me.'

'Okay, well we can't give you any information on the case, only to say that a social worker has been there and assessed the situation and we have no concerns.'

'So, so, that's it? Nothing more can be done?' I felt my gut wrench at the thought of the poor child next door.

'No, because as I said we have no concerns.'

'But the crying? They never let him out.'

'If that's all then? Okay, thank you, goodbye.'

And she hung up before I could finish my sentence.

I felt the rage build and I looked at my work in front of me. I just needed to throw myself into it. That was what I was here for anyway. But instead I flicked my phone onto Instagram and looked for a recent post from Mrs Clean. I knew this would calm me the way it had been doing so well. She had uploaded a post and a couple of stories. I settled down on a stool and began browsing them. Her latest was a picture of the end of her bed, showcasing a new throw. *NOT AN AD*, she had written in bold writing.

It was something she had picked up from Ikea.

She was talking about how cheap it was, yet how effective. I had to agree. It looked good on the pure-white bedsheets.

Even Russell agrees, she went on to say as half of her ragdoll cat was in shot.

As usual I looked for the negative comments, and then halfway through I found one from lucybest65.

She should be able to afford a lot better on the money she gets in sponsorship.

I imagined she was right, but wasn't one of the purposes of the account to show people what you could get for your money and how to dress a house without having to pay out thousands?

I could write that in in the comments if I wanted to, but I had been put off responding after the cryptic message I received from Lucy.

I looked at Mrs Clean's Instagram stories: one was a boomerang of her watering her plants, another one was the cat walking past her perfectly manicured foot as she sat in the garden.

I could have imagined her living alone had I not seen that toddler boot. Had I really seen it? But, of course, there was no other evidence of any child in any of her photos. And now I would never be able to see the image again as it had gone for good.

I put my phone down and found that half an hour had passed since I had taken my materials out of the drawer and become distracted. But it was a good distraction.

I placed my phone down on the desk and decided I would focus fully on the work I had come here to do.

Before long, I had fully immersed myself in the fabrics. I enjoyed working with the glue and the sewing machine, adding piece by piece to the coat that would be a statement artistic piece, not really something practical and wearable. But it would play its part in the whole exhibit, which would focus around my autumn theme.

Time passed in a haze of reds and yellows and oranges, with the sound of the sewing machine buzzing gently and lulling me into a meditative state.

Eventually, I looked up at the time. I needed to use the toilet. It was almost nine. I had about an hour left to use the room. I downed tools and hopped off the stool and headed off down the corridor to the closest ladies' toilet, which was at the very end. The sole of my Doc Martens were squeaking against the lino floor with every step; it started to form a little beat in my head, and so I went out of my way to move my foot outwards slightly as it landed to make it squeak even more. As I did this, I was sure I could hear another squeak on the off-beat. I looked around quickly, but the corridor was clear. There were bound to be cleaners doing their rounds, but I had yet to see one. The door to the toilet made a loud screeching noise that I would never have noticed during a busy college day, but now made me flinch at the sound. A small stirring within me drove me to lock and unlock the cubicle door six times. Then I used the toilet and when I came out I stood at the mirror, looked down and washed my hands. I looked back up and for a second I saw movement from the corner of the mirror. I looked behind me to my right. There was nothing there. It was late. And I was starting to feel weary from the concentration.

I dried my hands with a paper towel. I walked back along the corridor and back to the art room, only to find the door locked and the room in darkness.

'Goddamn it.' I patted my pocket, but I already knew I had left my phone in there.

I started to feel the panic rising inside.

'You are okay. The room has only just been locked – you are going to be okay. Nothing terrible is going to happen,' I said aloud to myself. The build of panic at something so silly was so strange and sudden. But I was overwhelmed with the thought of feeling out of control, not being able to call anyone, or have my purse to get the train home. I was literally stuck.

Then I remembered, Will had told me where his room was located in the college, should I ever get lost. I made my way back to the main reception and main hall where he said his classroom was situated. But it was so late, there was no way he would be there.

I popped my head around the door whilst giving it a little knock, and I almost jumped out of my skin when I heard Will's voice.

'Yeah?' He looked up and saw me. 'Regi!' He jumped up out of his seat from behind his desk and was at the door greeting me.

'Have you been staying late to start your piece? How's it going?'

'Well, it *was* going, but I popped to the loo and the bloody cleaners seem to have locked the door, locking all my stuff inside.'

'What? Surely not, they know they have to leave all the rooms unlocked until last thing, someone was obviously trying to get ahead of themselves. Come on, I can help you.'

'What, but no, you're busy.'

'No, not busy as such. It's just quieter here than... than where I live.'

I was intrigued by Will's hesitation. What was it that he wasn't telling me?

'Follow me.' We left the classroom and headed to the main reception. Will jumped over the desk and crouched down and unlocked a cupboard to the left.

'All the keys to the art rooms are kept here.' His voice was muffled and strained. 'It was Textiles 1 you were in, wasn't it?'

'Yes, how did you know?' I was slightly unnerved.

'I only say that because it should be the only one they keep open – I wasn't stalking you or anything.' He turned and jumped back over the counter, clutching a key with a flat rectangular wooden key ring. 'There we are.'

'Great, thank you.' I felt relief pour through me.

We walked the few minutes back to the art room and I began to make small talk. Now the anxiety had lifted, my body tuned in to the nerves I felt at being alone in the school with Will at such an hour.

'Your hair.' I touched my own hair to demonstrate where hair was as though perhaps he wouldn't know. 'It's different.'

Will tugged at the small amount of length that was left. 'Oh yeah, I had my ears lowered.'

I smiled at the expression, which never failed to amuse me no matter how many times I had heard it.

'Suits you.'

'Er, well, I couldn't get my usual barber and this one got a bit trigger happy with the old scissors, if you know what I mean. If I hadn't been on the ball, he would have chopped my whole bleeding barnet off. I like it a bit longer, you see.'

'I see,' I said as I turned to look at some of the displays along the corridor walls.

'Right, here we are,' he said as we arrived at the door. He put the key in the lock. 'Let's hope this works...' He gave the key a quick fiddle and it opened.

'Thank you so much.'

Will turned the light on and I walked into the room to find all my things as they were.

Then he was behind me, looking at the scrapbook I had open on the bench.

'Looking good. Work-in-progress, obviously, so I won't ask too many questions.'

'No, it's fine. I have it all pretty much mapped out now. But I don't suppose there's much point carrying on today. I was only going to stay another hour and I've kind of lost my flow now.'

'Right, well, then, I mean, you can say no if you like, seeing as you've turned me down a couple of times now, but that offer for a drink is still open and, well, I'm pretty free now.'

I looked at Will's face, taut with anticipation.

'Okay then,' I said.

We found seats in the bar that Will had told me about. It was not full of students and there was a certain chic to it, which I liked. I would almost go as far as to say that I felt comfortable. Will brought us both a bottle of pear cider with ice and I gulped mine as though it were a soft drink, realising I was thirsty.

'So what is it that is keeping you here so late then?' The alcohol loosened my tongue almost immediately.

Will cleared his throat and looked down. 'It's a bit complicated.'

'Okay,' I said and looked around to get a feel for my surroundings.

'Actually, no, that's bullshit, it's not complicated. I just said that because, well, I feel awkward talking about it, which is not the same thing at all, and you asked me, so the straight-up answer is I am going through a divorce and my wife is still in the house at the moment. We've been living in limbo like this for about six months now. There has been a delay at her end, so we've sort of been stuck with each other.'

'Okay, well that's a bit awkward and annoying, I guess.' I felt both shocked and weirdly relieved to hear that Will was going through a divorce.

'So I sometimes hang on longer at school to catch up on my work, work through the holidays, you know time I would normally be spending with my wife.'

I nodded.

'Although to be honest, I made a specific effort to stay behind tonight because I knew you said you would be taking advantage of the extended classroom opening times, and so I purposely hung around a little longer. I had every intention of popping down to see you, and then, there you were.'

I felt a swell of something inside and I tried to conceal the smile, but it escaped, and I felt my face light up.

'And I managed not only to see you but to finally blag you to come out for a drink with me.' He smiled on one side of his mouth, his eyes sparkled.

'Yes, you did.' I laughed.

I finished the cider and Will headed off to the bar and returned with two more. We chatted about my project and I found myself opening up to him about the work I was doing and the inspiration behind it, and we also talked a little about my living arrangements and how I was beginning to notice the age difference between me and my house mates. I could feel an energy building between us as we occasionally spoke over one another, both keen to keep the conversation going.

I looked at my phone at 10.45 p.m. I had missed the last train home.

'Any chance of a lift?' I asked.

'Thank you for having that drink with me, Regi. I had a nice time getting to know you a bit,' Will said in the car as we pulled up outside the house, and my mind was thrown back to dates that ended with boys in cars and those electric moments seated next to one another, not knowing if the other would turn and try to kiss you. I opened the door and quickly stepped out.

'Thanks, I'll see you soon.' I gave him a small wave.

As Will drove off, the feeling of what could have happened in the car lingered with me. It was nostalgic; there was nothing like the sensation of a new relationship blossoming, and that was the part I would always remember the most.

23

The bruises from the last beating faded, but I knew they would be replaced with new ones soon enough. I had to up my game. I had to get smarter, find a way of doing it all. Plenty of mums managed to raise a baby and keep a house. But our house was bigger than any house I had lived in before, and although I hated to admit it, it was too much for me.

I had tried to make it my own in the small ways I could, but it was rare that I was in town and could meander the shops. I had to plan so far in advance and even then, D was so controlling, never allowing me to spend more than an hour out as he waited impatiently in the car, texting me every ten minutes asking me how much longer I was going to be. I ordered a lot of stuff online. Boxes and packages would arrive and were my only comfort and delivery drivers my only company as D's trips away grew increasingly longer. He had begun to travel for his work, and he was earning a lot more money. I didn't know how much and I was never given access to any accounts, just one debit card to order food and essentials with or occasionally a small pile of cash would appear on the kitchen surface the morning he left on his latest trip. There was a temptation to stuff it all under a mattress so I could take me and Baby Boy away somewhere one day. But I allowed those thoughts to evaporate when I imagined what would happen when he found me. And he *would* find me.

Although D was absent for much of the time, when he returned he would flip between needing me and wanting to knock me into the middle of next week.

I felt as though I was just bumbling through each day, trying to make the best of what was around me. I guessed that I was strong because that was what strong women did, didn't they? They could manage to stay in a relationship where they weren't always treated fairly and equally. That too I had learned from films, as well as watching my own mother put up with more than her fair share of abuse. For all the time my dad was there and I witnessed the endless fights and boxing matches, she would pick herself up, slap on the make-up and get on with her day. It was only after he left that she started to fall apart. It was as though the energy that he brought into the house, as negative as it was, was the only thing that fuelled her and gave her the courage to carry on.

Baby Boy, who was now three months old, smiling and gurgling and trying to roll over, gave me my courage. He was too young still to see the abuse, and I told myself that by the time he was old enough to understand, things would have calmed down. D and I would fall into a calmer existence. I knew he had it in him. I just had to help draw it out of him.

I wasn't to know that what I really should have been doing was looking at the future without him. If I had the foresight to know that things rarely got better, that they only got worse, then I would have told myself to run, take Baby Boy and go far away. Find someone somewhere, a refuge, anything where we would be safe.

* * *

The beginning of the end was when D brought home the other guy. At the time I had no idea who he was or what he did, but very soon I would come to know how he would change my life forever.

'This is my new business partner, babe, Fabrice.' D looked pleased with himself.

Fabrice was a stocky man, about fifty, with a Mediterranean look about him. I could smell the alcohol and cigarettes on him. He was wearing a dark-brown coat that was too heavy for the time of year, and his balding head twinkled with beads of sweat. Fabrice walked boldly over to the crib and picked up my sleeping baby. Then he cooed and stroked his cheek until Baby Boy began to stir. I stood rigid, frozen to the spot, unable to put into words what I was feeling, and even if I could articulate it, I knew it was best for everyone, especially me and Baby Boy, if I stayed silent.

'Ain't he a natural?' D said as he squeezed my arm, the pressure as always was too firm.

I flashed a smile that felt more painful than the arm squeeze. 'He is.' I pressed my other arm against my body, I felt the tingle in my fingertips, my heart pounded. I wondered if both men could hear it. I knew they could sense it, that they could smell my fear. I had learnt that people like them fed off it.

I wanted to ask Fabrice if he had experience with children; if he was a father himself. Perhaps then he would give me some sort of clue as to who he was and what sort of role he was about to play in my life, as he was giving nothing away. Maybe I should have said something, asserted myself. But I stayed silent until finally Fabrice walked towards me, his eyes half closed as though he were stoned.

'I think someone's ready for a feed.' His top lip glistened with sweat as he approached me, his large hands held my son, one around his head, the other cupped under his bottom, as though he were offering him to me for a baptism. I looked him in the eyes, making sure I wasn't reading the situation wrong, then I slowly reached out my hands, took Baby Boy and pulled him close to my chest. Immediately he began rooting, even though he had only been fed an hour ago.

'Ah, yes, I thought as much,' he said with a crooked smile, revealing two gold teeth on the right. 'We'll leave you to it.'

D gave Fabrice a friendly slap on the arm. 'Let's go and talk business then.'

They disappeared outside, taking a bottle of whisky with them.

Baby Boy had a quick comfort feed and went straight back off, but I did not dare lay him back in his crib. I didn't want Fabrice picking him up again. I held on to him and even used the toilet with him still in my arms.

I kept hold of Baby Boy, I kept him on me for the rest of day and all night, listening to the whoops and laughs coming from the garden. I clutched the baby to my breast where he stayed content and happy until I heard Fabrice stumble out of the house towards the sounds of the chugging engine of a waiting taxi.

I clutched my baby son tightly to my chest. Still so young, being on me was where he was happiest, but that day we bonded more than ever. Which was what made it so much harder when I finally had to let him go.

Instagram post: 14th May 2019

I feel happy tonight, guys, so I'm having a cold glass of bubbly in the back garden. I bought these glasses from Oliver Bonas about three

years ago. I couldn't resist how beautiful they looked with the
gorgeous gold design. And who doesn't love a bowl-shaped cham-
pagne glass – they are so retro, I feel as though I am in the 1920s. I
am teaming up with Oliver Bonas when I decorate the spare bedroom.
I just love the retro feel of their products and the colours are going to
look so great against the grey and white background in the bedroom.
Once I begin, I will post a before shot and have you guys help me out
making all the choices for which key pieces to use in there. It's going
to be such great fun and I can't wait to get started. Until then, chin-
chin, and have a great evening.

Mrs C x

#champers #champagne #oliverbonas #mrsclean

178,223 likes

parfait91 Aww enjoy your day.

lucybest65 Bit sad drinking on your own. Where's your family? Any
friends?

happyhev I would be quite happy for everyone to leave me alone.
Especially mardy trolls like you @lucybest65.

jerico88 Have a great day, you deserve it.

plainjane00 What gorgeous glasses, I need to get some of those
right now.

lucybest65 Hello, is no one listening, this woman is weird? There's
something not right…

alanheeks_1 There's something not right with you, love, @lucybest65.
She just said she's happy – give the girl a sodding break.

24

NOW

I was starting to wonder if Karen was right and that maybe I needed to think about some more therapy. I had felt as though I was turning a corner, having some sort of awakening. But now all these emotions and feelings were igniting inside of me, anger, frustration, contentment, like old friends crawling out of the woodwork. Could I trust them after so long? I had been sleep-walking through life, and if these feelings were resurfacing, then I needed to make sure I was fully equipped. I would never forget. I would always live with the regret, the guilt, but maybe the fear could be replaced. Maybe I needed a little more help. Just a final push to get me there. Which was why I picked up the phone the following morning after my impromptu drink with Will and heard the soothing tones of my psychologist's voice on his recorded answerphone. I left a message, knowing he was always busy in the morning with his clients, but confident he would call back promptly.

As I was leaving a practical lesson that afternoon, my phone rang, and I saw Joe's name on the screen.

'Hello,' Joe said, his soft Scouse accent poured through the receiver like honey. This man had saved my life. When I wanted it all to end, when I could not wake up one more day feeling wretched and unable to breathe, Joe was the one who slowly but surely brought me out of myself. I wasn't perfect afterwards – I had developed a series of behaviours and compulsions that I had to perform throughout the day when I felt a spike of fear rise within me – but at least I felt as though I could wake up and not be beaten down with the heavy guilt that crippled me and made me wish I was no longer alive.

'Joe,' I said. Already my breathing, which I hadn't realised was laboured, started to feel lighter.

'How are you? How's the college course going? You did start it, didn't you?'

'I did, yes and it's going well, thank you.'

'Good, good, then I know you're not just ringing to catch up, so what can I do for you?'

'I wondered if you could fit me in for a couple of sessions. I've been feeling... different recently, and I just wanted to make sure everything was okay. '

'When you say different, how do you mean?'

'I mean, different as in, I've started to feel things. Whereas before I felt, well, sort of numb, now I feel actual feelings, like anger, frustration, and, on one or two occasions, actual happiness.' I felt a laugh bubbling in my throat.

'Well, this all sounds really positive, so why do you feel you need to see me? I mean, I'm happy to see you, I'll never turn down the work.' He gave a soft laugh.

'I know it sounds weird, I just don't want to mess it all up, you know? I just want to know that this isn't a trick.'

Joe paused and I heard the click of his pen. 'I'd be happy to chat it through with you, when can you come in?'

* * *

I made an appointment for the following Tuesday morning and then on my way home from uni I decided to stop at Waitrose and pick up the dinner which I had failed to cook the other day after the jogger incident. I allowed a small smile to creep across my lips as I realised that although it wasn't Tuesday, it was Whatever Wednesday, and because we hadn't eaten tacos yesterday, I thought I would make them today.

As I meandered the aisles of the supermarket for cod, avocados, limes, mangoes, red onions and green chillis for the *pico de gallo*, a small spark of joy ignited within me. There was a song playing softly through the supermarket speakers that I recognised and I heard myself humming along. In the next aisles I grabbed some crunchy taco shells and a couple of bottles of Pinot Grigio.

I stood in line at the till, mentally preparing the meal, how I would serve it and what dishes I would use, when I felt a chill and I knew someone's eyes were on me. I looked up and saw the face of my neighbour, the flash of her short, bleached-blonde hair. She was right in front of me, having just completed her shop. Now she was staring at me with venom in her eyes. She moved towards me and I tried to take a step backwards, but it was almost 4.30 p.m. and the supermarket had got pretty busy. There was no room for me to go anywhere with three other shoppers and their trolleys behind me.

'I know it was you,' she spat in her European accent. 'You called social services, you think I cannot look after my own son.'

I looked around. Eyes were boring into me. I could feel my public guise being stripped away, that spark of joy extinguished.

'I see you – you think I don't see you? I see everything. Just because I forgot my purse, you think I can't buy my son medicine.

I have plenty, you know nothing.' She pointed a chipped red nail towards my chest, turned back to her trolley, which was full with packed bags, and stormed towards the exit.

I cleared my throat, looked behind me at the queue of shoppers and to either side of me; it seemed everyone had paused what they were doing or saying to stop and listen. I took a few steps forward with my basket and began placing my items on the conveyor belt. I looked awkwardly at the young lad behind the till and gave him a lopsided smile.

He gave a quick sniff. 'Would you like a bag for that?'

* * *

I walked home at a hurried pace, the bag digging awkwardly into my fingers. I wished I had taken up the offer of a second bag to distribute the weight of the wine. But at the till I had felt the inner me slowly being exposed to the other shoppers, so I had quickly stuffed all the items into one.

As I walked, my fingers burning from the tightness of the plastic, the idea of cooking for my house mates was quickly evaporating. At least this time I got as far as buying the food.

I couldn't stop thinking about what she had said and the way she had said it. She was right, of course she was right. What the hell did I know? But why would the child be so unhappy all the time? It broke my heart that I had no control over the situation.

The urge to just go home and crawl into bed was fast becoming the favoured option. But I did not want the girls to know that there was something wrong. I was trying my best to be a good house mate and I had drawn far too much attention to myself recently and not in a good way. It was time to rectify that. I would get on and cook the damn tacos and act as though everything was fine and that for once I was just a normal woman getting on with my life.

* * *

I took my time to chop and prepare the *pico*, and just as I had everything prepared, the girls started to filter through from various parts of the house. Finally Steve arrived – through the front door having rang the doorbell and then knocked far too aggressively.

'Wow, this looks great,' Mini said, getting up close. 'How colourful does that look?' She pointed at the *pico*, then pulled out her phone and snapped a photo.

'It's the salsa, it's called *pico de gallo*,' I said, feeling a smattering of the joy I had felt in the supermarket returning.

'*Pico de gallo*. Wow, you're spoiling us, Regi,' she said, looking down at her phone as she quickly altered the colours to make the *pico* look even brighter than it was.

'It's the sort of thing I learned to cook a few years ago. Up until then, I didn't have a clue about flavours and what not. I would just cook stuff out of packets, pies and chips, that sort of thing.' I thought back to the days when I would sit down to eat at the table alone, the seat opposite me perpetually empty.

'Well, you've got the hang of it now, girl. I'm salivating, I really am.' I looked over Mini's shoulder as she posted the *pico* photo to Instagram with a hashtag. #tacos

'Great. Well, tell the others as it's ready.'

Everyone, including Steve, gathered around as I brought everything to the table in little separate bowls so they could help themselves.

I watched as a perfect sequence of table etiquette unfolded in front of me; dishes were passed, and quiet mouthings of appreciation evolved into enthusiastic approval; even Karen managed to mumble a few complimentary words.

'This is literally the best non Taco Tuesday or Whatever Wednesday we have ever had,' Mini said.

'Good shout on the fish,' Steve said, taking a bite of his overly stuffed taco. I had made extra knowing his appetite would cover at least two people's.

I hadn't really been taking much notice of Sophia, but suddenly I saw she had only a small portion on her plate. She hadn't loaded a taco and she was just picking at the pico and moving the fish about her plate.

'Are you okay, Soph?' I asked quietly.

'I don't know, it all smells a bit funky.' Sophia pulled a funny face.

'I know, it's great – I have never had fish tacos before. I just love the crunch of the tacos muddled with the softness of the fish.' Mini grinned.

'All right, Mini, you're not Greg bloody Wallace,' Karen said, taking a bite of her taco.

'Well, I think Regi's cooking is *MasterChef* standard – it's truly delicious.' Mini was undeterred as usual by Karen's negativity.

Suddenly, Sophia stood up and pushed her chair back too quickly so it fell backwards. Steve was up on his feet as though he was back in the army and the enemy had just arrived. He swept Sophia's chair back up again as though it had never happened. By this point, Sophia was on her way out of the kitchen, her hand over her mouth mumbling something about having drank too much at the weekend.

'Oh my God, how dramatic,' Karen said and carried on eating.

'I didn't see her drink that much at the weekend,' Mini frowned.

'I did,' I said quickly. 'I saw her disappear to her room with a bottle of wine when you lot went to bed.'

Karen pulled her mouth down in disgust and shook her head. 'We've all done it.'

'Well, that'll do it, drinking right before bed,' Mini added.

Both of them were oblivious to my lie. I had suffered the symptoms and seen it enough times to recognise the early signs of pregnancy. Now I knew which of the three house mates the pregnancy kit had belonged to. I kept my poker face. But who could be the father?

* * *

I stayed at college late for the rest of the week. Will had had a word with the cleaners for me, and so there was no repeat performance of the door being locked with all of my stuff inside. We exchanged numbers – he said to save me walking all the way across the college to reach him if I needed to again. Once I had his number in my phone, I felt a sudden urge to text him something small-talkish and flirty, but the longer I thought about it, the more it made me cringe. What I wanted to say to him would never be properly executed because I had absolutely no experience of being cool or flirting or any of those things. I hadn't perfected those skills in my late teens or early twenties the way all other girls that age did. Whilst they were making endless mistakes, moulding themselves into the people they were to become in their later life, my life was leading up to making one of the biggest mistakes in my life, one that I could never recover from or could be rectified.

25

I really began to throw myself into my work for the remainder of the week. Will had suddenly become elusive. Yet again I considered sending him a text but bottled out at the last minute. I decided to try to use the quieter time in the evenings to focus on myself. I did not need to be wondering what Will was up to today, or if he was wearing that trademark denim jacket with the hoody that made him all the more appealing, or how looking at his shiny eyes and listening to his easy voice loosened my breathing and lifted the weight from my heart.

I was, however, worried about Sophia. I knew her parents were affluent – employed staff on their countryside weekend residence kind of affluent – so I knew she would be set financially. But I was worried that she had got herself in trouble; with no mention of any male friends, her pregnancy could only have been the result of a silly one-night mistake.

I didn't want to think any more about my neighbour and her child. The more time I spent at uni, the less I would hear the crying. The incident in the supermarket would occasionally creep back and bother me. It was usually just as I was dropping off to sleep when the finger of shame would tap me lightly on the shoulder and remind me to feel a little more mortification.

On Friday I arrived home from the art rooms to the lingering smell of fajita. It was gone 10 p.m., and I was absolutely starving. I hoped that someone had the foresight to leave a plate of food out for me. I placed my bag down in the hallway and headed for the kitchen. I stopped when I heard hushed whispers coming from inside and stood behind the closed door. The hallway was in darkness – someone needed to replace the bulb and I felt a surge of annoyance that it would probably be left to me.

I could hear a female voice and a male voice. It could only be Steve and Karen arguing again. They had been doing a lot more of that recently. I was intrigued to know what they could be discussing at such a late hour outside the privacy of Karen's bedroom. What had happened to love's young dream? They had once been joined at the hip, now there was a tension in the air whenever Steve was around. The cracks were starting to show.

It had suddenly gone very quiet, and so I thought I would leave them to it, pop back for my fajitas when they had come out. I was about to turn around and pick up my bag and head upstairs when Sophia almost collided with me as she came racing out of the kitchen. Even in the darkness of the hallway, I could see she had been crying.

'Oh, hi,' I said. 'I was just going to see if there were any fajitas left.'

'There's some left in the fridge, just reheat them in the microwave.' She was already heading for the stairs.

'Great, I'll...' I was about to say I would pop up and see if she was okay in a minute but she was already taking the stairs two at a time.

Next out of the kitchen came Steve.

'Guess she's still got that sickness thing,' he said and, again, he hurried past me, up the stairs and I heard him open Karen's door and go in.

I stood in the dark hallway for a few seconds and let the reality of what was happening sink in. Sophia wouldn't have had to go anywhere to get pregnant. It had been happening under this very roof. All those days when Steve was here and Karen wasn't.

Suddenly the thought of leftover fajitas was no longer enticing.

* * *

Over the weekend a heavy tension increased like a thunder cloud after a heatwave. I heard plenty of raised whispers from Karen's room and Steve left the house several times only to come back half an hour later on each occasion. Sophia spent the whole time hibernating in the bedroom.

By Sunday morning, Steve had gone and Karen was sat at the kitchen table sipping a coffee, looking deeply sorry for herself.

'It feels like summer now,' she said to the room, even though she knew I was in there, clearing through the fridge, getting rid of the old food and giving it a good wipe down. I had seen a post that morning from Mrs Clean and she had been doing the very same thing. It inspired me to keep up the momentum. So many germs breed in the fridge. I had taken a picture beforehand and I was even thinking about doing my first tap-to-tidy post and tag Mrs Clean in it.

'I love the summer. I was so looking forward to the summer with Steve.' She pulled her legs up to her chest as she sat on the chair and pulled her sweatshirt down over her bare knees. She was wearing what looked like a pair of Steve's boxer shorts. Her hair was pulled tightly into a ponytail. 'I don't think we'll last that long though.'

I stopped my cleaning and turned towards Karen. She had a wad of tissue in her hand and for a moment I thought it was for her hay fever.

She put her legs on the floor and spun towards me.

'I think he's fallen out of love with me.' Her voice broke and tears spilled from her eyes. 'He left this morning, said he wasn't sure when he would be back, said he needed "time" to think things over,' she said, accentuating and almost spitting out the final words.

I edged towards the table, unsure whether to sit down and try to comfort her.

'Time, time for what? Did he say?'

'No, that's just it, it's a bloody cryptic quiz with him. I literally cannot get a word of sense from him. I don't think he even knows what he wants. All that time he was coming here when I wasn't here, I thought it was because he loved being here so much, because it made him feel close to me or something. When you said that he was here as often as he was, I had no clue. I only gave him a key for the odd occasion he may need to let himself in. I really felt we were moving on, going places. How can he go from being that keen, to this, leaving and not saying when I might see him again?'

It made sense that Steve and Sophia had become so close so quickly if he was here when Karen wasn't. I moved to the kitchen table, peeled off the Marigolds, took a deep breath and tentatively placed my hand on top of Karen's, hoping this would offer some sort of comfort.

'I don't know is my answer. But I really think you need to

speak to him properly and make him be up front and honest with you?'

She looked at me with panic in her eyes. 'Why, do you know something I don't?'

I gulped. 'God. No.'

'Cos I saw you in the summerhouse the night of the party.'

'We were just talking. I don't really remember, to be honest, anyway. The point is, if there is something he has on his mind, it's only fair he shares it with you. Tell him he has a couple of days to mull it over and then he has to be square with you. Life is too...' I stopped myself from saying the final word. I hated it, I hated admitting that life was too short when I had experienced how short it could be. 'Life should be spent with the person you know loves you as much as you love them. I can see you love Steve a lot and if he doesn't love you, then he needs to make that absolutely clear and not mess you around. Do not let him mess you around,' I said and got back up and carried on cleaning the fridge.

Karen let out a long sigh.

I had just picked up the spray gun and was about to clean the final bottom shelf when I heard her softly say, 'Thank you, you're a good friend.'

I felt something swell inside of me, a sort of gratitude. I knew I hadn't felt the same closeness with Karen as I had with Sophia and even Mini, so it felt good to know I wasn't just a source of her continued grievance.

I was just thinking of something suitably friendly to say back to her when the doorbell rang through the hallway. I looked at Karen.

'I can't go looking like this,' she said. Sophia would still be in bed – she didn't seem to rise before nine these days. I had no idea where Mini was.

'Right,' I said and I went to the door. *Don't do it*, I heard the words from my past. But I would do it anyway, to be on the safe side because the uncertainty of not knowing who was behind the door had made my mouth go dry, so I unlocked and locked six times before I opened the door and found myself face to face with Will. I must have exhibited a myriad of expressions as I tried to fathom why he was here before 9 a.m. on a Sunday. I knew I must have looked like hell on a stick and that, oh my God, I lifted my hands and saw I was still wearing the Marigolds. Will began to laugh. I realised how much I had missed that laugh and that smile. It had been over a week since I had last seen him.

'Very fetching. Have I caught you at a bad time? You didn't have your hand down the loo or anything?'

I laughed, despite myself.

'No, not quite that rank, just giving the fridge a once over.'

Will sucked in his breath. 'Well, as riveting as that is, I wondered if I could drag you away to join me for a coffee at the new artisan place in town. I was headed there myself – they do great coffees and pancakes, so I'm told.'

'New artisan place? I haven't heard of it.'

'Trust me, it's real. I wouldn't make it up just to pull you into the streets this early on a Sunday morning.'

I heard a scuff on the floorboards behind me and I threw a glance over my shoulder. Mini was standing wide-eyed with a wry smile in duck-egg-blue cotton pyjamas, her hair tousled up on her head.

'Hello,' she said in her most angelic voice.

'Oh, hi there, I'm Will.' Will gave a quick wave. 'Sorry to disturb so early.'

'Don't mind me,' she said unable to stifle the giggle that came out as she scooted off towards the kitchen to gossip about me to Karen, no doubt. But Karen would be in no mood for gossiping about men.

I looked around awkwardly to make sure no other house mates were loitering where they shouldn't be.

'I just need to, um, freshen up. I'll be five minutes, do you want to...' I gestured towards the house.

'No, no,' Will said firmly. 'I'll wait out here, I'm enjoying the fresh air.' He stuck his hands in his pockets and looked around enthusiastically.

I widened my eyes and gave a small smile.

'Okay, great. Gimme five.' I closed the door and immediately ripped off the Marigolds. What must Will have thought of me in them?

I raced up the stairs, dropping the Marigolds on the way. I knew I would need to perform the full repertoire of behaviours after the shock of Will turning up unannounced. I brushed my teeth, counting to thirty-four even though I was sure I had done them already.

The bedsheets hadn't been stripped, so I ripped off the day-old sheets and threw them in the corner. I swapped my T-shirt and leggings I had put on this morning to have a good cleaning session in for light-blue skinny jeans and a baggy white T-shirt. I sprayed on some deodorant, ran a brush through my hair, rubbed some tinted moisturiser into my face and applied a little lip gloss. Will said there was a chill to the air, so I pulled on a grey chunky cardigan. I took a deep breath. There were a few pound coins on the bedside table, so I quickly lined them up, then closed and locked the door to my room six times before letting myself out. It was the most behaviours I had ever performed in such a short space of time, and I felt full with satisfaction. Nothing bad could possibly happen now.

Once downstairs, I tried to bring my heart rate down as I took slow breaths. I had already gone over the promised five minutes. I opened the door and saw Will leaning casually on next door's front wall, his hands in his pockets. I stole a look towards the top-floor window and saw the flicker of a blind.

'Come on,' I said as I began walking at speed.

'You look fab.' He stood up, leaving his hands in his pockets as he fell into stride next to me. 'Blimey, someone's keen.'

* * *

The café was already starting to fill up, even though it was only nine thirty. Early-morning dog walkers and parents with tiny babies strapped to them and toddlers in tow. It wasn't the ideal place with so much going on, and I felt my mouth go dry as I looked around at the amount of small children I was suddenly forced to share the vicinity with. But I did what I usually did and began to phase their chatter out. It was a finely tuned process, but with a little perseverance and concentration, I eventually succeeded. I began by making conversation with Will, asking him about his weekend so far, how he found out about this place, what his favourite brunch dish was until, finally, the sounds of the children were a murmur in the background.

When our coffees arrived, along with our pancakes, I sat back and sipped it gratefully.

'Sorry for throwing your morning into disarray by turning up at such an ungodly hour.'

'You're forgiven. This place is lovely.' I looked around at the décor of copper and distressed wood.

'I think so. How's your coffee?' Will asked as I took another sip of my decaf with coconut milk latte. I didn't feel confident to relay my preferred coffee style to Will just yet so I threw caution to the wind and ordered one from the menu. It had felt liberating.

'Delicious,' I said, feeling a sense of betrayal towards my local café. But now Heather had left, I really had no reason to visit there any more. Maybe this could become my local haunt? Maybe, just maybe, I could meet Will here from time to time. I knew he lived fairly close by.

We ate our pancakes in almost silence, occasionally making an appreciative noise. I surprised myself at how comfortable I felt eating next to him.

Will put his knife and fork next to one another in a neat line, and wiped his mouth with a napkin.

'Fabulous. I'm officially a regular.'

'It was great,' I agreed.

Will cleared his throat, looked down at his lap and then up at me. Immediately, I sensed a question forming on his lips.

'Regi.' He cleared his throat again. 'I hope you don't mind me asking, and tell me to mind my own if you like, but I wanted to ask... I say ask... I had rather hoped you might share with me, any problems you are having at the moment, or maybe whatever it is that you are running away from. You see' – he edged himself forwards in his chair – 'I like you. Very much. But I can see there's pain in your eyes. And I don't mean this to sound wanky, so please receive it as sincerely as I mean it.'

I looked at Will for a moment, then tore my gaze away. My eyes prickled with tears, but I would not allow myself to cry. Even though I wanted to weep, knowing that he had truly seen me for who I was and he still wanted to date me.

'I mean, listen, you don't need to tell me anything today. I think what I am trying to say is that I would like to try, at least, to get closer to you, and I believe from past experiences – one that I am still dealing with, in fact, but which I hope will be wrapped up very soon – it's best if two people, who seem to share an avid interest in... coffee and pancakes' – he gestured to the table – 'and who might like to get coffee and pancakes again, maybe one day might like to only get coffee and pancakes with one another and no one else.'

I couldn't help but break into a small smile at that.

'What I want to say is, I want you to know that if you like me as much as I like you, then, when you are ready, you can talk to me about anything you like. There are no judgements here.' He held his hands up in surrender.

I looked down at my feet as I felt the emotional tears burning my nose and throat.

'I'm here. Just... I want you to know that I'm not just looking for an easy catch, which, by the way, you most certainly are not. The next stop for me is forever.'

I looked up and my smile morphed into a laugh.

'God, did I just say that?' Will put his hand on his forehead.

'You did.'

'Oh hell, I just stepped over the line into official wankiness, didn't I? I think I need to call Richard Curtis. I think I just nailed a line for his next blockbuster. My God, I'm so cheesy.'

'I don't mind a bit of cheese.' I sniffed out a small laugh. It was probably what I needed more than I knew.

'Good, cos I have been known to dish it out on occasion. Only when it's necessary, mind.'

'Like just then.'

'Like just then.'

I sniffed out another nervous laugh and cleared my throat. 'Right, I think it's time to walk off those pancakes.'

* * *

That night in my room, I opened the window with the intention of only leaving it open a fraction all night. I stood and waited. I waited for the racing heart, the dry mouth and sweaty palms. Something that would urge me to feed the beast with repetitive locking and unlocking. But I lay down in my clean sheets and allowed a small breeze to come in through the window and wash over me.

When I woke early at around five the following morning to the lively chatter of birdsong. I looked to see the window was still open. I smiled to myself and fell back to sleep and dreamt of Will calling me by my real name.

Just before Baby Boy turned six months old, I reminded D we hadn't yet registered his birth. He spat out an insult, ripped a sheet of paper from a notebook and wrote a name on it. He shoved the paper in my face, and when I didn't reach to grab it, it dropped onto the floor. I looked down at the paper and saw a first and middle name and D's surname.

'That is my son's name,' he called as he walked away.

After that D didn't once refer to him by his name and I continued to call him Baby Boy.

* * *

When Baby Boy was eight months old, D came home from work or wherever he had been one afternoon, and came through the door, followed sheepishly by a petite woman with a mousy-brown sleek bob.

'This is Olga – she is here to help you out, babes.' D waved his introduction and began rooting through the fridge for a beer.

I looked at the small woman with a lost expression in her eyes, then I looked at D with confusion.

'What do you mean, help me out?' Baby Boy was sitting right up on my hip, clutching on to my T-shirt, occasionally rooting for the boob. D looked on, a frustrated expression flashed across his face. He had not got used to having to share me with the baby, and I knew he was expecting me to give up breastfeeding him very soon. But I had no intentions of giving up; feeding my son was the only control I had.

'Well, you're my girl, that's my baby, and this is our house. I want you both to be happy and not worry about anything except making yourself look pretty and keeping the baby alive. No more cleaning for you.' He winked. An act I hadn't seen him do since we first started dating. I looked at Olga. She shifted uncomfortably. I wondered if she already knew his behaviour was all an act.

'So what am I expected to do with myself all day?' I could hear the agitation rising in my voice as I looked at this Olga woman that had arrived in our house. I was grateful for the help, but to just bring an actual person into our lives without discussing it with me first was disturbing to say the least. What was more disturbing was that Olga's repugnance at being here was palpable.

'And where will Olga be living?'

D approached me. Olga physically shrank backwards.

I knew D was daring me to push him a little further. I knew what was in store for me if I did, but something uncontrollable within me spurred me on anyway.

'Olga will be staying with us. In the spare room.' D's voice was high and stretched. He knew I was testing him, and he didn't like to be challenged. But I wasn't sure how he would react with another woman in the house. Something urged me on.

'And would you like me to organise Olga's room or will she be doing that herself?'

By this point D was almost at my face, so close I could smell his skin, which reeked of stale alcohol.

'I think it might be nice if we do that for her seeing as she is our guest.' He spoke through gritted teeth.

'We?' I said it so fast I hadn't realised it had fallen out of my mouth, but knowing it would be me who sorted the room while D drank himself to sleep with a bottle of whisky, I couldn't help myself. Quick as a flash Baby Boy was ripped from my arms and thrown at Olga who barely had a second to think about what had happened but who managed to catch him by the arm and pulled him, red-faced and wailing, into her chest. I didn't have time to thank her as I was dragged into the bedroom with only Olga's shocked and worried face in my mind's eye and the screams of my baby ringing in my ears.

27

A mere few hours later, I woke to the sound of screaming. I had been dreaming again. I was stuck between sleep and wakefulness, and the sounds of crying were ringing in my ears. I started to grab around me, to pull him close to me, but I woke to empty, flailing arms. I looked up and saw the window had been left ajar. For a second, I panicked; how had that happened? Then I remembered. I had left it open after the serene sense of calm that had followed my date with Will.

But now the open window that brought me so much joy last night and only a few hours ago at 5 a.m., plagued me. The sounds of the child had entered my dreams and made me wake with a pain in my chest and a gut so tight it hurt. I jumped out of bed and opened the window a little further just to look out. The birds were still tweeting their morning chorus; the sun was already warm and it was going to be a lovely day. But the beautiful morning was marred; I could hear the now muffled cries of the little boy next door. I couldn't bear it any longer. It was pure torture. I was going to have to deal with this, to speak with her directly. If she refused to speak with me, I would put in another complaint to social services.

As a way of pain relief, I opened my phone to Mrs Clean's account. I was instantly soothed by her easy tone and aesthetic symmetry. I could feel the pain in my gut easing as the sound of the cries faded.

* * *

The usual Monday-morning routine of everyone getting ready to leave the house was in full swing by the time I got downstairs.

I hadn't seen or spoken to Karen since our little chat at the table before I went for brunch with Will. I think she had spent the rest of the day in her room, and I wanted to catch up and check in with her before I went to my seminar. I didn't think I would be very good at harbouring Sophia's and Steve's secret. The weight of their lie hung heavily within me.

Karen wasn't downstairs, but Sophia was. Her skin looked pale and shiny.

I wanted to speak of her pregnancy outright, but the words wouldn't form properly. I had hoped she would have said something to me by now, but that hadn't happened either.

'Morning,' I managed and sat at the table.

'How are you feeling after your hot date yesterday?' I had seen Sophia and Mini when I came back and was subjected to half an hour's grilling over my 'mystery man'.

I smiled at Sophia who was trying her best to sound chipper but I recognised the strain, the way each word came slowly and with effort. I had experienced the worst kind of morning sickness. I wanted to put my arm around her, to tell her it was okay, but I would have to wait until she spoke to me.

'Well, it wasn't a date,' I said, taking out some fruit from the fridge, which still filled me with a surge of delight whenever I opened it to reveal sparkling shelves and everything sitting snugly in its home.

'Yes, it was.' Mini strode into the kitchen, looking fresh and funky in tight, blue trousers and a red-and-white-spotted shirt, her long, dark hair was freshly washed and blow-dried.

'Wow, Mins, you put us all to shame,' Sophia said, looking her up and down.

'Yeah, well, you'll get your mojo back, Soph – you're just feeling a little out of sorts.'

How was it that Mini had not yet managed to work out that Sophia was suffering from pregnancy sickness? Unless perhaps the two of them were in cahoots about the whole thing, and perhaps they thought I was none the wiser.

'Anyway, are you still feeling high after the brunch?' Mini looked excited.

'Well, I was, and then this morning, the damn child next door was crying again.' I spoke boldly and then noted how Sophia and Mini exchanged a brief look; Mini's was something that resembled despair.

'So will you do anything about it?' she asked.

I shrugged. 'I don't know. I sort of want to go round there and have it out with her.'

'Do you think that's wise? If it's a social-care matter, then leave it in their hands,' Sophia said.

'But that's just it, they are telling me there is nothing to be concerned about – they have assessed the situation and they have no concerns.'

'But you still think there's something going on?' Sophia asked.

'Perhaps. I don't know. It doesn't bother you guys?'

'I haven't heard a thing,' Mini said.

'Me neither,' Sophia said.

'But you know there's a little boy living next door, don't you?'

'I couldn't say for certain.' Mini looked again to Sophia for reassurance.

'Nope, never seen him,' Sophia said. 'But then your room does look right over their garden, so that gives you the advantage there. Or rather, disadvantage in this case.'

I shook my head. 'Maybe I'm just letting it all get on top of me.'

'Have you got your psychologist's number?' Sophia said.

'I have an appointment tomorrow.' I felt the familiar wave of serenity wash over me when I imagined myself speaking freely with Joe.

Mini and Sophia looked at one another again, this time Mini's face looked hopeful.

* * *

I sat on the train on the way to uni and looked at Mrs Clean's most recent post. It was a photo of a potting bench, something I had never heard of before. It was a normal workbench, but a little taller and more elegant. I presumed you would stand and pot your seeds on it. She had written that she had been wanting to get one for ages and she was over the moon with it. On the worktop were a few tiny pots and packets of seeds.

Underneath, there were the usual fifty thousand or so likes and a string of comments. As usual I went straight in to sift through to the negative comments, but more specifically I wanted to see what lucybest65 had to say on it. And there it was.

Are you telling me this woman is buying all this stuff herself? She has clearly been gifted it – at least have the courtesy to tell us that.

A few people had replied to her; a couple agreeing, only to egg her on, several others just to tell her off. Questions about lucybest65 tumbled through my mind and I was interested to know what she had been up to since the last banal photo she had uploaded.

I clicked on lucybest65's profile and I was taken through to her grid which boasted a handful of photos. There was a new image, so I clicked on it. She had taken a photo of a window, all I could see of her body were her feet, which were up on a stool. A large window was in front of her and through the open blind, on the opposite building's rooftop, was a large cinema screen. There were about fifty or so seats full with people all facing the screen. I zoomed in on the photo and saw it was a screening of *The Greatest Showman*.

Sat in my lounge and I have the best seat in the house.

Although the photo was grainy and a little out of focus, she seemed to have captured a moment in time that many would be envious of. She had only a handful of followers, and no one ever commented on her posts. I felt an urge to comment, to say something about being set up in the most perfect location to watch a film for free. But more than that, I was suddenly intrigued. I wanted to know more.

I was being given access to a window into someone's life – in this case, literally her window. I spotted a few familiar items in the background of this photo, things I had seen in her previous images: a blue vase on a small table, a small Dalmatian dog ornament and occasionally what looked like a cat's litter tray in the corner of the room. This was certainly her home, if not somewhere she resided frequently. It occurred to me that if I knew where all the rooftop cinemas were in London – and there surely couldn't be that many – there was a chance I could know where lucybest65 lived. And that notion created a tingle of excitement that rippled through my body.

* * *

By the end of the college day, consciousness had become an aching weight and had consumed me. I was already thinking about my bedtime routine, but I knew I had to get on with utilising the time and space to finish my piece for the exhibition. There had also been a suggestion from Will that he might be able to sidle down the hallway and drop me off home.

Since the first night when the cleaner had locked the door, I had begun setting up on the bench closest to the door, my work spread out across the entire bench. I believed that if something happened once, there was a good chance of it happening again.

I had moved on to the next phase of my project and was now working with more fabrics. I quickly became absorbed in the cutting and sewing, and I was pleased to see the coat taking a more solid shape. So far the flamboyance that I had planned out in my head and on the sketch pad wasn't quite right, but it was starting to feel like a proper project and so I allowed myself a flutter of excitement at the prospect of completing the first creative thing in many years. This was a milestone, something I should feel proud of, but anxiety had a cheeky way of never quite letting you stay in that happy place for too long.

The room by now was losing quite a lot of light. It was nearly ten and the sky was almost black outside, and I had only one small lamp on the bench and all the blinds were drawn tight.

I stood up and went over to the corner to hit the main lights when the whole room plunged into a murky darkness. The lamp on the desk went out and the corridor outside went dark. I grasped around me for something to help me gain my bearings. I could just about see the bench a few metres in front of me, but there was no other light feeding through, which must have meant that the lights around the campus must have gone out as well.

I took a few steps forward until my stomach hit the bench. I tried to push away the panic that had begun to constrict my throat, but before I knew it, I could feel a tight grip around my wrist. I began twisting from it, trying to escape, to pull myself free.

'Let me go,' I said into the blackness. I started to grope around on the desk in front of me for my phone, but my hands just collided with one another. The panic was dialled up a notch as my thoughts began to spiral out of control. I dropped to my knees and tried to focus on just breathing in and then out for a longer breath, but the darkness had consumed any rational thought.

But amongst the chaos of my mind, I could hear footsteps; they were coming closer and closer until they stopped just outside the room.

Then I heard someone calling for Regi, but it was getting lost amongst the noise in my head.

There was a surge of light. The brightness was overbearing. I blinked at my surroundings from my safe place under the bench. I hadn't realised I had found my way there. I turned around on my knees and saw two figures illuminated in the doorway by brighter lights in the corridor.

'Regi,' came the voice again, soft and feminine. I began to crawl out from under the bench at the same time as the figure came towards me. I rubbed my wrist where I could feel the lingering sensation of someone's firm touch. I looked to the bench where my phone was sat next to my scrapbook, exactly where I had left it. I stood up, then turned and saw who had come into the room.

'Sophia?' I was confused. From behind her emerged Steve.

'Guys?' I couldn't understand why they were both here. 'Is everything okay?'

Sophia rubbed her face with her hands and sank into a stool opposite.

'No, it's not,' she squeaked through her fingers.

Steve stepped forward and stood in front of me with his hands in his pockets.

'It's not, not okay. It's, it's a bit messed up,' he said awkwardly.

I looked between them both, trying to bring my breathing back to normal.

'Did you... was there a power cut?'

'The lights went out for a second just then,' Sophia said, and then she pulled her hands away from her face and looked at me. 'Are you okay, Regi?'

I sucked in a big breath and blew it out. 'Absolutely fine. I couldn't find my phone when the lights went out. Just a bit disorientated. And tired.' I shrugged off her concerns.

'We wanted to tell you about us,' Sophia said.

'It's okay.' I waved my hand. 'I know.'

A small wail escaped from Sophia.

'Oh, you do?' Steve went rigid.

'Yes,' I said, still slightly breathless. 'I wanted to say something to you both, well to you, Sophia, but I didn't know how.' I thought about the pregnancy test. I would wait until they mentioned that.

'Okay, well.' Steve's shoulders relaxed. 'We wanted to come and say to you, here, tonight, away from the house and prying ears, we wanted you to know that we have every intention of telling Karen. You see, the thing is, Regi...' Steve shifted his feet and looked around, perhaps for something of comfort to lean on.

'The thing is, we are in love.' Sophia looked at me, her eyes wide. Waiting for me to respond.

She said it so dramatically that I wasn't sure I had understood her correctly. I had presumed it was a one-off, a mistake.

Steve smiled. 'That's right and I'm going to finish things with Karen properly and we're going to move into Sophia's parents' house. You see, Sophia is pregnant.' Steve paused and I realised he was waiting for a response.

'Oh, oh wow, pregnant,' I said, looking at Sophia. She nodded and smiled. I didn't feel it was the right time to recall my nocturnal adventures of rooting around in a wheelie bin at two in the morning and discovering a pregnancy test.

'So we'll stay there until she has had the baby, and then we will save up to buy our own house,' Steve continued. 'I'm going back into the army at some point – there's an opportunity for us to move to Dorset to some barracks there, so we have a few choices.' Steve looked at Sophia with a warm smile and she looked back at him, with an expression on her face I had never seen before and I realised it was admiration. It wasn't like any look I had seen exchanged between Steve and Karen. I watched them both for a second, then Sophia turned to me.

'We wanted you to know, Regi, to be the first to know. We respect you a lot, and I know you and Steve never really hit it off—'

'No, it wasn't that,' I tried to defend myself.

'It's fine, Regi, you don't need to pretend. I wasn't happy with Karen, so I wasn't really projecting my best self. I had wanted to talk to you about it for such a long time, because you're older and wiser. I thought you might understand, but every time I went to say something, I lost my nerve. I would go out of my way to try to catch you on your own sometimes, so I'm sorry if I creeped you out. I'm sorry. I don't really know how to be myself around anyone, really. Except Soph. All those extra days I was there, at the house, well, we became close very quickly. I was confused. It wasn't supposed to happen this way.'

I thought about how I had treated Steve, how his presence had unnerved me. I had felt that tension and uneasiness about him, but it had triggered other thoughts in me.

'Well, I'm really very happy for you guys. It's wonderful news.' I moved closer to Sophia and squeezed her arm.

'Hey, what's this? Did I miss a party?' Will appeared in the doorway. 'I heard there was power cut this end. Is everyone okay?'

'We're fine,' I said quickly. Will stood for a moment and then launched into the room, his hand outstretched towards Steve. 'Hi, I'm Will, I'm a lecturer here and also a friend of Regi's.'

Sophia looked over at me and gave me a small smile whilst Steve and Will shook hands and exchanged pleasantries.

'Hi, I'm Sophia, I'm Regi's house mate,' Sophia said as Will moved from Steve to her and shook her hand as well.

'Are you okay?' Will looked at me.

'I'm good.'

'Great, then I think it's time for a drink at the pub. Anyone?'

Steve and Sophia said their goodbyes – Steve was going to drop Sophia off at home, and, apparently, they would be telling Karen at the weekend. I decided I would have to make myself scarce when that happened, but for now, I decided to take Will up on his offer of a drink.

It was busier than the last time we had visited the pub but I found I could relax a little easier and found us some seats whilst Will bought the drinks with some cash I had assertively stuffed in his hand after he tried to wave it away.

He arrived at the table with a round tray with two bottles of cider and two glasses. He sat down opposite me and pushed a bottle and a glass my way. I poured the cider out and took a long drink.

Will began asking me about the Sophia and Steve saga. I had briefly mentioned it on the way over to the pub and now in the comfort of the tub chairs with the buzz of the alcohol creeping into my system, I felt ready to share a few anecdotes from my time in the house: from my discovery of the pregnancy kit to the way Steve had made me feel uncomfortable. Will laughed long and loudly at my description of myself wading through the bin at 2 a.m., and he told me it was perfectly understandable that I would feel a little insecure with a guy who you didn't really know that well coming and going from the house all the time. The conversation was steered back to his family again and his sisters. He was going to visit one of them at the end of the summer term and was looking forward to the break.

'Any siblings, Regi?' he asked casually, and sipped his cider.

I shook my head. 'No. Only child.' I felt a ripple of apprehension that he would quiz me further. Will looked at me over his glass, waited a beat for me to continue. When I didn't he put his glass down and said, 'There's a pool table round the back there, fancy a game?'

* * *

After Will beat me three games to one, we walked out of the pub and back to the uni car park. The night air was a cool contrast to the warm pub and was refreshing against my bare arms. There was a cosy feeling between us as we strolled; one I had forgotten could exist between two people.

'You want my coat?' Will offered.

'No, it feels nice on my skin,' I said, gazing up at the starry sky. I felt Will's eyes on me, but when I looked at him he looked away.

Will drove me home and pulled up outside the house, turning off the engine.

'Don't want to alarm your house mates,' he said.

I looked at him and we held each other's stare for enough time for us both to realise how charged the atmosphere was and then look away. We both went to speak at the same time and then we laughed coyly. But there had been something in that look that both of us had felt; an energy had built around us, magnetising us towards one another. I opened the car door and brought us away from it, making whatever had been building fizzle and evaporate. I hated myself the second I did it, knowing I had pushed away feelings that were natural.

Once I was inside and in my bedroom, I began my night-time routine with brushing my teeth. I was a few seconds in when I realised I had forgotten to start counting to thirty-four. My mind had been replaying a conversation between me and Will where I must have said something funny, which made Will look at me with endearment. When I got into bed, my thoughts were buzzing. But not in the usual way. The fear and panic I had felt in the art room were now replaced with a happiness that I hadn't felt for such a long time. It made me get right back out of bed again and fling open the window as wide as it would go.

I arrived at Joe's house on Tuesday morning, where he ran his practice from a three-room extension round the back. Marion, his receptionist, smiled warmly at me when I arrived and offered to take my coat and make me some tea. I accepted a chamomile and a few minutes later Joe was ready to see me.

He greeted me as warmly as he could without breaching patient/counselling boundaries, with a grand smile, taking my tea and placing it on the coffee table next to a chair. Then he gestured to where I should sit and when I sank into the seat, it was as though no time had passed at all since our last meeting.

At one point, when the pain was so raw and breathing was so laborious, I had wondered whether I would always be in therapy. I had checked myself into A&E so many times with chest pains and heart problems that I knew the staff by their first names. Of course, there was never anything wrong with me – not that they could see from looking at an X-ray anyway. Joe had said there was always the possibility that I would find myself back here and that I was always welcome.

'I thought I was just getting on with stuff,' I began.

Joe pulled his usual nonchalant face. He never liked to butt in when I began talking; this was something I had noticed from the beginning. At first I thought he was a total charlatan, and that he was expecting me to just monologue for an hour and take my money, but after a few sessions I began to see the pattern; he would slowly talk more as the session went on, always allowing time for me to formulate the words and sentences at my own pace.

'As I said on the phone, I've started to feel different. A whole mix of emotions. And I have been busy. I have certain behaviours now, do you remember, we discussed them via Skype last year? – I know I shouldn't – but they help massively.'

Joe nodded and smiled.

'I mean, they don't affect my life or anything.' Joe nodded, and I knew I sounded as though I was trying so hard to justify them. I knew it was what all OCD sufferers said, how every compulsive behaviour bore no infliction on their life. But I honestly didn't see how a few minutes of repetitive action made any difference to mine or anyone else's life.

'But just recently, there have been a few occasions where I just forgot to do them.' I carried on, 'I wondered if that was normal for a start. Then there's the anxiety. It comes and goes, and when it's not there, I'm scared it will return. And, of course, these feelings that are surfacing, I'm feeling them all from anger to frustration to, sometimes, happiness.' I cleared my throat and stretched my legs out. 'Sometimes, recently, I have been feeling these pangs of...' I could barely say it. 'Maternal instinct. I hear my neighbour's child crying a lot. I was really concerned at one point, and I'm ashamed to say I called social services and now my neighbour hates me. It turns out it's all okay according to social services, but I'm still concerned.' I gave a small smile and looked around the room. 'Hardly serious psychotic behaviour, I know, but I just wanted to know if, well, like I have always said to you, if I'm... if I'm going to be okay?'

Joe took a long breath in, as if preparing himself to speak. But he didn't. He just waited. Because he knew I had more to say.

'And I see him, you know, all the time. He comes at me, and he grabs my arm, and he tells me I can't run away. I don't know if I'm delusional, but I know I don't want to keep seeing him.'

'I take it when you say "him", you're referring to your husband?'

I sucked in a breath and looked at my finger that once held a wedding ring.

Joe looked at me and waited.

I swallowed and blew out the breath.

Joe gently stroked his chin with his thumb and forefinger. 'Let's just focus on the child next door for a moment. You said you were worried about him.'

I gave a firm nod and my stomach lurched as I waited for his next statement.

'We know from experience this isn't the first time this has happened.'

I looked down at my hands as the past sessions in this room came flooding back.

'You do know what I am talking about?'

I nodded again.

'You've allowed yourself to become emotionally involved with children who all bore some resemblance to—'

'Don't say it. Don't say his name.' My nose burned with the tears that I was holding back.

'I wouldn't say his name. Not until you say it first,' Joe said quickly.

We both stayed quiet for a few minutes as I let the reality of Joe's words sink in. I had done this before. Twice before. Once just three weeks after it happened, and the last time about a year later. They were both boys. Around four years old.

'Although there is the other thing to consider,' Joe said eventually.

'I know what you're going to say.' I looked away. I could feel the stinging sensation of tears now prickling behind my eyes. Joe was the only one who could extract this sort of emotion from me.

'I know you know what I'm going to say, and I think that's why you are here, why you have said that you have had all these feelings recently again. I think the real reason you came, the real reason you wanted to see me and assess your emotions, was because you needed someone else to say it. To verify it.

'I think you are ready to be a mother again. I think you want to see him again, your other son. And I think you know he is missing you. He's what? Fifteen now? I think it's time.'

Olga, it turned out, was a nice woman; a good egg. She was incredibly helpful and didn't ever overstep the mark. She was polite and always checked with me if something needed doing before she did it. When I finally got over the shock of her presence, I began to ask her some questions about herself.

She said she was twenty-five, yet she looked so much older, as though she had been through so much already. I tried to extract more information from her, such as where she came from and what work she had done before, but she was good at holding back information. I even had the courage to ask her how much D was paying her. Her face went pale and she said, 'He has been very generous.'

Her answer made my blood run cold. Was she offering him services separate to the housework, or was he taking advantage of her? Even though I hated him for every bruise he had given me, he was my first love. I still felt a spark of something for him, some kind of ownership. He may have been cruel and flawed in many ways, but he was all I had.

D was away more and more, and so we women fell into a

routine of waking early with the baby. I would chat away to Olga whilst she mopped and tidied. She even took over the cooking, which, in a way, was a relief, but it also meant that I never really learned how to cook; something that made me quite sad. I had wanted my husband and then my son to look at me with gratitude when I presented them with a hearty meal.

I suppose it was a blessing when Olga arrived. It would have been so lonely with just me and the baby otherwise. It was nice to have someone in the house with me, day and night; someone I could rely on to be consistent with their behaviour. When it was just us girls in the evening, we would pour ourselves a small glass of sweet wine, wrap ourselves in cardigans and blankets and sit out on the patio under the gas heater. We would giggle about stories we had seen in the news or TV programmes we had watched. I enjoyed having a girl around that I could relate to. I was so young, even though I did not feel it at the time. The saddest part was it made me realise I had never actually had a girlfriend before. I was so busy being there for Mum and then the first time I moved out, it was to be with D, so friends had always fallen by the wayside. There weren't any siblings or friends who were doing the domestic-bliss thing that I could relate to. It was just me. I knew deep down that there was something fundamentally wrong between me and D, that this wasn't the usual set-up; this was not how families worked. I even knew then I should have been fearing for the safety of my child more. I knew he wasn't safe, and yet I did nothing to protect him. I stayed. I don't know why. I suppose I had nowhere else to go? If I left and went to my mum's, he would only come for me and how would my mum – as frail as a ninety-year-old woman at just forty-five – protect herself and two others? I would not want to put that stress on her. She deserved a quiet life. She had suffered enough already.

* * *

One day, D came home and found Olga and I stood at the kitchen island laughing so hard over something that had begun with an unusually shaped vegetable and evolved as the wine took hold of us.

I froze when he walked into the room. His jaw was set hard, his eyes fixed on me; he was ready to pounce. I could feel my heart pounding hard in my throat. But Olga was up and round the other side of the island, talking quickly at him. First, a string of compliments about the house, how much she had settled, how grateful she was. Then she told him to get himself comfortable in the lounge. She told him how I had been assisting her with his dinner preparations and it was almost ready. I watched in wonder how the tension in his jaw slackened and his eyes were drawn away from me and towards the cold beer Olga was handing him. He shuffled out of the room, clutching his beer, to the sofa where he would probably drink himself unconscious later.

Olga returned to the island and busied herself finishing the meal. She must have felt the weight of my gaze as I stood looking on, not knowing how to discuss what had just happened and what hadn't; how she had potentially saved me from a beating, and, thinking back, I realised it wasn't the first time she had managed to deflect his behaviour. Eventually she turned to me with a sadness in her eyes. She understood the narrative of my life and she knew she couldn't save me. She could only occasionally distract him.

I had both hands laid out on the island, waiting to be of assistance. Olga reached across and pressed her hand into one of them. I felt a collision of shame and regret wash through me like a tsunami. I wished I could have been a stronger person and that we could have met in better circumstances. All of these unspoken words hovered between us, each of us understanding the other perfectly.

Olga let out a long breath and picked up a peeler and the knobbly carrot. We both laughed through our noses. We shot a precautionary look towards the kitchen door then back to the island, where we tittered away like schoolgirls, preparing a meal for the man in my life that I secretly hoped he would choke on.

30

NOW

I sat on the train and could think of nothing else except the session with Joe. It had been so long since I had talked about my big boy, my firstborn, and doing so had brought a tidal wave of sadness. I looked around the carriage of the train as I pressed my eyelids closed and pinched my thighs to stop the tears that were threatening to erupt and never stop. The guilt was crushing me. I had neglected him. What must he think of me? But he would remember what I had done, that I was certain of. How the beautiful sibling he once had was no longer with us, and it was all my fault. Of course, Joe was right. I had been living out some sort of fantasy, every time the feelings reared themselves and the pain became too much, I would look for him, and I usually found him in another child.

But I was still a mother. But did he need me? Would he want me? I couldn't face the rejection. I had been hiding from the truth for so long, I wasn't sure how I was supposed to feel any more. I glanced around on the train at the other afternoon commuters who were all going about their days, perhaps with issues of their own, but you would never know or be able to tell from looking at them. I held on to these feelings of regret and hopelessness all day every day. I wondered if anyone else felt the same. I felt as if I was riding this journey of grief all alone.

I had just about managed to suppress the tears, and as I continued looking around the carriage my eyes finally rested on a copy of the *Metro* on the table in front of me. I picked it up and began to flick through it. Nothing much kept my attention these days except for my textile work or Instagram, so I knew this magazine wasn't really going to hold my interest for long enough. I was considering throwing it back on the table when I saw a flash of something that looked familiar. I couldn't have been sure then what it was, as I began frantically turning the pages back, until I found what had caught my eye. It was an image of a rooftop cinema. The angle was slightly different and there were a few more people seated, but there was no doubt that it was the same rooftop cinema that lucybest65 had taken a photo of from her armchair at home, claiming she had the best seat in the house. I looked at the text under the image. It was a short advertisement piece – but the words that stood out were those that told me exactly where it was. I felt a rush of heat run up my neck as I looked around the train carriage, certain someone would jump out from behind a seat any moment and catch me out; tell me it was a joke, just a test, and snatch the magazine away. But they didn't. It felt too good to be true.

The conversation I'd had with Joe, about meeting with my elder son, had been playing on a loop in my mind. But for now I would shelve it away into the dusty corners of my mind, where I could forget about it again for a while. I had this image in front of me, showing me that the rooftop cinema was only a few streets from my college campus.

It occurred to me that perhaps lucybest65 was more obtainable than Mrs Clean with her million-plus followers, and I had always been interested to know why lucybest65 had such a vendetta against her. It would be a perfectly reasonable coincidence if I happened to be on the same street where lucybest65 lived, or even outside her house. Perhaps I would catch a glimpse of her coming out of her front door. Maybe I would engage in a conversation to find out if it was her, without her knowing that I followed her comments on Instagram. The idea that I had access to this kind of information about a complete stranger caused a rush of excitement to course through my body.

Instagram post: 21st May 2019

Hello, cleaners, how are you all getting on? Are you enjoying this lovely weather we've been having lately? You all know I have been spending a lot of time in the garden and also thinking about decorating my spare room in association with Oliver Bonas. So I have been sent images of these beautiful key pieces and I just wanted to share them with you. I'm really excited to get cracking.

Today I am going to start with the mirrors. Here are a selection of four mirrors. Quite honestly, I love them all, so now it's up to you guys to vote for which one you would prefer to see in the spare room.

At the end of this project, Oliver Bonas are offering you all a 10 per cent discount – I will post the code later, as well as offering one lucky person a chance to win a £250 voucher to spend online or in store. I know!? I'll reveal the winner later today. It's a quickie competition so get your skates on. It's a way for us both to say thank you for helping me decorate my room. It may look as though I know what I'm doing, but even I need a bit of help sometimes.

I'm really looking forward to hearing your thoughts!

Mrs C X
#win #freebie #competition #mrsclean
145,733 likes

LucyBest65 she gets a whole room decorated and we get 10 per cent discount. That sucks ass.

I arrived home from my appointment with Joe in the early afternoon with a restlessness within me that I couldn't suppress with
my usual behaviours. I lined up coins, opened and closed
windows and doors, even washed my hands for thirty seconds but
nothing would shift the maddening sensation growing within me.
As I packed a rucksack with an apple and a couple of satsumas,
water and a few other snacks, I began to think about the distance
between the college and where lucybest65 lived. I had already
looked on the map on my phone and I had seen the route. I tried
to push away the thoughts and instead focus on the exhibition. I
needed to finish my piece so I would be ready for the end of July.

I put a sweatshirt in my rucksack and then looked at my
phone. It could do with a charge, but I could do it once I got to
the art rooms. There was a train to the uni in a few minutes and if
I hurried, I could catch it.

I performed a few hurried locks on the front door as I left,
before stepping out into the street and straight into the path of
my neighbour.

'Ahh, it is you.' She looked me up and down. 'Are you going to

ring social services again, tell them what a wicked mother I am?'
Her lips were turned down in disgust.

'I... I—'

'No, I thought not. You think you can just go around saying
what you like about whoever you like? I am a good mother, I am a
good mother.' Her tone changed from antagonistic to desolate
and she seemed to almost go weak at the knees and her body
slouched to one side as she grabbed at the wall.

I instinctively reached out to catch her.

'Get off me.' She pushed me away. 'You have no idea, do you?
You think you can look over the wall or hear something and you
make your mind up? Nothing is as it seems from a distance. You
see a snippet of my life and you make your mind up. Always,
people make up their mind without knowing.'

'I'm sorry, I really am. I thought I was doing the right thing.' I
felt the panic surge through me. What had I done to this woman?

'He is ill,' she said eventually, leaning all her weight against
the wall. She was wearing the long thick black jacket she had
worn when I saw her at the shops, even though it was warm
enough to go without. I could see her skin looked pale, she had
make-up caked into the wrinkles around her eyes. She had on red
lipstick, perhaps to compensate for her tired face, but it only
accentuated her paleness.

'I'm sorry.' I reached out my hand to touch her, but she waved
it away.

'He cannot go outside, if he does, he could risk picking up
germs, and I hate it, I hate that he cries, that he doesn't understand, that he is curious, that I have to tell him no, no, no.' She
used her finger as though she were scolding a child.

She stood up straight, looked me in the eye once more before
walking away in the opposite direction. I wondered if I should go
after her, to try to explain to her my reasons for presuming her

son was in danger. But I just watched her reach the end of the road and turn the corner.

Realising I would almost certainly be late, I began running towards the train station in the opposite direction.

I just caught the train as its doors were closing and as I took a seat, I couldn't stop thinking about what my neighbour had said to me. I had been given an opportunity to be a good person. I could have rung on her doorbell, checked in on them, offered to make them a meal. Instead, I construed her child's frustrated tears for abuse. I was overcome with regret for what I had done. And the familiar compulsion began growing within me. I needed to do something to rectify what I had done. If I didn't, something terrible was sure to happen.

I thought about lucybest65. Perhaps she was confused, frustrated, lonely. Perhaps all the comments she put out about Mrs Clean were, in fact, mirroring her own thoughts and behaviours about herself. We live on a small overpopulated planet where we are more connected than ever before, yet we feel lonelier than ever. I had found great comfort from Instagram, and finding my way into Mrs Clean's world.

Suddenly, it occurred to me that perhaps Lucy had given that information away about where she lived on purpose. And perhaps there was a reason. I had to find out and my mind would not let me rest until I had seen it through.

* * *

By the time I had arrived at my stop, I had already made up my mind. Although I had been looking forward to spending some more time preparing my exhibition piece, an urgency was building inside of me. All I had to do was go there, see where lucybest65 lived and the monster would be satisfied.

But that didn't stop me from checking in with myself. I had made the wrong choice with my neighbour – it was human contact that was the most natural thing in the world. Instagram had become my new compulsion and with it I had discovered a world where the connections weren't wholly organic, and forgotten about connecting to reality.

I needed to do what I hadn't done with my neighbour and check-in with lucybest65. She was, I supposed, a virtual neighbour of sorts. I had been observing her and what she projected out through Instagram for many weeks, and her negative comments hadn't sat right with me. I wasn't sure what I would do when I found her house, but I knew more or less where she lived. I couldn't just ignore it; I had to do something with that information.

I stepped off the train and for a few uncertain seconds, I stood absently in the middle of the platform as people hurried around me. I looked for the signs that would lead me out onto the street, suddenly unfamiliar with a place I had been coming to almost every day for weeks now, and slowly started to follow them.

I had taken a photo of the rooftop cinema advert on my phone and I looked at it now, where the address was underneath the picture. I put it into the maps app on my phone and began to follow the route, which said it was a ten-minute walk away. I couldn't take in my surroundings as I was glued to the map, not wanting to a miss a turning that would take me to where I needed to be. Once I was there, I would need to suss out which building would have the full-on perfect view of the rooftop cinema screen. This would be where lucybest65 lived. I would worry about that when I got there. For now, I just needed to concentrate on walking straight without bumping into people; already I could hear the tuts and sense the frustration from my fellow pedestrians. The words of my neighbour rang in my ear and urged me on.

She was right, I knew nothing about her life and why would I presume to? I knew nothing about lucybest65's life either, but maybe she was reaching out, conveying her loneliness through her posts. Would it be so impertinent to simply knock on her door and ask if she was okay?

I pushed my way past people in the street until finally the maps app told me what I needed to hear. I had reached my destination. I put my phone into my rucksack and looked around me. There were tall buildings all around us in different styles, and I couldn't work out which one held the rooftop cinema from this level. I began to turn in circles, trying to get some sort of bearing. I pulled out my phone again and looked at the photo of the rooftop from the picture I had taken of the newspaper. It did not offer any more clues.

'Excuse me.' I turned to a man in a suit who was making his way past me. 'Do you know where the rooftop cinema is?'

He shook his head. 'Sorry, love, no.' He carried on walking.

'Excuse me,' I said to a young guy with huge headphones. He pulled the cans down as he saw my lips moving. 'Do you know where the rooftop cinemas is, please?'

He shook his head and pulled the cans back on and carried on walking.

I asked another five or six people and no one knew. It really was an elite little enterprise. I was beginning to think I was going to have to start walking into all the buildings one by one and asking, when I spotted a small sign across the road. I checked the traffic and walked over the road. I had obviously seen it somewhere else subliminally because I instantly recognised the words *Blue Moon* that were printed above the doorway. I looked at the photo on my phone. I couldn't see the logo there. I went into Instagram and looked for the image that lucybest65 had posted. Next to the large screen was a huge pull-up banner with the very same logo words printed on it. *Blue Moon*. This must be the company who hosted these rooftop events. I felt a tingle of anticipation as I realised that I was standing very close to where lucybest65 lived. Very soon I would be standing at her door. Somehow I imagined she would be in. From what I had gathered online, she seemed to be the kind of person who enjoyed staying in, looking at other people's lives.

I began to look around as I tried to work out where Lucy would have had the best view from, but it was no use. I didn't know which way the rooftop cinema was set up, so I couldn't possibly know which street to start to with.

I took a deep breath and rang the buzzer next to the Blue Moon sign. There was a crackle and then a woman's voice came through the speaker.

'Hi, can I help you?'

'Oh, yes, hi.' I quickly thought on my feet. 'I'm here about a potential group booking? I was told if I was in the area to just pop in?'

'Oh, right, sure. Come on up. We're on the second floor.'

The door buzzed. I pushed it open and took the stairs two at a time until I reached the second floor and saw the sign for Blue Moon.

I entered a small, beige room where a slight girl in a high red chair was applying a sticky-looking gloss to her lips. To her right was another desk, which was empty. These two desks appeared to be the sum of the entire business.

'Hiya,' I said breathlessly.

'Hi, did you say you had booked an event?' She smacked her lips together as she popped the lid back on the gloss.

'No, I wanted to book an event for a... birthday, sort of thing, like a birthday party. Is that the sort of thing you do?' I began looking around the room for another door that would lead to the roof.

'Yes, anything like that, work dos, hen nights, we've even done a few weddings. When were you thinking of booking for?'

'I was hoping to get a look at the rooftop, to see if it would be suitable for the—'

'Your party? Right, well, unfortunately I'm on my own today, and I'm not insured to be up there. My colleague is out assessing other potential sites and I can't let you up there alone – health and safety and all that – so did you want to make an appointment to come back and view it another day? Also, I can show you the floor plan here.' She pointed to an open pamphlet on the desk. 'Or you can view the website, which has many images of that particular rooftop—'

'That's great, but I really need to see the rooftop. Are you sure you can't escort me up there?' I pointed to the ceiling.

She shook her head. 'I can't, I'm afraid.' She pulled her mouth into a tight smile and I knew she wasn't going to budge.

'Right, okay then.' I looked down at the desk. 'Can I grab a couple of these then?' I pointed to the pamphlets.

'Of course, take a handful, spread the word.' She handed over a pile with an inordinate amount of keenness.

'Great.' I stuffed them into the outside pocket of my rucksack.

'Just give us a call and I can get you booked in for a viewing.'

'Okay, will do, thanks.' I turned and walked out of the small office and headed through the door to the stairway, I placed my hand on the bannister and looked upwards. This building was about another two storeys high. There could possibly be a door to the roof if I carried on up. The receptionist was unable to take me, but although I wasn't supposed to, there was no one stopping me from heading up there by myself.

I looked behind me to check that I was I alone and that I

could make the move and leg it up the stairs, before anyone caught me. I decided this was one of those moments when you just had to take the opportunity that was being presented. I needed to feel the fear and do it anyway.

I took a deep breath, swung one last look behind me at the closed door, then headed up the stairs. I walked up two more floors until I reached the top where there was one final door. I stood and caught my breath as I read a sign that said: *This way for the rooftop screening.*

I crossed my fingers, pushed the door and to my relief it opened.

I stepped out into a glorious otherworld. I looked down to my left and dragged a large pot plant to the door to wedge it open; I didn't need to be stuck out on a roof top with only one route out. I took a moment to take it all in. It was as though I had stepped into a fairy tale; there were huge potted trees all around the perimeter, white seats were in the middle, each row raised slightly more than the next. There was a bar with a Caribbean-style thatched roof, and outdoor heaters were placed in the corner of the seating and also in the centre.

I took a quick glance behind me, sure that someone must have followed me, that I couldn't have this magnificent haven all to myself. Then I reminded myself why I was there. I needed to find the opposite end of the rooftop to where the screen was facing to see the view that Lucy would have and to try to work out where she was living and posting her comments from every day.

I walked to the back of the rooftop, which was heavily secured around the sides, and even then, when I looked over the side, the drop was only a few feet to a fire stairway. But still, I felt a surge of uneasiness. Something terrible would happen. With nothing to hand to take away the stress, I closed my eyes and imagined I was at home brushing my teeth; I counted out loud to thirty-four. I opened my eyes and blew out a long breath. I looked out over at the row of buildings directly opposite. I took out my phone and looked at the photo again, as if it might give me more of a clue, but, of course, it wouldn't, she had taken it from the inside, and I was standing on the outside looking at three or four buildings that could all have an equally central view of the rooftop. I did, however, know that it would have to have been taken from a higher part of the building, meaning that she either lived in an apartment or she was extremely affluent and owned an entire four-storey house.

Assessing the possibilities, I knew I would have to go and ring every house and apartment until I found her. I took out my phone, went into Instagram and found the image of lucybest65 looking out of her window. I looked longingly at the photo once more, willing it to show me something more. Then I double-blinked as I spotted something. It was a purple flower, just peeking up from outside the window, and there were two silver brackets attached to the inside of ledge. Of course, it was a window box. She has a window box! I looked up from my phone and across at the houses, scanning back and forth. I spotted two, the first one was a silver box with a flurry of yellow and orange flowers, not a speck of purple in sight. No, that couldn't be it. My eyes reached another house, and on the top floor was a window and outside, clutching the bottom of the white frame, was a window box bursting with purple flowers.

'Hello, lucybest65,' I said as I put my phone into my back pocket.

32

THEN

I woke up one Saturday morning and sensed something was different. D was home, so that was one reason, but even with the heaviness that he brought to the air, it was what was missing that alarmed me.

I couldn't hear any of the usual goings-on in the house. Olga would usually be up by now, emptying bins, moving furniture around to sweep. Even though she performed these tasks with a gentle easiness, I would always wake to hear her making her way from room to room. But this morning there was total silence.

I knew Olga was gone. Even though I knew it to be true in my heart, I still had to check. Whilst D snoozed in the bed next to me, I lifted Baby Boy, who had been stirring in his cot, and went off to search the house for her. Her small collection of belongings in the spare room were gone. The house was eerily silent.

I found that I could not control the anger that raged up inside me. I put the baby safely in his playpen in the lounge and ran into the bedroom, the fury burning in my chest, with no regard for the consequences. He could kill me for all I cared; he had taken away the one bit of joy and variety to my life except for Baby Boy. He brought her into my life just to take her away again because he thought he could. I had been plagued by his cruelty for too long. I wished he were dead.

I ran at him on the bed as animalistic growls came from my throat. He shot up, ready to defend himself. I was shouting at him. He grabbed my wrists and restrained me; his strength always surprised me. He flipped me so he was on top, and he was looking down on me. I began to kick out, pushing my arms with all my strength.

'What. Are. You. Doing?' D shouted in my face.

I was out of breath from running and now the anticipation of what was to come was stirring up a familiar fear within me.

'You knew how much her company meant to me,' I said as calmly as I could manage.

He let out a loud snort and to my surprise, he rolled off me and over onto his back. I lay very still, waiting for what would come next.

'I thought something bad had happened.' He turned onto his side, facing away from me.

'This is bad? Olga, she was... my friend.'

Then he laughed, a malicious demonic laugh that penetrated right through me. I had prepared myself for a beating. I had anticipated it so much that to be lying there listening to his laugh was worse than having him physically assault me. I almost wished for the latter to take away the feeling of nothingness that he had left me with.

'Why? Why did you do it?'

He let out a blast of air from his lips, disposing of air the way he had disposed of my friend.

'Haven't you got something better to be doing?' he murmured. I lay there, feeling my heart rate return to normal.

'Why?' I said, but it was barely a whisper.

Now I knew he no longer even cared enough to punch me in my arm, throat, gut or anywhere else I had received his fists. But, of course, I knew he had, in fact, never cared.

I took myself out of the bed and went back to Olga's room, where the scent of her perfume still lingered in the air. I lay down on the bedsheets and inhaled the sweetness of the pillowcase, putting my hands under the pillow. As I did my fingers found a piece of card. I pulled it out; it was a photo. In the picture were three children, all very young, no older than five. The one girl was the spit of Olga, and I knew these were her children she had never spoken of. I could forgive her for leaving. But where was she now? I prayed she was safe and with her family, but I had no way of ever knowing. I couldn't forgive D for bringing her into my life, knowing she would never be able to stay. But mostly I couldn't forgive him for all the things he had done to me, to make me this weak, needy and vulnerable person who's only friend in the world was a woman that I would never see again.

Instagram post: 21st May 2019

Hi guys, thanks for all your selections on the Oliver Bonas post. I can confirm I have a winner! @wendyseaman_34, the voucher will be winging its way over to you soon.

I will post an image of all the pieces that you have chosen for my room once they arrive! Nothing beats the arrival of new goods. I love the feeling of when I've ordered something and then it finally arrives. There's nothing like it!

But, to be honest, guys, it's not all it's cracked up to be. This job that I do, it can sometimes feel lonely. I mean, I'm grateful to you all for being there for me, all one million and something of you. But I do wonder when the day will come when I will hang up my Marigolds for good, because this won't last for forever. That's one thing that life has

taught me. So enjoy every day that you can, be kind to one another
and remember, keep cleaning!
Mrs C x

hairymother Is she okay? She sounds as though she's flinging in
the towel.😂
wendyseaman_34 As long as I get my prize before she does lol!
Thank you. Mrs C! I'm very excited.
seventhheaven I imagine being an influencer can be taxing and lonely
at times. That's a lot of expectation on one person. Hope you're okay,
Mrs Clean. We love you.
lucybest65 The end is nigh.

I careered down the stairway of Blue Moon's office building as fast as I could and burst out onto the street below. I blew out a breath as I leaned against the wall and absorbed what was about to happen. I knew which building it was. Now I needed to find it and work out if it was the whole house or just a flat that Lucy had. I was just about to start walking when my phone began to ring. I pulled it from my back pocket; it was *the* number. I felt the familiar sensation of panic rise through me as I let it ring out. I didn't need to answer it.

I carried on veering around the corner and then back on myself until I reached the back of Blue Moon and immediately looked up for the window of purple flowers. There was a row of five four-storey townhouses. Most of them I could see from where I was standing had intercoms next to the door, but the one house with purple flowers in the window box, the one in the middle, the one I believed Lucy Best was residing in, had no intercom, meaning it was a house and not a flat. I walked across the road and stood at the bottom of the steps that led up to the main door. I paused outside, looking up at the grandness, wondering if being here was indeed the right thing. To my right were steps that led down to a white basement door, framed either side by black iron railings. I stood and thought for a moment, assessing the situation. I eyed the steps down to the basement. I thought back to what I had already achieved in the last hour, what I had managed to do; a daring task I would never have envisioned myself doing a few weeks, or even a few days ago. But things were rapidly changing in my mind. Maybe it was because I knew I was running out of time. As if my phone was wired to my thoughts, it began ringing. I yanked it out and cursed at it as I saw the same number ringing. I made an instinctual decision and turned it off.

I walked up the steps and approached the large, black door. I rang the doorbell and heard it trill through what I imagined to be a huge, sparse hallway. I stood on the doorstep. I felt a chill in the air as the afternoon cooled. All the walking I had done had made me hot, and now I was starting to cool down. I pulled my sweatshirt out of my rucksack and put it on.

A minute or so had passed and no one answered. I considered ringing again. Either I was being ignored or no one was in.

I looked around, beginning to feel paranoia seep in as people passed by. I wondered who was looking, who was making a note of my hair colour, height and what I was wearing so they could accurately relay it to the Crimestoppers' line later.

I shifted uncomfortably from foot to foot and shivered at the chill that was absorbing into my bones. I suddenly realised I was a long way from home. I thought about my phone, which was switched off. Maybe I should turn it back on? But the consequence of that would be more detrimental than the feeling of aloneness.

I had now been standing on the doorstep for a good few minutes and so I began to edge back down the steps. I took a quick look down the stairs at the basement door, and as I did, I thought back to the stroke of luck that allowed me to take my chance getting to the rooftop of Blue Moon. I thought back further about how I had found the advert for the rooftop cinema in the magazine. So far it felt as though I had not arrived here by chance but by a series of events that had all been carefully aligned. I felt as though I had a purpose; standing here on the doorstep of a total stranger actually seemed to me to be the first thing to have made sense in a long time.

As I arrived at the bottom of the steps, I automatically began the descent to the basement. Walls surrounded me on either side as though I had just stepped into an empty swimming pool. I peered through a small window to the left of the door and saw nothing but darkness. I knocked hard. I stood, shifting my feet from side to side. A minute or so passed. I glanced up at the road, then placed my hand on the doorknob, turned it and to my amazement, it opened.

34

The door let out a gentle squeak and I cast a tentative glance behind me before I stepped over the threshold and closed the door. With no one else around and a dread burning up my chest and into my throat, I took a moment to rapidly open and close the door another six times.

There was a musty smell in the room I found myself in that suggested it wasn't used for much other than storage. There was a shard of light coming through the small window, and I could see a closed door at the top of a flight of steps. I stopped and looked at the stairs. All my doubts and fears came thundering down on me at once, and I almost turned and ran back out of the door. But I thought about how I had been driven here by social instinct. About how far I had come. About my neighbour. About lucybest65 and how I needed to check she was okay.

There were about twenty or so different-sized boxes piled up on one side of the room; they were fresh and clean and didn't look as if they had been opened. I was intrigued as I walked past them and I brushed the top box with my hands, as though just a slight touch might tell me what was stored in them. The rest of the basement held a lot of old furniture: a couple of old sofas, dining chairs stacked against the wall, a round dining table half-covered with a sheet, a couple of mirrors and an open box filled with empty photo frames.

I suddenly became very conscious that I was in the basement of a stranger's house and I had just walked in uninvited. My palms began to sweat and my mouth became dry. The wise decision would be to leave. But the monster wasn't satisfied. Before I could leave, I had to make it to the top of the basement stairs and open the door. Nothing was going to let me get away with not doing it. I could just turn around and go home; come back and try to knock on the front door another day. But as usual, the fear was building into something impenetrable and unfathomable. Opening the door at the top of the basement stairs was the only way everything was going to be okay.

I took a deep breath and made my way to the bottom step. I looked upwards. Just ten or so steps. I could do this. I would be up and at the door in a matter of seconds.

Despite my thundering heart and legs that shook uncontrollably with adrenaline, I placed my foot on the first step and walked to the top.

I felt the sweat on my palms hit the cold metal of the brass knob. I wiped my hand on my jeans and this time I turned the handle. To my surprise, yet again, this door was unlocked. I pushed it all the way, all the while expecting someone to jump out, to tell me I was trespassing and to call the police. I had done it. I could close the door and leave now. But I had already seen a flash of hallway, and I stood for a second as my brain made the relevant connections and translated what it was I was actually seeing. And once it did, a thousand thoughts and images came racing towards me and my head began to spin so much I stepped backwards. I misjudged where the step was and then I was falling.

35

Ever since Olga had arrived in my life and then left so suddenly, things felt like they were spiralling out of control. I knew most of my life was in D's hands: finances, where we lived, what we ate, where I shopped. I didn't like it. D could sense I didn't like it, but it was never really in my hands. I had begun a life with a man who I thought would change my life for the better, only he was very much going to change it for the worse.

As I lay in bed, I instinctively listened out for Baby Boy. But I couldn't hear him fussing for me. He was almost a year old now, and in the mornings he was usually chattering away contentedly in his cot. He had never been a whining baby – we had remained too close for that. He received all the nurture when he needed it. He didn't have to ask for a thing.

I got up and pulled a long sweater over the T-shirt I had worn to bed and padded out into the hallway; from there I began to hear the small sounds of my darling baby. He sounded happy and for a few precious minutes I thought to myself how nice it was that D had got him up before me. It occurred to me that now he was almost one, perhaps D didn't feel as though his son posed so much of a threat to him; soon Baby Boy would be weaned and wouldn't rely on me so much. He was also becoming so much more sociable; perhaps now D could relate to him better. Perhaps this was the start of their relationship forming.

D had been hurting me less and less. The beatings had ended; he was still rough and pushy, but nothing near how he used to be with me. Perhaps this was a new start for all of us.

I was sat on the toilet when it hit me, what I had seen in my hazy, just-woken state. It hadn't really occurred to me that it meant anything. But of course it did, it meant everything.

I hurriedly finished in the bathroom and raced back into the bedroom and saw that the cot had been stripped of the blankets and toys. Perhaps Baby Boy had an accident and D was washing the sheets. Highly implausible. My heart skipped fiercely and I clenched my fists as I looked around for other evidence. I was stalling for what I knew was coming, what I knew deep down had been coming for a long time.

I walked slowly down the stairs, feeling my heart thudding so hard I was sure it could be heard in the lounge. My palms were sweaty on the bannister and my mouth was now so dry I wasn't sure I could speak if I needed to. I rounded the corner in the hallway and began making my way to the lounge. Nothing was going to prepare me for what was coming. As I entered the room, both Fabrice and D looked up at me at the same time as Baby Boy did. He was chewing a rusk; it was spilling all down his Babygro. Neither man had thought to put a bib on him.

'Ahh, here she is,' D said, and I felt a flicker of relief as I strode towards my son.

'He's going to ruin his Babygro with all that muck,' I said with a wobble to my voice that I couldn't disguise as I bent to pick him up; his sticky hands were outstretched ready to greet me. But D was on his feet and there before me, picking him up. Baby Boy squirmed a little and reached out towards me, his chunky little hands covered in rusk residue. Then Fabrice was on his feet and I watched as D handed the baby to him. Fabrice took out his car keys and handed them to Baby Boy, who could never refuse a jangly non-toy. D explained what was happening. But everything began to slow down and I could barely hear what he was saying to me. The animalistic screams that came from my mouth that I had tried to suppress for so long to protect my baby were now coming out in one long primal sequence. Fabrice moved towards the door, carrying a small holdall, and I lunged forwards to grab at whatever I could. I ended up scratching Fabrice's face. Then I felt the familiar feel of hands restraining me by my wrists as D pulled me backwards and Fabrice left the room with my darling baby boy propped on his hip. I managed to pull myself forwards with D still clinging to me, and I made it to the window just in time to witness my baby being put in a car seat by a woman I had never seen before. Was she someone official? Was my baby being taken away because I was a bad mother? Then both she and Fabrice got into the car and drove away.

I collapsed onto the sofa, shaking uncontrollably, too shocked to cry real tears.

I sensed D hovering in the room and without saying a word to me, I felt him leave.

* * *

By lunchtime, my breasts had begun to harden with the milk that was now redundant. By dinnertime, they were beginning to feel engorged. D had tried to speak to me a few times, but I couldn't hear him; his mouth was moving, but I could hear nothing.

At bedtime, as I finally let my weary body rest, I heard D's words come to me through my half-slumber.

'This is for the best. It won't be forever – you can still see him. I will bring him to visit you. If you love our son like you say you do, you will do this little job for me. And all will be well.'

Then he touched me, ever so lightly, on the arm before he left the room. It was the first time in a long time I could remember him doing anything so gentle, and I wondered for a split second if this had affected him too, if he felt pain at our child, who wasn't even a year old, leaving us both today.

I touched my stomach where my baby had grown as I clung on to the one blanket I had left of his. I thought of the first baby, the one who had only been able to cling on for a few months, and how D hadn't shown any remorse when I lost it. Now my second child was gone as well, and D was responsible. Where he had rested his arm for a second, I felt my skin burning because I knew now that the man was poison. And so my body began to fill up with feelings of regret, rage and devastation. They all became muddled into one hardened mass of contempt.

I had failed my son and I had lost him.

36

NOW

I woke at the bottom of the stairs. The light from the hallway was cascading down the steps, illuminating my crumpled body like a spotlight in a theatre. My whole body ached. There was a searing pain through my arm and my ribs. I heaved myself to standing and found that I could just about manage it; my backpack had cushioned some of the fall. I wondered if my phone had been damaged. I needed to speak with someone immediately and explain to them what I had discovered up there in the hallway and how none of it made any sense. I also needed to confirm it for myself. I must have been mistaken. I must have imagined it. Perhaps it was pure coincidence. I pulled out my phone and turned it back on. After a few seconds the apps came to life, ignoring all missed calls and text messages I headed straight into Instagram because that was where I needed to check first. Amazingly, I had missed a couple of posts from Mrs Clean, even though it had only been a few hours since I last checked. My eyes scanned the penultimate post; she was writing with a heavy heart and people were commenting, checking if she was okay. But wait, what was this comment from lucybest65?

The end is nigh.

It was a lot of information for me to take in, and none of it really made any sense yet, but the one thing I did know was that I had been duped. Everything that I thought I knew wasn't true. And the only way I could fit all the jigsaw pieces together was if I went back up the stairs and confronted it head on.

I noted there were three more missed calls from the same number I had been avoiding. I also acknowledged there were voicemails. This was new. He had never left a voicemail before. I knew I had been running away for too long now, and so maybe now it was time I stopped.

* * *

Instagram post: 21st May 2019

Hi, guys, sorry about my last post. I was having a contemplative moment. We all have them, don't we? I'm only human like you, after all. I wanted to thank you all for your lovely, kind messages. They mean the world. It's just so nice to know that you all have my back no matter what. I feel a hundred times better after reading your kind words. I read every single one of them as well. Phew, I'm exhausted now.

Thanks for checking in on me again. You really are all fabulous.

I say it all the time, I know, but I want you to understand how much I appreciate every single one of you and even though I cannot see you, I have felt your presence and you have all been a huge part of this journey with me. I will never, ever forget you.

Keep on cleaning.

Mrs C x

99,656 likes

hopeliveson Oh no, it sounds like she is having another episode.

rowandameansbiz Hope you're okay, Mrs C. Keep on cleaning.

dennis89 Should we check on her?

pennyslife No one knows anything about her. She's kept her identity a secret.

mechanicmaniac It sounds like a cry for help to me. Someone I know once wrote something similar right before she topped herself.

dennis89 I definitely think someone should call the police then. Anyone?

pennyslife You do it if you're so terrified!

dennis89 I don't want to cause a fuss? Or waste police time. I don't even know the woman.

workwally But you follow her life on here? What's the difference between seeing her in real life or through a box on a smartphone app?

dennis89 Is anyone else worried? Maybe we should wait to see if she replies to any of these messages first?

lucybest65 Or maybe she'll be dead by then.

37

I played the answerphone message over and over. But the only words that I could hear were his final words.

'*I know where you are. I'm coming to get you.*'

I shuddered at the sound of his voice. It had been years since I had heard him speak to me directly. It still surprised me exactly how it all worked, but he had always been a clever man, my husband. Even though I could not love him in the end. Even when the very thought of him laying a finger on me made my whole body shudder. I went to turn my phone off, but it was no use; he had managed to track me on it. I thought I had been so careful. I thought I would have been able to hide myself away for longer than just a few months. I knew my time was up. It was time to face him.

But first I needed to get myself back up the stairs and into the main part of the house. At least I would have time to do that before he made his move.

I put my phone in my rucksack and put it on my back, then I took slow, painful steps until I reached the top of the stairs. I took a deep breath and stepped over the threshold and into the hallway.

There I found myself standing in front of what I had seen the first time I arrived up the stairs.

Three large monochrome prints: one volcano, one beach and one waterfall scene.

I pulled out my phone again. I went to Instagram and found my way to the account I was looking for. The account I had been following for so long. I navigated my way into a room that was just off the main hallway. I stood in the centre of it and then flicked to another image on the Instagram feed.

There was no doubt about it. I was standing inside the house I had been looking at online for weeks. I had followed a trail from lucybest65's account. I had seen a photo of her in a room looking out over the rooftops at the very building I had just come from. I saw the purple flowers in the window box from there and that tallied up with the flowers on this window. On this building. I couldn't possibly have gotten any of this wrong.

This wasn't lucybest65's house. This was Mrs Clean's house.

I edged my way further into the hallway, all the while my mind was awash with disbelief. I half expected someone to jump out and tell me I had been part of some kind of social experiment. I felt as though I had just walked onto the set of a TV show. The hallway remained disconcertingly quiet. A house this size should have been filled with people coming and going, a loud raucous family like the one I had imagined having myself.

Before I knew I had done it, I had managed to walk to the room directly opposite and realised I was in standing in Mrs Clean's lounge. There was the grey sofa in all its glory with the bright geometrical-abstract-printed cushions. I had looked at this sofa so many times on Instagram it felt incredibly surreal to be standing right in front of it. A bit like meeting a celebrity for the

first time, having watched them in your favourite movies all your
life.

I looked around the room and felt a shiver across my neck.
The difference between seeing a celebrity on television and
seeing them in real life was usually the immense sense of disappointment when you realised that they looked nothing like they
did on the screens. In real life, you could see the cracks and the
lines and the imperfections. I looked around the lounge, the
lounge I had seen so many times before on Instagram. And it was
as though I were looking at the same picture-perfect image.
There wasn't a sign of life. The living room was totally unlived in.
I backed out of the room and headed past the stairway to what I
could see was the kitchen at the end of the hallway. On my way
there, I passed an open door. I pushed it so I could step inside
and realised it was the downstairs bathroom I had seen on Mrs
Clean's feed. I had purchased the very same candle that was
perched on the windowsill, which still hadn't moved or been lit.
Again, the room was spotless, like a hotel bathroom when you
first arrive. I couldn't believe anyone could live this tidily, exactly
the way she played it out on screen. Absolute perfection.

But why had lucybest65's photo brought me here? I needed to
know for certain whose house was I in.

I moved from the washroom to the kitchen, which was the
next room on my left. I entered, and immediately I was transported back to the endless days of gazing at the images of this
room. It was exactly how it was in the photo, only so much bigger
as well. I felt as though I had walked into a well-loved children's
picture book.

I looked around at the surfaces, which sparkled to perfection.
I couldn't see a speck of dust nor a tea stain; there wasn't even a
droplet of water in the sink. It was wiped completely dry.

I edged around the perimeter of the kitchen, feeling the

smoothness of the surfaces with my fingertips. I stopped suddenly next to a large white fridge. My fingers itched to open it, but even before I did I felt a surge of doubt that suddenly the image I had built up in my head of the perfect Mrs Clean was about to come crashing down on me.

I put my fingers on the fridge door. Already I knew that my fingerprints would be over everything I had touched. It was no good trying to go back and cover them up. He was on his way soon anyway.

I pulled at the door and looked inside, expecting to see an empty fridge, to match the empty rooms, but instead I was as greeted with four shelves packed with clear bags, each filled with white powder.

I blew out a long breath. Either Mrs Clean was developing her own brand of talc, or this house was a drug den.

My senses were suddenly heightened and on full alert. I slowly closed the fridge door and stood statue still. I could sense it; a spectre of a human presence. There was someone else in the house. I was not alone.

38

I crept out into the hallway, wondering what it was that my senses had picked up on. A smell or a noise? I could not put my finger on it.

I realised I could no longer feel any pain in my body from the fall; adrenaline had numbed me.

Every fibre of my being told me to stop, turn around and walk back out of the door. I had done what I came to do. I had suppressed the beast. But my feet overtook my mind and walked from the kitchen back along the hallway, past the basement door where I should have turned right, gone back down the stairs and left the way I had come in. Instead, I found myself at the foot of the stairs to the next floor of the house. There I stood, holding my breath and looking up. Along the walls leading up the stairs were more tiny abstract prints I recognised from other Instagram posts. I let out a breath and put a foot on the first step. I listened again to see if I could hear anything that would give me a clue whether there was anyone in the house. But there was just silence. Silence and extreme tidiness like I had never witnessed before. By the time I reached the velvet-like carpet on the landing at the top of the stairs, my heart was about ready to pound right out of my chest. There were three doors to my left, which were probably the bedrooms and a large bathroom ahead of me. Then the stairs continued to the right to a final top floor, and if I was right, this would be where lucybest65's photograph would have been taken, from one of the highest rooms in the house. I contemplated the idea that lucybest65 was a lodger here. But why would she write such awful comments on Mrs Clean's posts? It made no sense, and I was yearning to know the answers to it all. I ignored the urge to peep my head into any bedrooms on this floor, and instead I took myself to the foot of the next set of stairs, where I was certain I was about to find out who was living here.

39

We drove in total silence. I stared out of the window for the entire journey, which took just over three hours. Just before we arrived at the new house, D said everything was going to be okay. All I needed to do was trust him and do what he asked of me. This was the best way, this was the ideal situation. Everyone would be happy. What he meant was that he would be happy. How could I ever be happy again?

There was a moment when he was in the shower the day after Baby Boy was taken that I heard him whistling. I felt a rage build inside me, I almost burst into the bathroom and pummelled his head into the glass door. In the three days since Fabrice and that woman had taken my baby, I had considered going to the police every second. But every time I went to leave the house, I would hear D's words ringing in my ears. 'If you try anything, I can't control what will happen to Baby Boy.' I knew I had no choice. If I was out of his sight for a second, he began to get very tetchy. I would hear him calling for me around the house, the tension growing thick in his tone. I would always appear at the top of the stairs or the doorway to the garden, just to reassure him that I hadn't tried to disappear and that he didn't have to give the signal to whoever to make sure I never saw my baby boy again.

We pulled up outside the house I would be spending my time in for the foreseeable. It was bigger than any house I had ever seen up close. D took us inside and I looked around at the space and the many rooms. He had placed my case down on the floor next to the stairs. I looked at it, sitting there by itself.

'Where's yours?'

'In the car.' He looked at me deadpan. 'I won't be staying here.'

I scrunched my mouth up and looked around at the vastness to the house again. 'Right.' I had been used to being on my own at the other house. This wouldn't be much different, except you could fit three of our old houses into this one.

'Where will you be then?' I asked, but not really caring.

'I can't say. Not far.' I thought for the first time he looked mildly sheepish, like even he knew that whatever crooked business he had managed to involve me and my baby in was possibly a step too far and maybe he felt a little out of his depth. But he continued.

'You know what to do? You remember the plan?'

I nodded.

'You stick to it for one year. Then we can look at... adapting things.'

I narrowed my eyes at him. 'And Baby Boy?'

'He is safe.'

'When do I see him?'

'You'll see him.'

I wasn't sure I believed him, but I cast my mind back to all the films I had watched, the happy endings. It was all a fabrication. I had bought the dream and fallen for the wrong man.

40

NOW

As soon as I reached the top of the stairs, I was hit by a wall of heat and a musty stench that could have been a mix of body odour, urine and unwashed carpets. The hallway was cloaked in darkness. The one window to my right was draped with a dark piece of mock-up fabric that wasn't properly attached; the sort of thing students do when they have no sense of what went with what or that a curtain pole could be picked up for next to nothing. My body was tense, ready to turn and head back the way I came. But some unknown force still drove me on. I turned left at the top of the stairs, passed a closed door on the right and headed straight for the end of the hallway where I stood in front of a closed door directly in front of me. I was sure this room would have a window that from the outside would boast a wonderful array of purple blooms and also look out onto one of London's finest rooftop cinemas. I realised I was now more terrified than I had been in many years. I was no longer trying to suppress a compulsion with a behaviour; I wanted to know; I needed to know. But I hadn't felt real genuine fear like this since the day it happened. Since the day my world fell from beneath my feet.

It took me a moment to realise that my phone was ringing. I pulled it out of my pocket and saw the same number. I had nothing to lose any more. I had to face up to what I had been running from all this time.

I slid my finger along the screen and put the phone to my ear.

'It's me.' My husband's voice was urgent.

I blew out a long breath. 'I know.'

'I need you to listen to me.'

The urgency in his voice had just increased by another 100 per cent. It was a tone I had heard him use a thousand times.

'I know where you are and you need to get o—'

The line went silent.

41

I pulled my phone away from my ear and saw that it was completely dead. I had meant to charge it properly when I got to uni, but as I had taken an unexpected detour, I hadn't noticed the battery life wasting away with every unanswered call. Now I had finally answered it, I had heard that tone that my husband would only use when he wanted people to take him seriously. When he knew that lives were in danger.

I jumped as I heard the sound of the front door slamming. I froze to the spot, barely able to breathe as loud footsteps made their way along the hallway downstairs. The tone of the footsteps changed into a higher echoey frequency, the sort of sound that a smart flat shoe would make on a pristine marble kitchen floor. It was too late for me to get down the stairs and get out, besides I had come this far. If there was anything on the other side that looked like the photo lucybest65 had posted on Instagram, then surely there would be somewhere for me to hide, or someone who could offer me some sanctuary, perhaps call the police. I decided I would take my chance with the unknown on the other side of the door. Whether it be Mrs Clean or lucybest65, there was only one way to find out.

I put my hand on the door handle and pressed down. The door clicked and I began to push it open. I could see the beginnings of a dark room, the smell that had hit me at the top of the stairs was originating in here. I put my hand over my mouth and nose to try to stop some of it penetrating my nostrils. I couldn't hear anyone coming up the stairs behind me, so I edged into the room and closed the door behind me. My hands were itching to reopen and close the door several times, but the need to assess the room I found myself in was greater. Immediately in front of me, I could see there was a large window with heavy black curtains drawn. A small slither of light was casting itself across the room in a thin strip. I grabbed the heavy black pieces of material and began to pull them apart. The late-afternoon light began to stream through. Since I had been in the house, the clouds that had brought with them a chill to the air had now passed and the sun was creeping through and bringing with it a cascade of colours as a prelude to the evening sky. I watched this technicolour erupt across the skyline for a moment and then I allowed my gaze to fall on the thing I had been looking for, the sight I had been hoping to see. There was the rooftop cinema, an image of beauty, and looking exactly how it had looked in the photograph that was posted by lucybest65 in her Instagram feed. She had been sitting right here, right behind where I was standing.

'Urgh,' came a groan from behind me, and I swung around to see a figure beneath a pile of blankets on a sofa, beginning to stir.

I moved cautiously back towards the sofa, where a head was barely peeking above. I saw a flash of dirty blonde hair, and as I approached nearer I could see a pile of vomit next to the sofa and to my right I spotted a cat litter tray that looked as though it hadn't been emptied for some time; this was what I could smell when I was coming up the stairs.

I held one hand across my rib cage where the pain from the fall was snaking its way back in.

I tried to speak, but I couldn't think what I should say. The words wouldn't form properly in my mouth.

So instead, I reached out my hand. As my hand rested upon what I presumed was an arm. I was suddenly catapulted backwards as the sleeping figure launched off the sofa and came straight at me. I stumbled backwards and my head hit the leg of a chair.

A deep, male voice penetrated through the walls and ceiling, making the entire room shudder.

'What the hell is going on? Don't make me come up there.'

I looked up and saw it was a girl. She stood frozen to the spot, a look of pure horror on her face as she took me in and we both heard the voice from downstairs.

Her face was pale. She looked young, maybe late teens, early twenties. She was wearing a tatty grey woollen jumper and jeans that looked as though they would fit a small child. She looked severely malnourished. She turned towards the door as though she expected it to open any moment, and then she looked at me, her eyes wide with terror. She opened her mouth, took a deep breath and mouthed the word, 'Go.'

I tried to scramble to my feet but I could already hear the deep thud of footsteps coming up the first steps of the staircase. I looked around to my left where I had just been pushed backwards and saw a long burnt-orange-cloth covering a small square table that was stacked high with junk: paper and pamphlets, toilet rolls and empty cartons of food. The tablecloth came almost to the floor, so I leapt towards it and squeezed myself into a gap between two boxes that had been stored under there.

'No, no, no.' I could hear the girl muttering, and my stomach took a nosedive as panic mounted in her voice. Who was this waif-like woman-child? Why was she hiding in the attic? And who was she so terrified of, who was now making their way up the stairs?

42

THEN

Later, when I was alone in the vast empty house, my mind was awash with emotions. I walked around the stark rooms, thinking it was a shame no one would ever fill them, and that it would only be me here, day and night. I imagined how a house this size should be full to the rafters with kids, running down the stairs and into the kitchen, demanding snacks and drinks. I ran my hands along the pristine surfaces that hadn't ever had a crumb spilt on them. It was all such a waste.

I had to sit down several times a day when the pain at having lost Baby Boy got me in the stomach. It was as strong as a punch from D, only with this pain, I would sit and cradle my abdomen, trying to recall my son's face, his smile, the smell of his skin. I wanted to live in these moments for as long as possible, clinging to the memories. But as much as I tried to hold on to them, they faded more and more each time. I would fall into fitful sleeps, waking regularly through the night, unable to breathe, grasping for my baby who wasn't there and whose face I could no longer remember.

I had never felt so alone. Each night as I drifted off, I would wake abruptly to the sound of crying. Baby Boy needed me. I would sit up in bed, my hands would fly across the sheets, waiting to connect with a small limb or a head. But next to me, it was always empty.

The days turned into weeks. The pain in my gut subsided and I became numb, waking only to wash and eat a little. I just lay on the bed staring at the ceiling.

D popped by from time to time, always alone. He would stand at the end of the bed, shouting at me to get up and get on with it. I would turn my back on him.

Then one day I heard the front door open and initially I thought I was imagining the high-pitched wail that found its way through the walls and ceilings and straight into my chest. I gasped for breath as I sat up straight.

It was Baby Boy. He was here, D had finally brought him to me. Suddenly, there was a power within me as the energy resurfaced. I raced to the top of the stairs, my legs trembling with anticipation as I tried to slow my breathing to listen. I could hear D speaking to him in that tone adults only use with babies and toddlers. Then my ears pricked up at a second voice. Another male. My stomach lurched. Who had Baby Boy been with and who had D brought here? I descended the stairs two at a time until I reached the hallway where I could see Baby Boy pulling himself to standing using the brass umbrella holder next to the door and taking a few tentative steps.

I let out a gasp.

'He can walk!' I said as I hurried towards him and scooped him into my arms and covered his face with kisses. He responded with smiles and a podgy fist on my face. It had been only weeks, but it felt like years.

D glanced backwards. 'Oh yeah, he does that now.' I had barely glanced at the other figure in the hallway, but now D was ushering him into the kitchen, where they closed the door. It was just Baby Boy and I left in the hallway. I was so giddy with euphoria that I hadn't realised we had been sat, playing and cuddling for a good few minutes before D came storming out of the kitchen, locked the front door and put the key in his pocket. He glared at me as if I had already done something to deserve his fury.

He pointed his finger at me.

'One hour,' he said before he headed back into the kitchen and slammed the door. I felt the force of his silent threat and decided I would make the most of my time with my son. If I behaved now, then he would bring him more often. If I showed him I could comply, then I could prove to him that I was capable of fulfilling my role in this house and taking care of my baby. I was sure of it.

I immediately stood up with Baby Boy in my arms, took him to the next floor and slowly walked with him on my hip from bedroom to bedroom, talking to him the whole time. I wanted to fill his head with my voice and words so he would hear them in his dreams and echo through his head when he woke.

An hour came and went, and there was no sign of D or his accomplice. I longed for the dried milk to return to my breasts so I could nurse him once more, just the two of us in our own bubble. We had found our way to the top floor when I remembered seeing a simple tote bag at the door; it must have replaced the nappy bag I had bought when Baby Boy was born. I kept him on my hip and went back downstairs to the front door to retrieve the bag. I could hear the raucous laughter of D and his colleague coming from the kitchen. Baby Boy had grabbed my hair and was sucking it, so I knew he was hungry. I rooted in the bag for food or milk. I found a few cartons of formula and an empty bottle, which was a sad replacement for the breast milk that had enhanced our bond. How could I maintain any bond when I didn't know when I would see him again after today? My heart ached for him and the confusion this must be causing him.

I rummaged through the bag and didn't find any snacks. I knew by this point he should be experimenting with food and I thought about what I had to eat upstairs in my bedroom: packets of raisins and some crackers, finger food I was sure he would love.

Back upstairs on the top floor, we became so immersed in our own world of games, kisses and laughter, that I hadn't noticed D enter the room. He had crept in so quietly that I wondered if he had been observing our primate behaviour. Perhaps it evoked some emotion within him. But whatever he had been thinking, it made little difference as I heard the words.

'Time to go.'

I looked at the clock on the wall. Four hours had passed in a flash.

I felt my gut tighten. I began to speak but my words came out panicky and stuttered.

'Maybe he could stay here. I know I haven't been feeling myself recently, but I have a hold on things now. I wouldn't let him out of my sight... I could easily do my job, in fact... I think I'd do it better—'

'Pass the bag.' D didn't look at me as he held his hand out. I stood up from the floor where Baby Boy and I had been lounging together, oblivious to the time slipping away from us.

I stepped forward with my palms pressed together. I was going to beg.

'Please, D, I need my baby, I need—'

The last part of the sentence was lost as D's hand swiped my face with enough force to knock me backwards. My thigh hit the small table, which wasn't strong enough to take my weight, even though there was barely anything of me. As the table shifted backwards, so did I until I had hit the floor. From where I lay on my side, I could see Baby Boy was crawling towards me. I reached out for him at the same time D stepped over me and scooped him up. He walked towards the door, then turned around.

'You have a job to do. Get on with it.'

I looked at the empty doorway and listened to the squeals of my son getting quieter as they descended the stairs. I heard the front door slam. I lay my head onto the cold, hard floor and stared at the spot where Baby Boy had been moments ago. A flash of red caught my eye. Just under the sofa where I had been sat with my back against it, bouncing Baby Boy on my knee, was one of his red leather slip-on booties. I crawled over to the sofa, picked it up and held it against my cheek. I closed my eyes. An echo of his voice still lingered.

I wasn't sure how long I lay there, but eventually something cracked within me. I couldn't keep fighting any more. I was broken. I had only one choice, if I wanted to see my baby, for however long D would allow, then I had to comply.

I walked from my quarters on the third floor down to the kitchen.

There on the side in the kitchen was the smartphone I had been allocated. D was monitoring me from another phone, so I couldn't use it to text or message anyone, as he would be able to see. He had clearly demonstrated how this worked when we arrived.

I no longer felt sadness or anger, just numb from a fight I knew I had lost.

I no longer had any choice. So I set up the smartphone on its tripod, set the phone to timer, snapped on a pair of pink Marigolds, picked up a mop and bucket and started cleaning.

I tried to slow my breathing the way I was taught but my mind was awash with thoughts, questions I couldn't answer, pieces of a puzzle I was rapidly trying to slot into place. Was this Mrs Clean or was this lucybest65? Who was the crazed man downstairs scaring the life out of this girl and why did she look like she was about to keel over? Most importantly, I needed to make a plan. I was stuck under a table in a house where several hundred kilos of cocaine was sat in a pristine fridge in a gleaming clean kitchen.

He was coming up the stairs and I was hiding under a table with no way out.

I needed to control my breathing. I thought back to my cognitive-behavioural-therapy classes and began to think outside of myself to distract from the fear and panic. The '5-4-3-2-1' technique. Right, let's do this. Okay, five things I can see: A chair leg; a table leg; a length of brown-and-orange tablecloth, matted and greasy at the corner; a dent in the wooden floor, where something heavy had been dropped; a small handmade wooden bear the size of my hand, wearing a hessian jacket. I looked at this object the longest. Clearly a child's toy, but in a house with no children.

Four things I can touch. Stay calm, stay calm. The hard floor beneath my knees, sweat on my forehead, a sticky patch next to my knee where someone dropped some jam or something similar, a cut on my right leg that I must have got when I fell down the steps and ripped my jeans.

Three things I can hear: a clock ticking, a fan oven cooling... footsteps. I hear footsteps. He's coming closer. He will be here any moment.

Two things I smell: the putrid stench of vomit mixed with a cleaning product.

One thing I can taste: There is blood in my mouth. I can taste blood.

44

I heard the door crash open and a man's voice. The same man from downstairs?

'Oh my God, what the fuck? It's disgusting in here. What the hell are you doing?'

I heard the girl let out a small wail as though she had been grabbed. From beneath the tablecloth I could just about see a pair of black boots, and the bottom of a pair of blue jeans.

'Clean the fuck up. You're a disgrace.'

And he turned to walk away. Then he stopped and walked back over to the window.

'I thought I told you to keep these curtains closed at all times? Are you mad, woman? We had a deal. I don't think you are sticking to your side of the bargain, are you?'

'You haven't stuck to your side of the bargain for nearly six months,' came her voice, weak and hollow.

'Don't backchat me, woman.' His loud voice was accompanied by a sharp slap that reverberated around the room. The girl let out a wail and I heard the door slam.

I counted to ten and then slowly I began to shuffle my way out from between the boxes, and I pulled myself to standing. The girl was slouched on the sofa, her hand across her face. I knew I was on borrowed time now.

'What's going on?' I finally found the strength to speak, but I whispered the words. She shook her head.

'You need to go, I don't know who you are or why you're here, but it's not safe. Please go.'

'I can help you,' I said. 'I just need to charge my phone. Do you have somewhere I can charge my phone? Or if you give me your phone, I can call someone to help us.'

'You don't understand, do you?' She let out a pathetic laugh. 'If it was that easy, I would have done that a long time ago.' She sounded as though she was speaking with a lisp and when I looked a little closer, I could see she was missing a tooth.

'Is that?' I pointed to her face. 'Did he do that?'

She touched her lip. 'Yesterday.'

I looked urgently around the room and walked over to the window to see if I could find a way out, even though I knew from looking at the window from the rooftop cinema, it was just a window with a sheer drop underneath. I pushed my hands through my hair.

'Help me help us. What can I do? Where is your phone?'

'I don't have a bloody phone. He takes it. I'm only allowed to use it for work. It stays downstairs. I only have a tablet.'

'When you say work, do you mean... Instagram? Are you...?'

But she couldn't answer me because the door swung open again and a man came storming into the room with his head bent.

'I don't suppose you'll close the bloody curtains, so I'll have to —' He stopped just before me. 'What the fuck is this? Who are you?' I looked into the face of a man with a shaved head, tight white T-shirt and bronzed, strong arms.

'I said' – he took another step closer to me – '*Who. The. Fuck. Are. You?*' He spat his words at me. Sweat glistened on his scalp.

'I, I, I'm here to help. Your wife – she's ill.'

He looked over at the girl with pure disgust. 'She isn't my wife.' Then he looked at me again. His eyes narrowed and he rubbed his teeth across his bottom lip. 'And you shouldn't be here.'

I lunged forward to make a dive past him, but he grabbed hold of me and pulled me into him so I was locked in his arms.

'But maybe it's my lucky day.' He whispered into my cheek. I could smell body odour and a strong stench of alcohol on his breath. His stubble was scratching against my skin. He was whispering something in my ear, words that made my body itch. I tried to hustle my way out of his vice-like grip, but he only seemed to tighten his arms around me further. He began to drag me out of the room, backwards and out onto the landing. I kicked out with both legs and lashed out with my hand towards his face. He kicked a door to his right with his foot so it opened and he continued to drag me into a tatty bathroom. He pushed the door shut with his foot and flicked my leg with his so I was floored. He stood over me, his eyes cascaded down my body, greedily taking me in.

I closed my eyes tightly, as though I could will myself away somewhere else. The idea of the '5-4-3-2-1' technique flew through my head, but there was too much stimuli coming at me at once.

I could smell and feel a damp bath towel, the sound of the whirring extractor fan, and strangely I began to consider its lack of functionality as my nostrils were overpowered by the stench of mould. I could feel every beat of my heart pound heavy through my chest and it only increased in speed as I heard the sound of a belt buckle hurriedly being removed. I squeezed my eyes shut tighter and planned my attack. I had a matter of seconds, so I lifted my leg and thrust it forward.

I felt it make contact with him, and I heard him stumble backwards against the door. I opened my eyes to see him righting himself to a half-stand, a crazed and angry look in his eye, but I was already pulling myself up ready to fight him. Only the next moment, I heard a loud crash, and the door burst open, sending him flying towards me. He fell to his knees, his face inches from mine, just as two armed police burst through, grabbed him and dragged him out of the door. I heard his shouts and protests from where I lay as he was hauled down the stairs. Then the doorway was full again, this time with a man I recognised. There was nowhere for me to run to any more.

'Hello, Meghan.'

I sat and leant against the bath and let out a loud sigh.

'Hello, Detective,' I said.

45

The room felt too small as he came further in wearing bulky, black body armour. His clothes rustled as he knelt down to my level. His walkie-talkie on his chest crackled and a woman's voice came through it. He twiddled a knob until her voice became almost silent.

'I have been trying to get through to you for a long time. Why have you been running from me?' He touched my arm. 'Are you okay? Did he hurt you?'

I looked at his black baseball cap, the one he always wore during any sort of raid.

'Lee, don't,' I said.

'Meghan, you're still my wife.'

I shook my head. 'I don't understand why you're here. I don't understand any of this.' I gestured to the room.

Lee let out a sigh and moved himself into a seating position.

Another policeman appeared in the door wearing black body armour and a cap. 'Sarge, we're taking the girl in.'

Lee nodded and as the policeman stepped back, I saw the girl being helped past towards the stairs, her matted hair falling across her sickly pale skin. Under her arm she carried a ragdoll cat. Mrs Clean, lucybest65? Who was she? I still didn't know.

Lee turned to me. I looked at his day-old stubble, knowing he could never stay clean-shaven for too long. It had probably been a long shift for him already, and I doubted he had slept in the last twenty-four hours. I remembered all the nights sleeping alone, the meals for one, never knowing when he could be home from work. I looked at the lines etched on his face; the ones that only I could read because they held the narrative to our lives. Years of laughter and joy, but also so much sadness that mirrored my own.

I thought back over the last sixteen years. He had always been in control in some way or another. It had started with the age. He was eight years older than me. I had watched my father walk out on me at fifteen and five years later Lee walked into my life, a confident man, heading towards his thirties and rapidly making his way up in the police force. By the time he had made superintendent, he had already paid off our mortgage with some help from his parents, and I was pregnant with our first son, Jack.

But there had come a day when I could no longer look at him and see the eyes of Toby, the child we had both lost, looking back at me. And that was when I had begun to run.

I made it to Norfolk, where I lived with nuns for a year. It was only meant to be a short stay, a week or so, to right my mind, help me heal. But when the week came to an end, I felt I didn't want to leave. There was work for me in the garden, weeding and planting, which paid for my lodgings. I worked and sat and slept. That was all. No TV, no phones, no internet. No distractions. I didn't deserve anything else. I had been used to spending most of my time in a room six feet by eight feet. In the nunnery, I felt protected. I felt that things seemed to make a bit more sense. I developed habits that kept me sane, behaviours that kept me safe. Every time I remembered the events that had taken Toby away from us, I became more aware of my surroundings and patterns evolved, behaviours I would play out so nothing like that would ever happen again. I was protected by the four walls of my room. Locks were checked and rechecked, coins were aligned and my bed was kept immaculately clean. One of the visiting priests, who I had become fond of sitting with from time to time when he was around , would occasionally catch me out before turning a door handle or a latch. 'Don't do it.' His words would echo softly around the concrete walls. 'I won't.' I would call back. But I did anyway, and I could almost feel the warmth of his smile as he walked away.

A year passed and the nuns told me it was my time to move on.

Money appeared in my account from the sale of the house that Lee could no longer bear to live in with only one son, and the ghost of another.

So I signed up for a textile course and moved to London. But as soon as I was back amongst the chaos of life, the old feelings began to rear. It was going to take some time to adjust, I reassured myself.

I didn't contact Lee to tell him I had moved on again. I knew he would expect me to see Jack. But I still wasn't ready to face either of them. But there was only so long I could stay hidden from a superintendent of the Met's organised crime unit.

'We've been watching this organisation for months, and today was the day we hit the joint.' Lee rubbed his stubble, a sign he was tired. 'I've been tracking your phone for a while now. But you knew that. And today, when I looked, you're at the same address. So if anyone is confused, it's me?'

'I've been following this girl on Instagram, Mrs Clean. She had a troll who I worked out lived at this address. I worked it out because I saw a picture she had taken from the attic window of the rooftop cinema opposite. It became like a compulsion, I got carried away. I didn't mean to come this far.' I felt relief pour out of me like a balloon deflating. Exhaustion was taking over.

Lee smirked, that smile that had knocked me off my feet all those years ago. But the last few years I had stopped noticing. Instead, all I had seen was his anger. His frustration at what I had done.

'Doing a bit of your own detective work, I see. I taught you well.' Lee looked at me longingly.

Our past sat between us like a heavy rock; we would never be able to shift it. It had been over a year since I had laid eyes on him. But I had felt him all around me. Sometimes only in my imagination as the horrors of the tragedy haunted me. But other times I was sure I had seen him. I was sure I had felt him.

'I need you to know, it was wasn't your fault. It was an accident. I was so mad with you, with us, at the beginning, that was just raw grief. My world was shattered too, Meg. I know it wasn't your fault. I need you to know that now. You can stop running from me.'

My shoulders shuddered as the tears spilt down my cheeks. Lee's hand reached for mine, and this time I took it and squeezed it hard.

I thought back to the days when I could barely look at him and vice versa. On the odd occasion he would try to touch me with care, I recoiled as though his skin was poison. Then I thought back to the fights, the screaming. The blame. The days and nights he spent away when I would be left with Jack, who was verging on becoming a teenager who needed his dad around, but all he had was a half-version of the mother he had once known.

We were a couple grieving the loss of a small child who didn't deserve to die that day. Nothing would build us back together again. Our relationship ended the day Toby died. I would carry the burden forever. But to look at Lee every day, to see the blame in his eyes, was too much to live with.

Lee was speaking again. I wiped the tears and snot from my face with my sleeve, an act I had berated my children for over and over again.

'I went all out to make sure a proper investigation happened. The landscape was crumbling – they shouldn't have been letting people walk along that cliff. I mean, you can't walk there now. It makes me angry that we lost our son. It's been three years, Meghan. I'm sorry I hurt you. I'm sorry I was so angry at times. I've had therapy.'

'I changed my name,' I said through a sniff.

'I know,' he said. 'It's my job to know this stuff. But don't think I'm about to start calling you Regina any time soon. You'll always be my Megs, even if it's not legally your name any more.'

I tried to smile at his efforts and I winced. The adrenaline had worn off and in its place a searing pain in my ribs and arms was slicing me in two.

'We need to get you to the hospital. Can you walk?' Lee started to stand.

I nodded.

'Right, come on then.' Once on his feet he held out his hand. As he pulled me up, I automatically found my way into his arms and for the first time in years, I stayed there, not moving. No longer wanting to run.

25TH APRIL 2016

We had been waiting for months for the weather to turn. November through to April seemed as though it had rained non-stop. Outside of pre-school days I had been constructing more and more elaborate indoor activities, from Lego towers to dens with different rooms and sections to obscure obstacle courses. The rain had been relentless – I was becoming convinced it would never stop – but we hunkered down, found ways to distract ourselves. We were safe and warm and dry. Then one day the clouds parted, the rain stopped and the birdsong had never sounded so sweet. We flung open the doors and let in the light and fresh air. I hung washing on the line and watched the sheets dancing in the breeze. Then a small hand was in mine, tugging at me, urging me to come outside. We took it one step further; a picnic was packed and we filled the car with our basket of good-ies, a picnic rug and a beach ball, buckets and spades. The air was cool, but the sun was warm, and once we had parked up, our little family skipped towards the beach. Steam was well and truly let off and I watched my two boys running up and down the dunes and making sand angels. Then the elaborate construction of a sandcastle began. I stepped back and allowed the moment to continue without me, and I laid out the picnic rug and began to put out the treats we had brought. A Spanish omelette I had made yesterday, a jar of gherkins as they were a current favourite, little tuna-and-sweetcorn sandwiches, a punnet of strawberries flown in from Turkey or Greece so not as sweet as the British summer strawberries I would have to wait another month for.

The sandcastle was built and hungry mouths arrived, waiting to be fed. We grazed on our mini feast, watching the gulls flock overhead, swooping down into the water and collecting their catch, then flying away with it. Afterwards, I packed up the picnic, shook the crumbs off the rug and watched the gulls flock to the debris. I looked upwards towards the cliff and suggested a walk. Strong hands were on mine, taking the picnic basket from my hands, then a bristly kiss founds its way to my lips. Heat and salt air muddled my senses. We walked back to the car to deposit the rug and picnic basket, then my hands were free again, but only for a second before I felt tiny hands, sticky from strawberries, on my mine. I looked down at the messy locks and the blue long-sleeve T-shirt with the huge rainbow, one of his favourites. We marched up the hill, a firm family of four, arms swinging, singing songs that had been recited time and time again at pre-school and were now making their way into the home as his confidence grew enough to belt them out. I began to tire and I slowed down, a firm hand was on my back, helping me on the rough terrain. I looked at the view, and I noticed how the cliff face grew into a path cluttered with thistles and purple heather. I veered off course and was dutifully followed. The view from this angle was better than where we had come from. You could see where the bay scooped round, where we had been playing just before. From here you got the full view, the sky, the sea, the sand. It was breathtaking. It felt like a new discovery, a place I imagined we would return to often as a family.

We plodded on and I felt a sense of pride at having discovered this spot for my family to enjoy. It felt like a safe haven away from the world. I was a curious soul, and I had inadvertently instilled that trait in my children. Tiny hands pushed past me and I watched little legs and a flash of wild, untamed hair rush past me. I turned and smiled into big brown eyes, eyes that held my own reflection, who had seen me change from girl to woman overnight as I gave birth to his children. But my smile slipped from my face as I heard the gut-wrenching sound that haunts every parent's nightmares.

My legs couldn't get me there quick enough, but when they did, I wanted to run off the edge of the cliff. I felt a hand on my wrist, it was so tight, and I was being pulled backwards whilst I used every piece of my energy to run forwards. I couldn't feel the pain in my wrists until afterwards when I was questioned and they asked me where I got the bruises. I couldn't remember, I said. The sensation lingered for years after, surfacing as the horrors replayed over in my mind.

'I did it,' my husband, Lee, said. His voice for the first time in his life was small and weak. 'I had to stop her from following our son over the cliff.'

The hospital was stark and hot. I spent one night in a ward with a woman who called for a Freida in her sleep every hour. I barely slept a wink.

As I suspected, I had broken two ribs and fractured my wrist. I also had plenty of bruising from the fall down the basement stairs. When Lee came to collect me the next morning at eight, he had all the information I needed to satisfy my endless questions.

'Her name is Hero Dante. Her mother was a Spanish immigrant, came over twenty years ago. Dead father. She is twenty-one years old. Moved in with Demetrius Angelos when she was nineteen. She was what we call a modern slave. She was put in that house to initially make them money as an Instagram influencer. There are about another twenty women who are all scattered around different venues around London, all working for them. About six months ago they started using the house as a drugs den. It was the perfect place to store them, they thought no one would bat an eyelid as there was plenty of stock arriving from the Instagram sponsors. They have one child between them, a boy, two years old, unnamed – his birth was never registered.'

'Where is the baby boy?' I interrupted.

'With social services. He was picked up in the early hours of this morning in a house in Eastleigh with three Eastern European women.'

'And Hero, how is she?'

'Not well. She is pregnant, suffering from hyperemesis gravidarum and is severely malnourished. Couple of fractured ribs. It's amazing the baby has survived this far.'

'Is the baby okay then? How many weeks pregnant?' My thoughts were only with her and the baby.

Lee screwed his face up and shook his head. 'Twenty-four weeks, maybe. I can't remember that bit exactly. Megs, listen, I got to speak to her briefly, and she wants to see you.'

'What?'

'Yep, once things calm down a bit and she's feeling a bit more up to it, then yes, she wants to meet you. Properly. To thank you, I suppose for taking an interest in this alter ego of hers... Lucy something.'

I paused and took in what Lee was telling me and the final piece of the puzzle fell into place. Mrs Clean *was* lucybest65.

'How?' I shook my head in disbelief.

'She created a separate account as a way to reach out, she hoped that by posting regular comments that were not of the usual calibre that Mrs Clean was receiving, that someone might take notice. And you did. All those years living with a copper. I suppose it was worth something.' He smiled.

Tears pricked in my eyes. I looked at Lee and felt the weight of our past slowly sinking away. We had been estranged for years. It was time for us to finally find some closure for both of us.

'It was worth everything.' I sobbed as my throat swelled up with all the words I had been meaning to say for years. 'You were my everything, my world, you, Jack and Toby. But I ruined it, and there was no getting it back again. I lived under a blanket of guilt whenever I was with you and the weight of it was crushing me.'

'I know, Megs, you don't have to explain to me. I was a pain in the arse to live with, and after Tobes, well... I must have been hell to live with.'

The memories of arguments that began when Lee came home from work and had so easily carried on through the night into the next day. Our grief morphing into nothing more than exhaustion and resentment for one another.

I shifted and winced at the pain.

'Do you need more morphine?' Lee asked.

'No, I had some just before you got here.'

'Okay then, we can get going.'

'Okay.' I swung my legs down from the bed.

'Megs.'

That tone, I knew it was coming.

'Jack misses you. Do you think you are ready?'

I looked at my feet. 'Last night I woke with a terrible pain, the worst kind of pain I have ever experienced. It wasn't my ribs or my wrist, it was my bloody heart. It felt as though it was breaking and it was a gut-wrenching pain that started down there and went through my whole body.' I looked at Lee, my eyes welling with tears. 'I miss him, Lee. I miss him so much it hurts. I didn't think I did. I thought he was better off without me, but I felt his pain last night. It was like I was experiencing all our pain at once, yours, mine and Jack's and Toby's—'

'Toby isn't in pain. He's at peace.'

'I know. I know. I had Jack so young. We made such a good team in the beginning. I could never have imagined anyone taking Jack from me then, and yet I left him.'

Lee took my hand and squeezed it. We both knew we could

never be together, the pain and loss we had suffered was bigger than both of us.

'He's had me. We've haven't done too bad. But I think it's time for you to see him now, don't you?'

I nodded. 'Yes. I'm ready.'

EPILOGUE

I raised my head to the sky and felt the warmth of the late-summer sun on my face. I looked down at the picnic I had laid out ready. Sandwiches, melon, crisps and fresh homemade lemonade. I hoped when everyone arrived they would enjoy my offerings. I wasn't much of a hostess, but I was learning how to be better at it. The same way I was learning how to be better at other things: like being a mother. Something I had thought I had forgotten how to be, or maybe thought I no longer needed to be. My phone pinged. And I opened the messages. It was from Karen.

Tell Jack happy birthday from me. Sorry I can't be there today. I hope you understand. It's a bit too soon.

I smiled and texted back that I understood. Sophia was now almost five months pregnant and living with Steve and her parents. They were both on their way, and Karen could not be around them just yet. It could take Karen some time to come round to the idea of them together. The same way it would take some time for my neighbour, who I now knew as Natalia from

Bulgaria, to come around to me and my mistake and no longer see me as a threat. Her son, Raff, had a primary immunodeficiency disorder. I had bought some toys for him and flowers for Natalia and dropped them off. I still felt a little hostility. But I wouldn't give up. I felt eventually it could be a friendship worthy of the investment.

I had met with Hero twice and met her son, Baby Boy as she referred to him, but who was now officially named Noah. She started up the account of lucybest65 as another outlet to the world, and it had quickly spiralled into another alter ego. The comments she posted as lucybest65 on the Mrs Clean's account were mirroring her own disgust at what she was being forced to do. When she received a few comments back she realised it could be a way to get a message to the world. My obsession with both women had brought me to the house.

This morning, Hero had given birth, three weeks early, to a baby girl and so, quite rightly, had to cancel at the last minute. I said it was perfectly okay under the circumstances and I was honoured to share my own son's birthday with such a special little girl.

I have just one question for you

She had texted back.

How would you feel if I called her Meghan?

I had taken a moment to think before I had replied.

It will suit her perfectly.

She sent an emoji heart back.

I knew I was leaving behind that chapter of my life; Meghan was the woman I was then. I didn't feel it at the time, but I had been strong. I had been stronger than I had known. But Regi was who I was now. Now I worked as a barista at the trendy artisan café that Will and I had our Sunday brunch date in. I work there by day and will start university in the evenings from September. I discovered I prefer studying by night. I have also discovered a new love for latte art. I won Barista of the Month several times in a row. Having a job has left me with less time to think. Less time to spend on Instagram.

Mini, who was still living with Karen and I at the house, was running late as some sort of disastrous date last night had set her back. I had arrived half an hour earlier than everyone else so that I could have the picnic set up. I had bought white paper plates with a floral design and matching napkins. I had made my own bunting at college on the sewing machines and erected a few short poles to which I attached it to.

I looked up towards the sun again and closed my eyes. As I did, something immediately blocked out the rays I had been enjoying. I opened my eyes expecting to see that the sun had gone behind a cloud and instead I saw the warm and familiar smile of the face that I had been seeing a lot more of these days.

'Hello, Regi.' Will beamed down at me.

'Hello, Will,' I said politely back, even though we had gone way beyond such formalities.

Will kissed me softly on my lips, then sat down and tucked straight into an egg-and-cress sandwich. I watched the way he ate the triangle in two bites, dusted down his jeans and grinned at me.

I thought about how far I had come in a few short months and how a lot of it had to do with Will. When I had explained everything to him, he was so understanding, more so than I thought any person could be.

I looked up and another tall figure loomed over me. I saw a man in the boy I once knew. It hadn't yet sunk in and every time I saw Jack, my heart skipped a beat over how much he had grown. He was so handsome, yet he was also a good soul. Kind and thoughtful. Lee had done a good job with him these last few years.

'Hello, Mum.' His voice squeaked where it was still trying to deepen.

I jumped to my feet and embraced him as hard as I had been doing for the last four months, knowing there was still another part of me that was living and breathing and that was worth sticking around for.

Will and Jack gave each other a friendly slap on the arm and Jack sat down and looked at the food in front of him.

'You can start,' I said to him and my heart swelled at his patience and manners. 'It is your birthday. Sweet sixteen.' I ruffled his hair, an act that still felt awkward for me, but I still craved it. Jack smiled not showing any signs of embarrassment.

Will pulled out some paraphernalia from his front pocket that was obviously causing him discomfort: his phone, keys and some loose change. He put it all on his paper plate in front of him and lay down on his side. I looked at the pile of loose change, and spotted several pound coins strewn around. I edged my way closer to the plate.

Suddenly I heard the words: 'Don't do it,' spoken in unison. I looked at both Will and then Jack, who I both adored and respected. I looked at the messy coins and felt the familiar yearning rear itself and then I looked back at the gentle kind faces next to me. 'I won't,' I said.

ACKNOWLEDGMENTS

Writing a book is a hard task at the best of times, but when the world has shut down, jobs are being lost, children have lost out on education and aren't socialising with their friends; when the world is paralysed with fear, then it became really difficult to write a book. Despite the hurdles, the emotional stress and the constant distractions of having three children at home asking for a snack every 17 seconds, I managed to formulate 90 or so thousand words into a story, which I hope you enjoyed.

There are the usual few to thank for helping me get my third book to publication, but during these exceptional times, the team at Boldwood did a fantastic job at keeping us writers employed! During a time when many were (and still are at time of writing) losing jobs, homes and businesses, Boldwood were taking huge strides to keep our books on shelves and Kindles across the world. I am extremely grateful to Amanda Ridout for keeping in touch regularly over the lockdown months and to Nia Beynon for doing all that she does (which is a lot) but particularly for working tirelessly with the designers to achieve that striking front cover. My favourite one yet.

When I decided I would write about a character with OCD I asked around on social media for anyone who could offer any personal experiences that would help shape the character, Regi. I am extremely grateful to Joanne Askew for stepping forward from the world of Twitter to give me an insight into the daily mindset of someone living alongside compulsive behaviours.

I'd like to thank Claire Duffy for her invaluable insight into trauma, PTSD and hyper-vigilance.

Thank you to Ella Proctor for passing on her knowledge on child protection.

I like to save the best to last. Thanks to my lovely family: Chris, Savannah, Bodhi and Huxley, plus the furballs: Ferris and Willow, for bringing all the lols amongst the chaos.

Finally, thanks to you, the reader, for picking up my third book and supporting my writing journey.

BOOK CLUB QUESTIONS

1. What did you think of Regi's neighbour and what did you think the outcome was going to be?
2. Instagram and social media overuse is a strong theme in the book. Discuss your experiences of 'overusing' social media in a way that may have had a negative impact.
3. There are several other themes running through the book, how many did you recognise?
4. Who was your favourite house mate and why?
5. Have you ever been a house mate, if yes, what kind were you?
6. For the majority of the book, was Regi's husband's presence real or purely in her imagination?
7. Why do you think cleanstagrammers are as popular as they are on Instagram right now?
8. Why do you think the unnamed narrator in the 'then' chapters stays with D and won't leave him?

9. By the end of the novel, did you feel Regi was on some sort of path to recovery? Or do you think she will always carry her tics and behaviours with her?

MORE FROM NINA MANNING

We hope you enjoyed reading *The House Mate*. If you did, please leave a review.

If you'd like to gift a copy, this book is also available as an ebook, digital audio download and audiobook CD.

Sign up to Nina Manning's mailing list for news, competitions and updates on future books.

http://bit.ly/NinaManningNewsletter

The Daughter In Law and *The Guilty Wife*, two other gripping psychological thrillers from Nina Manning, are available to order now.

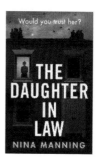

ABOUT THE AUTHOR

Nina Manning studied psychology and was a restaurant-owner and private chef (including to members of the royal family). She is the founder and co-host of Sniffing The Pages, a book review podcast. She lives in Dorset.

Visit Nina's website:
https://www.ninamanningauthor.com/

Follow Nina on social media:

twitter.com/ninamanning78
instagram.com/ninamanning_author
facebook.com/ninamanningauthor1
bookbub.com/authors/nina-manning

ABOUT BOLDWOOD BOOKS

Boldwood Books is a fiction publishing company seeking out the best stories from around the world.

Find out more at www.boldwoodbooks.com

Sign up to the Book and Tonic newsletter for news, offers and competitions from Boldwood Books!

http://www.bit.ly/bookandtonic

We'd love to hear from you, follow us on social media:

facebook.com/BookandTonic

twitter.com/BoldwoodBooks

instagram.com/BookandTonic

Printed in Great Britain
by Amazon